PRAISE FOR *THE BLOOD ZODIAC* SERIES

"Meticulously plotted and expertly paced. With *The Bull*, Crockett has proved once again that she is a fully capable and professional storyteller. Highly recommended!"

- David M. Brown, Editor-In-Chief, 5th Dimension Comics

"Erica Crockett burst onto the literary scene in 2014 with her debut psychological suspense novel, *Chemicals*. Now she is quick to follow up with an episodic serial tour de force worthy of *True Crime*, proving she is also on her way to establishing herself as a master of the thriller genre. It's hard to believe that such an accomplished talent is only just getting started."

- Vincent Zandri, New York Times and USA Today Bestselling author of *The Remains* and *Everything Burns*

"Erica Crockett hones in on investigating the paranormal aspects of her pagan roots as a storyteller. In *The Blood Zodiac*, there are daring dissections of the mirror world and the paranormal. While the series maintains a dark and somber atmosphere in dissecting the primal aspects of the labyrinthine human mind, its essence is a vibrant, hopeful energy for those characters who know how to wield their spiritual clout. And that's what makes it special."

- Benton Rooks, author at *Disinfo.com* and *Reality Sandwich*

BOOKS BY ERICA CROCKETT

Chemicals

***The Blood Zodiac* Series:**

The Ram

THE BULL

CYCLE 2 OF
THE BLOOD ZODIAC

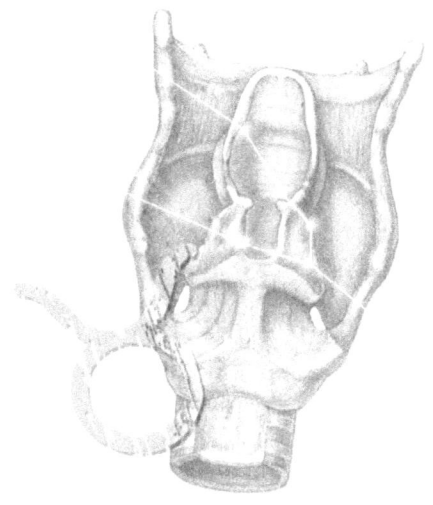

ERICA CROCKETT

Corral Tar Media

Printed in the United States of America

ISBN 978-1-942300-05-2

First Printing, 2016

Cover Design by Jenny Flint

Published by Corvid Tear Media
Boise, Idaho
www.corvidtearmedia.com

FOR THOSE BORN UNDER THE SIGN OF TAURUS

Adoring the gold coins, lustrous vitriol, lacy shells, simple carbon: all precious.

-    Peach Barrow

MONDAY, THE 20TH OF APRIL, 2015

01   PEACH

She can't get the blood out of her blond wig.

The natural hair must have been tinted the hue of honey by the wig-makers, because the blood seems to cling to it, color it. She convinces herself that hair exposed to peroxide might be subject to discoloring. Whether or not she's correct in her assumption, the locks appear ruddier now. If this is simply her imagination and the hair is unchanged, she cannot see clearly. Perhaps she witnesses some mysterious afterimage of the red liquid instead, a specter of that glorious act.

The wig in her hands meant to hide away her shorn scalp, the new tattoo at the base of her skull, these are potent, physical reminders of what she did to the tattooist just an hour ago. She had killed him. And she doesn't think of her action as wanton murder.

It had been a premier sacrifice.

While most of his blood—Roman Saucedo's blood—ended up on the vinyl floor of the tattoo parlor, some of it splashed onto the seat of the barber chair. That was where she'd cast off her hairpiece, leaving it an insentient witness to the violent thrusts of her heel on the face of the man who had inked her with the sign of Aries. She scours the strands with a nail brush in the shape of a hedgehog and generous dollops of liquid dish soap. Her hands are white and puckered from the water and friction. A pool of pink liquid sloshes over the side of the kitchen sink, escapes the tub of dyed hair and suds, and plunks in steady drops on her bare toes. Twenty minutes into her task, she wonders why she doesn't use shampoo.

The young ram bleats from the living room, his cries a plea for milk and attention.

"Wait, baby," she coos to him.

After a few more minutes of scrubbing at the blotches of light strawberry marring her wig, she gives up, leaves it to soak, and pulls out a chrome-legged chair at her little mid-century dining table. Her body feels heavy, the adrenaline nearly spent. It's only now she'll allow herself to think of what she's done from the perspective of a common human, one taught to consider all the unsavory realities of homicide. She's killed someone, a man who had a family, debts, a car. And she's taken his energy in the process. The rituals had guaranteed it. She places a hand over her pelvis, the spot near her belly button which flared with sensation as the man's life left his form and some of his vigor zipped into her. All her work for the masters of Aries culminated in taking the man's life. His death was the capstone, the bookend, the maraschino cherry. Necessary. The work incomplete without it.

Though she tries to feel sorrow, she possesses no remorse, no fear of retribution or punishment. Peach still understands killing indiscriminately is wrong. If she allows herself to think of killing other people—those not vetted and sanctioned for sacrifice—the emotions of regret and disgust bubble within. But not with the replay in her mind of Roman's demise: the tattoo gun shoved in his left ear canal, the hole she stomped in the center of his face. She intuits the man had his part to play in her story. He was the first human sacrificed to bring Perfect Peach to life. He'll always hold that distinction and Peach figures his death, aiding her in ways she has yet to ferret out, was the very pinnacle of his existence.

She looks at the shriveled flesh on her fingers in the dim light of the kitchen, the still of deep evening all around, and promises to make the tattooist a saint for the part he's played. Not a saint for the god of the Christians and Jews and Muslims, but for her. When it's all over, when her work is complete, she thinks she will decorate a wooden panel with his sacrosanct visage in rich dollops of vivid, oily paint. Sacramental robes exchanged for a high-buttoned plaid shirt, his hands lifted while preaching her glory, tattoo gun in one fist, ink pot in the other. Roman Saucedo will be a transcendent idol. He will stand as an example for the others.

A bag sits on the table across from her. It's a beige plastic sack with a green alien logo printed on it. The creature's eyes are black almonds. She meets its gaze and knows it cannot see her, cannot see the special contents within the bag. Peach is too tired to do anything with it right now other than note it's something necessary to deal with. And deal with soon.

Another weak cry and she remembers the lamb still waits. She pushes herself up from the table and goes to the refrigerator. She heats up some of the unpasteurized goat milk she gives the lamb and closes her eyes, listens to the whir of the microwave plate spinning the liquid around and around with the occasional clunking sound as it catches on the revolving base. There's no need to test it on her wrist anymore. She has the heating down to a science. The scent of cream hits her nose.

The lamb continues his bleating and Peach goes to him, swinging her legs over the grating to enter the fenced off area of the living room. He rushes her thighs, bumps her with his soft forehead and rubs the lanolin from his skin onto her red dress. When he pulls away, she can see his white wool smudged with a bit of blood. She looks down and can't see the red liquid on the crimson dress. How much of the tattooist's fluids has she managed to track into her car and her home? She'll have her work cut out for her with clean up. She recalls the last time she left flecks of red around her space, after the night she spray-painted deep ruby Vs onto major street intersections throughout Boise.

Peach attaches a nipple to the bottle and bends down to offer it to the lamb. He snatches at it with soft lips and rivulets of milk slip out of the corners of his mouth. She drops to her knees and holds the bottle while regarding the blotch of blood on the lamb's head. Both the animal and she have been marked by blood. She has the tattooist's blood mixed in the fresh ink on her scalp. She hadn't planned to massage his life force into her open pores but she'd been called to claim it and her tattoo as trophy. In the scant light, the blood on the lamb is merely a dark smear. It could be anything: soot, soil, oil. But Peach knows what it is.

It's power.

She pats the lamb on his back and closes her eyes again, the weariness taking over.

"I'm sorry I took your flock downtown," she says. The lamb slurps away. "I'm sorry your mother had to give birth to you in such foreign and stressful circumstances. You should have been born on grass, cold and yielding and green. I'm sorry for you, and for your mother and for your sister."

She calls to mind the work and planning it took to get the hundreds of sheep into downtown Boise. She remembers the warm slime on her arms plunged deep into the lambing ewe, pulling the second of two lives, a second lamb out of the sheep. She'd left the female with the mother and absconded with the male. She leaves the memory alone and comes back to the present, feels the glass container jerk against her palm as the

5

baby takes his sustenance.

And Peach thinks nothing of her empathy for the lamb and her apparent inability to empathize over the spent life of the tattooist. Then she remembers the lamb still doesn't have a proper name. And then it comes to her.

He finishes the bottle of milk and she pulls the flexible nipple away from his mouth. She plants a kiss on his black nose, her lips coming away wet. The smell of animal and sour liquid permeates the back of her throat.

"Your name is Roman," she tells him and cups her fingers around his soft, warm ears. "You're named after a saint, a sacrifice, a helper of Perfect Peach."

02   RILEY

He must have slipped into sleep.

Riley shoots up, the vertebrae in his spine cracking as they stack, and looks around the room for a clock. When his eyes locate one, digital numbers glowing in lime green, he sees it's just after 2am. The bedroom in which he finds himself is foreign. Heavy, dark drapes keep the room free from any light from outside and the headboard of the bed smells of cedar. An amber glow emanates from a night light shaped like the Sydney Opera House. He looks to his right and sees Nell Hyde, the stripper from Blaze Lounge he pursued and bedded, passed out next to him. Her form is splayed out at sharp, joint-bending angles and her sequined, black booty shorts are missing. Her neon green tube top is tucked under her large breasts. A sizable mole just above her right nipple rises and sinks with each inhalation and exhalation.

Riley immediately thinks of escape.

He's still drunk, but he's not so drunk to be experiencing

brown outs—those stints of lost time and unrecorded awareness that aren't severe enough to be labeled as black outs. He recalls the sex he had with the stripper. Rather, the bouts of sex they'd had. Their rutting had been unusual, even when compared to the backlog of Riley's varied and robust sexual experiences. She'd express moments of rapture, holding tight with her knees as she rode Riley. And then she would go slack, her limbs soft, and the spark of light in her eyes would dim. In this state, her body would automatically go through the motions of sex but he knew her mind was adrift in different seas. She'd murmur something about fire and the Australian town of Coober Pedy, train tracks and childhood monsters.

Though his hands are tingly, his vision slightly blurred, he's sober enough to realize something is wrong with the woman. And he has no desire to stick around and take the blame for her blitzed, drugged-out mind.

Riley rocks his hips around on the bed, testing to see if Nell will wake when he moves. Her body remains corpse-like and he stands in one fluid motion, pokes around the floor for his pants, stumbling only once. Upon finding them, he pulls them over his bare buttocks. He can't locate his shirt; his hands sweeping over the thick carpet and around the base of the bed produce nothing. There is a lamp on the bed stand but he won't risk clicking it on.

On a small armchair in the corner of the room lays a lump of something. Riley can't make it out so he goes over to it and feels at it. It's soft, knit. He holds it up close to his face, forgetful of what he wore to the strip club that night. The fabric is threadbare in some places and it smells of musky antiperspirant. He throws it back down.

The shirt belongs to Sev, the Australian poet with control issues. Nell's boyfriend.

"Shit," he murmurs to himself. "I'm in the asshole's bedroom. If I'm here, where the hell is he?"

Logic and fear should partner in this moment, act to push

him toward the exit of this unknown home and away from his dastardly doings. The thought of Sev returning, finding him leaving the jersey sheets and the embrace of his paramour should make him fly faster. But instead, Riley is torn. The reasonable part of Riley tells him to get out, go home and sleep off his drunk in his own king-sized bed. But the part of him that desires the wildness of life wins over.

Riley goes back to the bed, takes Nell by the shoulders, and shakes her until she bats at him with limp hands. She keeps her eyelids closed and he leans over her with his face close enough for them to bump noses.

"You want to fuck again?" he asks and she answers with a nod, her head flopping around on her neck.

His callous, self-important screwing will need to be quick. Riley is hard from knowing he's in Sev's bedroom, having sex with the girlfriend Sev fought so hard to protect from Riley. The poet could open the bedroom door any moment and find himself a cuckold. This widens Riley's smile. Nell releases quick, quiet grunts while he works on her with his fingers, never opening her eyes to look at his face. He nearly enters her without a condom but then remembers to suit up before pushing in and spending millions of futures inside of her. He leaves her lying with her ear snuggling her shoulder, her ribcage cocked up and off the mattress. She looks to be in a strange sort of yoga pose: The Marionette du Riley or Congress of the Stripper.

"Get some sleep," he quips, but she doesn't respond. He can tell she's already passed out, from tiredness or chemicals or both. Her navel slowly sinks back down to the fitted sheet. On his way out of the bedroom, his whole foot—his good foot with all of his toes—catches on his lost shirt and he scoops it up and tucks it under his sweaty armpit. He sniffs and catches his own body odor and the funk of sex permeating the air in the room.

There is no desire to stay and poke around Sev's domain. He leaves the house, passing through as few rooms as possible to reach the exit. The night air is bracing; the flesh on his bare chest prickles and rises. Yet he doesn't put on the shirt. He feels raw and untouchable.

He looks back at the front door he's just shut behind him. It's a dusty brown color with a welcome mat at its base made of woven plaits of colorful fabric. He's happy he'll never see it again.

He tries to imagine Nell's face but it's already fading—her sharp A-line haircut, her fake tits. He's taken what he wanted from her. The pursuit of Nell had been undertaken to make Riley feel more manly and in control. The booze in his blood makes his memory of this night murky. But he knows he got her away from Sev and completed what he set out to do.

He won. He screwed. He now feels remarkable and accomplished.

There is a smile on his face as he walks to his car.

"Been there, fucked that," he says to the night.

03   PEACH

"I apologize for my lack of focus," she tells the new client. He's a man in his early forties, with sloping shoulders and wide hips, and he wears a pair of thick-rimmed glasses at the tip of his nose. With each release of breath, a slight wheeze rattles out of his narrow nostrils. Peach resists the urge to reach across her desk and push the spectacles up to the sloping bridge in line with his eyes. He levels her with an observant stare and keeps his hands neatly folded in his lap.

She plucks a tissue from a box at her side to calm her fidgeting and dabs at the corners of her eyes. The Kleenex are there for her counseling patients, to sop up the effects of sadness or those quick, streaming tears which come with released anger. Now she uses a tissue herself. Her eyes tend to water when she's low on sleep and befuddled by tiredness.

"You slept, what, three hours last night?" the man asks while Peach wads up the soft paper and drops the tissue in the garbage.

She doesn't display the shock she feels at his keen guess. He's dead on. She curled up next to Roman the Lamb for a few hours of dreamless sleep before rousing with the early light and taking a few hours to shower, clean her kitchen, and dry her wig before heading into work. She still believes the blood left a light tint on a few strands of hair. This does not seem likely, perhaps not physically possible, but her eyes still note marred locks. If others notice the splotches of pinkish-red, she'll pass it off as dallying with temporary hair color while drunk. She considers that's the sort of thing people do when drunk. She wouldn't know, never having downed a full glass of booze in her life.

The man continues, unprompted. "Your body displays all the signs of exhaustion. And if one knows what to look for, those signs can demonstrate how fatigued a person is—whether that tiredness is due to stress, physical exertion or sleeplessness. Your face, for instance. It tells me sleep is the culprit. Shows up in the droop of your eyelids, the lack of healthy color in your cheeks and on your chin and your brow. Not enough sleep. Three hours, I'd guess."

Peach doesn't know what to say to the man. His face is slack but he keeps his body upright with a rigid spine. He wears a sweater vest in drab brown and there is a tiny feather peeking out of the knit weave at his shoulder. It's downy and white at the base, but then flares from cream to electric pink at the tip.

"Can I have that?" Peach asks and points to the feather protruding from the man's clothing. He turns his head and eyes the small thing and plucks it from his attire. He hands it to her and she twirls it around in her fingers by its hollow quill.

"It's from one of my birds. I've got fifteen. Mainly budgies. I can't afford more than a few macaws. That feather came from my galah. She's my gorgeous girl. Lerna."

The enthusiasm he feels for his avian friends is apparent in the slight upturn of his lips and the quick cadence of his speech. Another wheeze escapes him and Peach wonders if the house full of mites and churned-up dust contributes to his labored breathing.

"Budgies?" she asks.

"Americans call them parakeets. But I prefer budgies. Sounds like buddies. They're my buddies. And they're all so smart. More observant than most humans. Like me."

She looks down to the fine quill in her fingers. The feather is so light Peach can't fathom its weight. The pink of the topmost fluff is more vibrant than the rose-colored cardigan she wears now. She holds the feather up to the garish fluorescent lights overhead and notes the stripes of white that burst between the wisps of cream to pink ombre.

She puts it down on the desk and forces herself to look at the man, look him in the eyes. It's easier than it used to be. To really lock gazes with people. And she wonders if it's because of the energy she took from the tattooist. She wonders if her transformation to a stronger, more powerful Peach is already underway.

"You're different than you used to be," the man tells her.

"You've never met me before. Today only," Peach responds and shifts in her chair.

"I can see you feel different about yourself. A big change of some sort. There are scientifically-observable signs."

"There are signs," Peach repeats and shuffles the papers on her desk so she doesn't dip into memories of the curly-topped Vs she painted on the Boise roads for Aries. She does it casually, looking for the general information sheet all the potential patients fill out. The sacrifice last night and the lack of sleep has her unable to remember the man's name. She's usually good with names and faces but not now, not with this peculiar guy.

"Take your time," the new patient tells her. He takes a turn at plucking up the feather from the desk, twirls it and lays it back down in front of her, neatly off to the side of the papers.

"And when you can't find it, you'll ask again for my name."

Peach takes her hands away from the papers and shows him her palms. "Okay, just tell me. Again, I'm sorry for being so disorganized this morning."

He reaches across the desk and taps the stack with a well-manicured finger. "Keep trying. People say no one likes a quitter. It's a colloquialism I'm not sure I agree with, though it's apropos in this situation. You're not a quitter. You'll find it."

Peach smirks. She wonders what it will take to get Camille or one of the other counselors in the office to take this man off her hands. She knows a problem when she sees one. And this one sits in front of her, refusing to speak his name.

04 RILEY

He wakes up sans top, smelling like artificial peach-flavored tobacco and cedar and sex. He eventually opens his eyes, afraid of what he might see, afraid he's in bed next to Nell, with Sev looming above him, a cricket bat on the descent. But he's greeted by tan carpet and oak baseboards and plaster walls. The overhead light fixture, absent of illumination, is the final thing indicating he's at home. He figures he passed out in his upstairs hallway before making it to his bed. He wipes at a little spot of cold drool on his cheek and shuffles onto his elbows.

The beating of blood behind his eyebrows leads him to the kitchen and the coffeepot. He comes alive at the smell of the whole beans grown somewhere in Honduras. He grits his teeth while he whirls them to a powder in an electric grinder and then he bends over the counter, watches the brown liquid drip into the glass carafe and prays for its speedy finish.

His eyes drift to the picture on his fridge, the one Tate Marchesi—the five-year-old boy who might claim Riley as his father—drew for him as a birthday present. The giant eagle still stands his ground in the pasture of bulbous cows. They look disabled, with lolling tongues and misshaped eyes. It might be his hangover, but the artwork comes off as creepy. Perhaps he should slip it inside a drawer in his den instead of letting it dominate the space over his ice dispenser.

Riley forgoes a cup and drinks straight from the glass pot, burning his tongue on the coffee but pushing through the pain for the sake of his caffeine intake. He wanders to his front window with the carafe in hand and looks out to his driveway. His Nissan is parked half on the cobblestone pavement of his driveway and half on his lawn. His right tire has flattened a squat, chartreuse arborvitae.

"Hell," he whispers and shakes his head. He puts the carafe down on the counter and hopes the neighbors haven't seen his parking job, a product of possible intoxication. Then he realizes the sun must be overhead outside, that it's a Monday, and everyone has seen his idiocy.

In his foyer he pokes around in his coat closet for his house slippers. He means to slide them on and go out and take care of the vehicle, but realizes he's still wearing his shoes from last night. Then he realizes he can't remember ever putting them back on his feet after sleeping with Nell.

Nell. That's where the smell on his clothes originates from. He pauses to replay some of the previous night in his head, but there isn't much there aside from the physical sensations of sex, remembrance of certain positions, the mole on her breast and the rousing rounds between her legs. He can't recall how he ended up getting from Blaze Lounge to Nell's bed. He doesn't know what happened to Sev along the way.

He laughs a little and closes the closet door. He pats down his pants and can't find his car keys. He looks around his kitchen and the upstairs hallway and decides they might still be in the SUV. It would be the most likely place to look before tearing up the house.

He's thinking of Nell and the way her thighs didn't jiggle at all when they were up by his ears. That's something he can recall about last night. He opens his front door and stumbles backward, stopping himself with his wounded left foot—the toes claimed by the farcical fall of an anvil at High Desert Trommel. He keeps himself from swearing and runs his hands though his ratty hair to push down the matted mess.

A police officer stands on his stoop. The man is tall, wide like a linebacker, with dark hair and dark eyes. There are two chevrons on his sleeve. He squints at Riley.

"Are you Riley Wanner?"

The cop doesn't wait for an answer. Instead, he turns his head and looks behind him at Riley's poor parking job. Then he leans forward and dramatically sniffs at Riley, running his nose from Riley's belly to his face. The cop's cheeks scrunch up and he grimaces.

"Been drinking? And what? Chewing on something?"

Riley suppresses the desire to be a smartass and just swallows the response about eating something all night long. Suddenly, his inability to recall much from the past night is no drunken boon. It's a terrible liability.

"Yeah, I'm Riley," he manages to say.

"Well, 'Yeah, I'm Riley,' get your jacket or a sweatshirt or something."

The cop eyes Riley's chest, his gaze on Riley's nipples, pert from the cold air wafting in from outside. Riley caps them with his palms and his left foot cramps in punishment for his misstep.

"We're taking a drive to the station."

05   PEACH

The Boise Towne Square Mall stands as a behemoth example of the urban sprawl Boise has experienced over the past few decades. Peach has seen it transform from a small box with four department-store anchors in the nineties to the sprawling beast with international chains it is today. Satellite wings blossom away from the busy epicenter like runners on strawberries.

She parks outside the department store known for throwing a Thanksgiving Day parade in New York City each year, locks up her Honda Civic and shuffles her feet over the sandy asphalt replete with pot holes large enough to hold several grapefruit or a clutch of eggs left by an errant goose. She figures the mall will provide her with the most options. She could spend the rest of the evening shopping around for a particular price or cut or look, but she's exhausted from her counseling and her sacrifice of Roman Saucedo. And she can hear that ticking clock. Her whole life is now. Now that she has started her transformation.

Inside, the Muzak on the overhead speakers is meant to be soothing, but Peach can't stand its insipid use of xylophone and lite electric piano. The air holds a sugary mix of floral perfume samples. She moves quickly to the jewelry section of the store and walks a zigzag around the glass display cases until she finds a selection of sapphires.

A woman in a tight-fitting blazer with cheeks subject to too much bronzer smiles at Peach.

"Can I help you?"

"Yes," Peach says, her eyes darting over the gems. "I'm looking for a sapphire. Pink. It must be pink. Maybe a ring?"

The saleswoman waves her to the next case over and here the pink sapphires outnumber the blue ones. She unlocks the back panel of the case and pulls out a tray of rings. Most of them are situated on silver settings, the pink sapphires flanked by diamonds. There is a dazzling selection of cuts in heart, marquise, emerald and cushion. The options are overwhelming to Peach; she doesn't touch any of them. Or slip them on her fingers to feel their weight. Or see how they will catch the light with their angled facets. She hovers her hand over the black tray, getting the sense that none of them are quite right.

"Are these all synthetic? I mean, fabricated? Like in a lab?"

The lady nods. "Most people want bigger and brighter for pink sapphires. And the price is an issue. The lab-created sapphires are cheaper. We do have natural pink sapphires. But they cost significantly more."

"Please show me," Peach says. The woman pulls a new tray out of the case, less impressive than the one already in front of her. The stones are smaller and the price tags larger.

Peach breathes in and draws her energy to her pelvis as she's teaching herself to do. She hadn't expected to get a bump of vigor there upon Roman's death. She has yet to figure out what it means for her and her work. But she nestles her attention back in this spot now and feels a pleasant pressure, imagines an orangey-pink light growing between the muscles and fat and skin.

Without thinking, she pulls a ring with a petite stone from amongst the offerings and slides it onto her right ring finger. The stone is a square cut, no more than a quarter carat. There are no diamonds or additional precious stones ringing the pink sapphire. It stands alone in its bezel setting, solitary in its beauty.

"This is it," Peach says and only then looks at the price. It's five hundred dollars. She'll have to scrimp to make rent. Maybe even ask Linx for help. But this is the stone. There's no getting around it.

She uses her only credit card to purchase the ring and asks the woman to put it in a black box and then put the box into a bag. Walking out of the store and into the common halls of the mall stretching a story above her, Peach doesn't hear the music anymore. The tiles under her feet radiate outward in shades of taupe and cream, treated with care to maintain a high shine. Her annoyance dissipates with the feel of the small paper bag folded over at the top against her skin, carried by her pinched fingers. Another step completed.

She enters a small bookstore, the last of its kind left in the mall. In addition to rows of popular fiction, cookbooks and the latest best-selling hardcovers, the store stocks Pokémon stuffed animals and board games marketed to adults. She makes for the Science Fiction and Fantasy section and her eyes skim over the offerings. She knows what she wants and smiles when she finds she can lift it from the shelf, pay cash for it, read it to take a break from her day job and her soul's job. Thumbing through the slim paperback copy of *The Merchants of Venus*, she smiles to see the cover is smooth and unbent. She takes it to the counter, purchases it from a mousy woman in an oversized blouse, and then heads out of the mall.

Once she's back to her car, she locks the door and pauses for a moment to enjoy the heat the metal-bodied Honda has gathered and contained. She takes the square, black box out of the bag and flips open the lid. It creaks a little and she stares at the small pink sapphire on a poufy bed of white satin.

She puts the box in her lap and reaches up to her chest. She unlatches the bloodstone pendant from around her neck and sets it on the passenger side seat. Once she's back home, she will tuck it away somewhere safe.

"Thank you, friend," she says to it. "I'll put you back on later. When this is all over. But for now, I've got to play with my new helper."

Then Peach slides the pink sapphire on her right ring finger and holds it up to the last of the late afternoon sun streaming through the windshield. She tilts her hand, angles it just so, to imbue her new friend with light.

06 RILEY

He's not passed off to just another cop, but to many others. It's like a game of musical chairs, with the chairs replaced by police officers. Though he doesn't sit on them as the rules of the game dictate, he does feel like a burden to be shuffled around because no one appears willing to bear his weight. Hours ago he was off-loaded by the man with the good sense of smell and Riley hasn't seen him since. Each new face offers coffee or water or little packages of pretzels or the Wi-Fi password. And it isn't until late afternoon that Riley gets plunked into the right office with the right officer.

Riley expects to see Detective Dauchaun, the detective who handled Double Al's truck fire, but instead he's with a plainclothes officer. He assumes the woman is a detective, but he's not sure. He's never really taken the time to understand the ranking system in criminal justice or the military. He chooses to stay ignorant as a personal protest against the memories of his past and his tribulations with the law. Now he wishes he could tell a sergeant from a lieutenant. He figures this way he would know how much trouble he has gotten himself into.

He's acutely aware of the smell of whisky on his breath. He'd kill for a toothbrush and some toothpaste before getting grilled by the woman in a monochromatic dress suit with her hair pulled back in a sharp ponytail. She's older than him by a few years, in her mid-thirties, the series of lines around her mouth and underneath her cheeks betraying her age. Otherwise she looks fit enough, and he can sense immediately that this woman will be a ball-buster.

"Riley Wanner, I'm Detective Mallory. Would you mind taking a seat?"

The woman waves to one of the two seats set out in the room. Other than the chairs, there is a rectangular table between them and a squat water cooler in the corner of the room. The walls are bare, made of cinderblocks covered in peeling yellow paint.

"Sure," he says and smiles, raising his palm to his lips to keep his rank breath in check. His headache is still present but he turns on the charm. "This is like an interrogation room you'd see on Law and Order or one of those CSI shows. Never thought I'd be in one," he lies. He has been in many. They usually smell of bleach or something else chemically and keenly caustic.

"Really," the detective says and plants herself in the other seat. Nothing about her voice or her posture makes Riley think she doubts his words. "I was sure I'd be in one. I was warming seats in these rooms before I turned ten. I was a bit of a juvenile delinquent. Then, when I got older, I figured I liked the rooms. But that I'd much rather be on the side asking the questions instead of answering them."

Riley doesn't know where to put his hands. They feel awkward in his lap so he shoves them down into his pockets. He's aware his movements might be giving him away as drunk or hungover or guilty. He doesn't know how to look or act casual and innocent. He's never had to act the part. He's only ever been innocent, clearly so, or guilty. And the times before, with the guilt, bravado, prestige and social power had carried him out of hard situations. That and his dad's clout.

"Seems like asking questions works for you. The power suit conveys...power? You've got my attention with that ensemble and those slingbacks," he ventures, eyes dropping to the woman's feet. He pulls his hands out from his pants and rests them at an odd angle, clasped, on top of the table.

Detective Mallory looks at his clutched fingers and smiles. "Relax, Mr. Wanner."

"Okay."

"I mean," she starts and Riley does his best to sit up as straight as possible, "I can see why you might be nervous. Some weird things have happened to you lately, right? Wasn't that your boss's truck someone incinerated downtown recently?"

"My ex-boss," Riley says, "with whom I was eating dinner when the truck was lit on fire. So there's that."

"There's what?" she asks, her eyebrow cocked high. The lines around her mouth deepen and Riley notes they look like dark arroyos absent of moisture.

"Um, my alibi?" he answers.

"Speaking of alibis," Detective Mallory starts and then loses focus and tilts her head back to the ceiling and yawns.

He doesn't know if the woman is tired, bored or feigning disinterest in what he has to say. Riley's mind feels like shutting down, going on the defense, but he urges it to sharpen up and shape up. He thinks of his Nissan parked back at home, tires over his flower bed and considers prosecution over a possible DUI. He knows people can spend hours in court and thousands of dollars paying for such a mistake. He can't afford the cost of a DUI right now. Not with his decision to forgo work and a steady paycheck.

Then it hits him. Riley wonders if he could have hurt

someone driving from Nell's place back home last night. Struck and killed a child, some teenager out past curfew, blasting music and cruising around on a learner's permit. Riley doesn't know how an alibi would come into play now, unless it was to point a finger and lay blame. Perhaps to outline the story of his act of manslaughter.

"Alibi," she says again, popping back to attention. "For last night."

"Okay," Riley says and then chokes on a bit of his own spit. His armpits are sodden; his wounded left foot comes to life with sparkling pain. "I'm going to ask you to stop so I can get counsel on the phone. I'm sure you've dug into my past, right? I was a lawyer. My father was, too. If we're going to do this attack and defend thing, I'd prefer a shield. Made out of a thick résumé in criminal law."

"No, no," the detective says and waves her hands at him like he's offered her dessert one too many times. "Just an alibi would be fine. Just a name."

"For what? For why?" Riley is with it enough to know he deserves some specifics. He won't put up with the general intimidation any longer.

She yawns again, so wide that Riley can see the black gap at the back of her throat. Once she clamps her mouth closed, she keeps it shuttered for a second before speaking. Now he doesn't assume her CPAP machine didn't work last night or that she had hours of sex, just as Riley had and the coffee never kicked in over the course of the day. Now he sees her true nature; she's a competent cat, well-muscled, able to yawn because she can take down prey whenever she fancies.

She rubs at her nose and sniffs.

"For murder, Mr. Wanner."

07   PEACH

She makes the drive to her apartment with her right hand at two o'clock on the steering wheel so she can see the light pink of the precious gemstone out of the corner of her eye. She's never been a big fan of the color but she doesn't have much choice in the matter. The color is dictated by the time, the cycle in which she lives. All she can do is follow what's already set by the gods and the stars.

When she gets to her door and rummages in her purse for her keys, she hears a crash from within the apartment. She freezes, feels the notched lengths of metal against her fingertips and debates whether or not she should go inside. Old Peach may have backed away and called Linx or fetched a neighbor and a baseball bat before venturing any farther. But not this Peach. Not the one who performs sacrifices.

She waits a minute before slipping the key in the door and turning the knob. She will defend herself with the silver metal between her clenched knuckles. Peach does not think of fighting the intruder with the intent to destroy him, but if it comes to that, she's certainly not opposed to killing for self-preservation. Otherwise, she considers slaughter anathema unless marked as sacrifice: murder, for the sake of murder, is inherently wrong.

She kicks the bottom of the door so the wooden panel swings fast and hard, smacking the inside wall of her apartment with a resounding thwack. And standing in front of her is Roman the Lamb, freed from his enclosure, a mess of broken pottery strewn at his feet.

"Roman!" she says and rushes in, shutting the door to keep the lamb inside. The baby animal responds to her voice and nuzzles her arms when she kneels down to embrace him. She looks to the living room and sees the kennel fencing knocked down. She admits to herself the corral wouldn't work forever, but she thought he'd be bigger before figuring out a solid head butt or forelegs lifted up and over would bring down the sides of his pen.

She stands and slowly finagles him back to the confines of the living room with one hand on the back of his neck and the other patting at his wooly side. It takes time, but she doesn't want to spook him by acting overly anxious or trying to lift him off the ground. Soon enough he's corralled in his part of the living room with the tarp Peach is forced to hose off each day and dry, swapping out a fresh one for a dirty one each morning. She latches the kennel back together and then takes a seat on her couch a few feet away and watches.

The lamb bleats and his nostrils work the air between the diamond-shaped holes in the barrier. Black eyes study Peach sitting outside his reach. Then he rears back and butts the lattice with his forehead. He does it again and again, until the entire structure folds in at its hinges and the victorious lamb trots over to place his chin on Peach's knees.

"So that's that," she says to him and pats his head. She reaches up and touches her own head, right where she hit the tattooist between the eyes with her forehead. Right where her smooth skin gave way to the sturdy elastic of her blond wig. Peach only now realizes it didn't hurt to bash skulls with Roman last night and it doesn't hurt now.

"I guess we'll have to find other options for you, baby," she says and then stands and moves to the kitchen to retrieve the lamb's evening milk. The bag, the plastic sack with the green alien visage emblazoned on its side still sits where she put it on the dining table. She eyes it and decides to take care of it. Tonight.

While the milk heats in the microwave, she pulls her wig off and examines the strands of hair. The stain seems to be fading; the blood didn't do too much damage to the sandy blond tresses or it never did except for in her mind, and she's happy for it. She reaches up to her raw, new tattoo at the base of her skull and prods it gently with her index finger. The skin is puffy and sore. She cannot see it, but imagines it's a ripe red color due to the needle, a slight infection, and Roman's foreign blood.

After feeding the lamb, she washes her hands, goes to her master bathroom, and digs around for some topical antibiotic cream to rub on the tattoo. She takes a small amount of bacitracin on her finger and spreads it thin over the sign of Aries. She does her best to crane her head around and look at the tattoo in the mirror, but she finally resorts to pulling a hand mirror out from under the sink. She stares at the V with the curling top for ten minutes. Roman did a remarkable job on the small tattoo.

It is indeed red and she is okay with the mild irritation under her skin. As she told herself when she started the work, to spill blood meant her blood might also spill. The skin around the tattoo was, is, the color associated with the cycle of Aries. She ruminates on the symbol's meaning. She thanks it for bestowing her with all it represents. It's a focal point, the visual culmination of Aries's power: supremacy, leadership, fiery temperament and drive.

When she's satiated with her appraisal, she moves to her bed. The freed lamb rubs his sides along the bottom edge of the bedspread. Back and forth he goes, leaning his full weight against the mattress. The friction makes him lift his head skyward in pleasure. Peach doesn't shoo him away. The entire apartment will have to do as a cage for now until she can figure something else out.

She pulls open her nightstand drawer and snatches up her teal Moleskine notebook. She sits on her bed, her back against the rectangular headboard, careful not to lay her tattoo against the padded wood. She flips open the book and dog-ears a page. She reads the name Nell Hyde out loud to the lamb.

"I'm glad I'll never have to see her again in such circumstances. Or put up with Sev and his lame come-ons. Or that dirty, sleazy strip club," Peach tells the lamb and reaches a hand down the side of the bed to scratch at his haunch. "Turns out I didn't need her in the end. I'm glad for it, glad it wasn't her. I was so convinced it was right, with the odd confluence of relationships between us. If I'd taken her as a sacrifice, I would have regretted it. Plus, *he* would have been disappointed in me."

"But I suppose I learned enough from the hunt, right? It fine-tuned my instincts so I was able to take what I needed from the tattooist instead."

Then she turns the page and reads silently. She does her best to center her energy in her pelvis and then use that energy as a lodestone. She reads the same information over and over until she can see the words in her mind and recite them from memory. Peach pulls the cream and pink feather she picked off her new patient from a pocket in her slacks and tucks it into the book as a place holder. Then she closes the notebook and rests it on her chest.

She begins to think about bulls, about earth and the smell of thick, fertile humus. Soon the image of a tall fir tree with sparkling eyes comes into her head. After that, a mountain made of bark chips and soft clay and the cross-hatched tops of acorns arises and she thinks she must climb the hill. At its base, a small, black cavern entrance bores into the mound and she thinks she must enter into the foundation of the earthen structure instead. And then a voice, not unlike her own, tells her that she's falling asleep. And though it's been a long day, she has more work to do.

Peach sighs, opens her eyes to see Roman sitting in repose at the side of her bed. For a moment, she regards him, notes the way he looks like a picture in a children's book or a Sunday school primer in three-dimensional reality. Then she thinks of the alien-logo bag and its contents in the kitchen and shakes herself back to being awake, back to life.

08   RILEY

"Who's dead? I mean, what murder?" Riley stutters getting out the question. What exactly did he do last night during his periods of unconscious revelry?

"Your torso does this clenching thing when you're nervous, Mr. Wanner. Like you're about to start shivering. By the by, is it cold in here? I'm a bit chilly. I could turn the thermostat up a few degrees? Good?"

He does his best to relax against the plastic back of his chair, to let out a deep exhale.

"I'm hot enough. Please tell me who was killed."

She grins, shows off a set of long teeth. The lines around her lips widen, deepen, until he can stare only at them, see them transform from small culverts to micro versions of Hells Canyon.

"It was Roman Saucedo. He was found by one of his coworkers this morning."

Riley thinks the name sounds familiar but can't place it immediately. Then the remembrance strikes him: the high-buttoned collar, the smell of weed, and the barely-begun tattoo on Riley's left foot, left incomplete because of thin, readily-flowing blood.

"He's a tattooist at Crucible Tattoo," Riley states.

"Right," Detective Mallory leads, "and do you recall you had an appointment scheduled with him? For a tattoo? I checked. I had money on you going for a piercing. Perhaps in one head or another."

"Funny. Of course I recall," Riley begins and then stops. The realization his appointment was scheduled for the previous night hits him, sneaks past his slow, alcohol-addled brain and reminds him of his failing to actually get to the appointment. He'd forgotten all about it once he'd had Nell up against the metal of his car, telling him about her astrological sign while he watched the sharpness of her nipples lift the green fabric at her chest. That memory of the night returns now and he feels the familiar tightness in his crotch at reliving it.

Another detective comes into the room. He slides a packet of unopened Twizzlers across the table to Detective Mallory and she stops them with her palm before they skid to the floor. She takes the time to pry open the plastic and then offers Riley a dark red licorice. He shakes his head no. The other detective—a man with short legs, long ears, and twenty years on Mallory—leans against one of the bare walls and looks at Riley.

"So the appointment, I had it scheduled for last night," he admits. He's happy to feel his ardor dissipating thanks to the arrival of the male detective in the room.

The police smile at one another. The man reaches over to the packet of candy, pulls out a twist, and sticks it in his mouth. He stays silent, excepting the sound of his jaw clicking when he chews the gummy licorice.

"Detective Sewell and I know," Detective Mallory says. Her partner's audible bites are background noise, nature sounds in juxtaposition to her sharp words. "And that's why you're here.

And that's why I'm asking about alibis."

Riley can smell the faux-cherry reek of the candy and his stomach does a small flip. He wills himself to keep from vomiting on the laminate table in front of him. He looks at the woman and then the man and knows he has nothing to hide. No longer thinking he needs to play innocent, he relaxes into the fact that he *is* innocent.

"I didn't show up at the appointment. I got lucky instead. She's my alibi, if you need one."

"Who is this she?"Detective Mallory prods.

"Nell Hyde. She works the pole at Blaze Lounge. Do you need to know how many times we had sex as well? Three, at least. Maybe four."

Detective Mallory raises her eyebrow and smiles at the man leaning against the wall. "Well, it seems like a girl lucky enough to benefit from that kind of stamina and attention would remember where you, ahem, *were* all night long." And then the woman lets out an awkward chuckle, an exhalation of air that sounds similar to the braying of a donkey.

Riley flips his gaze to the other detective but the only mirth the man betrays is a skewed smile. It seems constructed, propped up from the inside with toothpicks and chewing gum.

"So am I an actual suspect? Seems to me I need that lawyer I mentioned."

Once the detective across from him gets her chuckling back in line, she does the same hand-waving she did earlier and purses her lips, the wrinkles there disappearing. "You aren't an *anything* for now, Mr. Wanner. Mr. Saucedo recorded you as a no-show in his appointment book last night. And while you could have made your way to the tattoo parlor to murder him after being rude enough to miss your scheduled appointment, we have nothing to suggest that's the case. Unless you did?"

"Did what?" Riley asks.

"Did you have a reason to kill Roman Saucedo?" And then

the woman's face sharpens, her lips pull back to show her teeth without turning upward and her eyes narrow to slits. No more donkey. Now more cat.

"No," Riley answers without hesitation. "I didn't know him. Just wanted the guy to finish my tattoo he'd started a few weeks back. Thought he'd be the best one for the job. Maybe the only one I could stand to do it, based on his online art samples I'd seen. I didn't want to end up with some blurred, off-centered bullshit on my foot. What I wanted was simple, but I wanted the best in town. He was supposed to be one of the best."

"And were you mad he hadn't finished it? Why didn't he finish it the first time?"

Riley almost answers truthfully, telling the detectives that he had been too drunk and his blood to thin for a proper tattoo session. But he knows although the pair of investigators in the room might seem odd and off-kilter, the entire conversation is likely an act. Besides, he can smell the booze on himself. So they can too. He figures he should keep his mouth shut for now, in case he gets branded as an alcoholic who may have murdered a man in a tattoo parlor.

Instead, Riley goes for a defensive approach.

"So what are you saying?" His voice rises noticeably and the male detective leaning against the wall pushes off of it, walks over to the table, and sits his wide butt on the edge. His legs are so short they dangle beneath him. "That you think I was so furious about not having a tattoo finished I went and murdered the only man I wanted to actually finish the tattoo? Huh? Come on, guys. Tell me. Do you actually have anything on me? A videotape? A signature on a piece of paper from that evening? Someone who saw me go into the tattoo parlor?"

Detective Mallory releases her lips back to center and leans back in her chair. She looks to her partner and then to Riley.

"We aren't at liberty to discuss evidence with you, Mr. Wanner."

He can't help but smile. "You mean you have nothing? Is that what you're telling me?"

"It *means*," the male detective finally speaks. He has a slight lisp and inches his way closer to Riley keeping his behind on the table, "that we might be checking into that alibi of yours."

Though he knows there is a good chance Nell doesn't remember the confrontation with Sev inside Blaze Lounge, the drive to her house or the hot, fast sexual bouts with Riley, he's willing to bluff for now and sort it out later.

"Go ahead," Riley postures. "Maybe she'll be kind enough to tell you both about her multiple orgasms. I can relate a little preview if you'd like."

"So I know you're full of shit? I know that now, Mr. Wanner," she says.

Detective Mallory pulls back her lips again to display her sizable teeth. Her mouth is like a bellows, opening and closing with regularity to expel hot air. There is no humor left in her now. The other detective is so close to Riley his leg brushes up against Riley's knee and Riley gets a mild static shock. The man picks up the bag of Twizzlers and sticks the open end in front of Riley's face.

"Come on, sir," he lisps, "take some for the road."

09   PEACH

The eyes of the deer are luminescent and yellow. They alert Peach to swerve away from the long body she cannot make out in the dark, in front of her car, as she winds up Highway 21 to the solitude of a conifer forest. The two dots of light keep her on the asphalt and keep the deer out of her windshield. Peach is not one for unnecessary deaths. Especially not the deaths of animals.

She exits the main highway and drives on a dirt road littered with rocks too big to be called pebbles and too small to be called boulders. Peach prays to the stars the undercarriage of her small car can clear the rough, jagged spots of earth. It takes her another half hour on the back road—pulling to a stop twice to fumble with a hand-drawn map, using her phone as a flashlight—to locate her destination. Once there, Peach parks on the shoulder of the road and snatches the plastic bag with the alien on it from under the passenger seat.

The mountain air is cooler and cleaner than what stews thousands of feet down in Boise. She's greeted by a great display of icy stars overhead. She takes a moment to crane her neck up and look at her friends. As she stares up, away from the lights of humanity, the fiery suns rotating light-years away dominate her vision. Her eyes acclimate to the dark punctuated by pinpoints of light. Until there is less black and more a spectrum of white which runs from dim swaths of milkiness to clear sparks of brilliance above her.

She makes her way down a slight embankment, the plastic bag looped around her wrist. Instead of using her phone for light, she trusts the illumination of the stars and finds she can see well enough. Peach counts her steps, factors in her speed, and does her best to find the plot of land she seeks on this spring night in the Boise Basin.

She stops when she comes to a slip of a creek. It's where she thought it would be and that fortifies her belief she's in the right place. The sound of water flowing over smooth rocks keeps her company as she puts the sack down and busies herself with finding fuel for a campfire.

The kindling isn't hard to come by. The tall ponderosa and lodgepole pines drop short branches capped in spikes of dead needles. And a downed, dried-out willow bush snaps off clean into lengths of finger-sized branches. Once she finds a splintered piece of Douglas fir as fat as her thigh, she arranges the sticks just so, creating a teepee with the dry willow. Then she digs a long-handled lighter out of the plastic sack.

It isn't the easiest fire to start, but Peach manages—and practices patience, one of the strengths of Earth—until the fire is full of ruddy embers. Certain that it's hot enough, she pulls the rest of the items out of the bag, excepting two objects she leaves alone. She rolls the pair up in the alien-faced plastic and moves the sack away from the fire.

Peach looks to the universe overhead and asks for its attention.

"These are just the first steps," she says to those above.

"And this is just the first mess to clean up."

She lays upon the fire a videotape, a consent form for a tattoo signed with the name *Hamal*, latex surgical gloves, a towel she used to wipe down surfaces, and the small bit of hair the tattooist shaved from her scalp. It all singes, smokes, blackens and turns to ash.

Peach waits an hour, stirs the ashes with a green stick flush with pulpy, new growth. When she's sure the evidence of her time with Roman is gone, she tosses the lighter into the dying flames. The plastic resists the heat for a moment, then the little tank of lighter fluid inside the handle ignites. Peach moves away from the fire when the pile of wood and evidence explode in a burst of blue and orange flames.

The intensity of the heat reminds her of the way the old man's Dodge Ram went up when the wool from her sweater caught the sparks from the fireworks. It was a glorious display of respect for Fire. Better than any 4th of July she'd ever experienced, even though she'd seen several grandiose affairs with molten metal cascading in vivid colors over city parks.

"But now it's time for Earth," she says to the smoldering circle of black debris. She kicks loose, sandy dirt over the entire site until the conflagration is completely smothered by soil and then makes her way back to her car. Her body presses for sleep. It's all she can do to get in her Honda and make her way back to Boise instead of nestling down on the forest floor, letting the stars overhead sing her to rest.

TUESDAY, THE 21ST OF APRIL, 2015

10   RILEY

Even though he held his own yesterday, even though he
knows he's innocent of murder, the detectives actually have
Riley scared. He's had to worry about repercussions from the
law before. Though he's had enough fun with drugs and women,
usually in innocuous yet questionable ways, his true lapses have
been with booze, gambling, fisticuffs and mean-spirited youth.
And there had been that one time, a time of great mistaken trust
in a vulnerable and disturbing situation.

All these events had occurred when his father was still alive
to help him through his transgressions. He's aware of the irony
that of all the times in his life to be suspected for some evil deed,
on the sharp edge of vilification, it's now. Just when he was so
certain of his choice to go wild again, to shirk his responsibilities
to Double Al and High Desert Trommel, to be a free-range Riley
Wanner. All cock of the walk or more realistically, of the
stumble, due to those five missing toes.

Riley is no longer so sure of himself. He holds his phone in his palm and sits on his bed, a down comforter compressing under his thighs. Outside his upstairs bedroom window, a soft cooing comes from a mourning dove or perhaps a young songbird left alone, hidden high in the ash tree near his back fence. He came into his room to change the wrapping on his injured foot, but his mind kept returning to his potential incarceration, and from there, to his potential salvation. He needs to call Nell and see if she remembers their evening together. But calling her would likely mean he would be explaining the activities of the night rather than reminiscing. And that would get Sev involved.

So he debates calling Double Al instead. The man has already called him twice since yesterday and both times Riley looked coolly at the screen on his phone instead of picking it up or sending it to voicemail. Double Al: former boss and perhaps future boss, working to get Riley a disability check and his bills covered by insurance, best friends back in the day with Riley's father. Yes, Double Al could be the key to saving Riley from himself.

"It's easy," he says to the phone. "Just call him and tell him you'll take the office job he offered that night his Ram got blown to shit. It'll show the police you're a man with integrity and an income. And you need the income, besides. Just dial the number. Dial it."

But his fingers don't move, the phone starts to feel like a heavy rock in his palm, and he tosses it over his shoulder onto the soft, green duvet. He eyes it, pretends it's an island made of lava rock, alone and sturdy in a miasma of algae-ridden water.

The oak dresser he took from his parents' bedroom is in front of him. He looks at the intricate cuts on the drawer panels. Twining ivy. He stands and pulls open the underwear drawer. Under a pair of seasonal boxers he never wears, their fabric dotted with candy canes and bells, he unearths the three cards he's received in the last month.

He opens them one by one and reads them again. There's the name. *Hamal.* And then he remembers how much he hates this man. Though he doesn't know him, and even though he swore to himself he would ignore the communications and just live his life in the spirit of fun, things had rapidly changed in the last day.

"I'm tired of being the villain," he says to the cards and splays them out on his bed. "Unless I can get away with it, of course. How about you be the villain, Hamal? And I'll play the hero. Just for once. Just for a little while."

11 PEACH

Work had been difficult since she was running on day two
of minimal sleep. But the evening air and smell of catkins off of
a golden locust tree revitalize her just enough. She sits in her car
with her window down, parked at the base of Simplot Hill near
the north-end of Boise proper. She plucks up a vinyl belt
holstering five water bottles, pulls the keys from the ignition and
steps out of her vehicle. There, on the left side of her Honda are
wild roses. The petals are a vivid pink so bright they defy the
darkening sky; center stamens and pistils are colored a warm
yellow. She uses her fingernails to break off one of the roses,
snags the tip of her thumb on a thorn, but sticks the prickly
beauty behind her ear anyway. She takes a whiff of it and finds
no strong floral scent, normal for an uncultivated, natural rose.
The fine, nearly translucent barbs cling to her wig. She sucks at
the thick droplets of blood pushing out of the puncture wound
and starts up the grassy hill.

Halfway up the grand knoll she's over the rooftops of some

of Boise's oldest homes, their porches and gables small and fragile from her vantage point. She keeps an eye out for other meanderers but she's alone on the manicured hill topped with its luxurious, uninhabited home. Queen in her solitude, she takes stock of her realm, the first peak leading into the rolling, tumbling brown of the Boise foothills.

Once she's up high enough to see the tall buildings of downtown, she stops and sits for a moment, her weight pushed back against the hillside. She's aware children slide down the hill on blocks of ice during the summer. Worn burlap between their butts and the ice keeps them from pitching off to the side as they zoom downward. The mound of earth is a bit of a Boise landmark. It's perfect for what she needs of it.

This night is one of the warmer ones yet this spring and she takes off the light leather jacket she's wearing and tosses it down on the grass. The climb was a little tricky in her leather boots, brown with white embroidery, but her feet don't ache too badly. All the same, she peels off her shoes and salmon-colored socks and digs her toes into the soft sod kept green and thick with gallons of city water. She heard somewhere it costs well over a hundred thousand a year to keep the grass green. She'd spend the money on something else for Boise: perhaps more parks or better public psychiatric care.

She steps a few feet away from her discarded clothing and looks out over the city, trying to judge the best angle of hillside facing out over the populace. Once she's happy with her location, she begins to squeeze out the liquid from one of her large, clear water bottles. She does her best to keep the flow of the line, to make her drawing big enough to be seen from far away.

Peach makes a circle with a radius of at least sixty feet. Then she caps it with the necessary lines, having just enough liquid in her last bottle to finish the job. She nods at her work and scoops up the belt of bottles. She walks back to her leather jacket, boots and socks, and sits down again. She pulls the boots up over the hem of her jeans and leaves the denim tucked inside.

She thinks of Roman the Lamb. She imagines him on Simplot Hill, the grass his alone to roll about on and consume. Peach wonders if she should have brought him with, on a lead, but she knows a baby lamb's joyful baaing would have caught someone's attention. Still, he could have been the jester to her queen, putting a smile on her face with his frolicking.

The night is not over for Peach. She stands, puts her weight into her heels on the downward walk, and checks to make sure the fuchsia rose still rides the top of her ear. She has one more stop to make in order to deliver a gift in proper time. She thinks of the lamb in her apartment breaking things, peeing on the floor, oblivious to the wonders of thick grass and sloping earth.

WEDNESDAY, THE 22ND OF APRIL, 2015

12   RILEY

It's not the new card which ultimately surprises him. Part of
him knew the three cards sent from Hamal wouldn't be all the
cards he'd receive from the mysterious communicator. What
catches him off-guard is the fact that this envelope doesn't have
any postage or a metered bit of ink showing its voyage through
the mail. This card has been hand-delivered. And while Riley
realizes obtusely that the person named Hamal knows his
address, he never believed the man would actually come to his
home and leave him one of his bizarre messages.

Riley is frozen on his front stoop and wonders if the person
is still around, watching him pick up the card he found tucked
under his welcome mat. Once his body unlocks and relaxes, he
walks out to his driveway and peers down the street. It's hard to
see clearly in the dying light of early evening and the streetlight
hasn't kicked on yet to shine down on the cul-de-sac. There
aren't any cars parked on the street he doesn't recognize. There
aren't any shady characters hiding their heads behind

newspapers, slumped down in bucket seats. He looks around a few of the larger bushes in his front yard, half expecting to see a pair of boots leading up to an overcoat swaddling a deranged man. But there is nothing and no one. He's not certain he's alone when he goes into his house and locks the door, but there's no evidence Hamal is still in the vicinity after delivering the note. The card could have been placed there early in the morning, even last night. Riley hasn't left his house all day.

He stops in his foyer, under the modern light fixture dangling from the ceiling. With the entrance illuminated, he gets a good look at the card. It's now he realizes there is nothing on the front of the card to indicate it's from the same person. This odd Hamal guy. In fact, there is no writing on the card at all. But when he turns it over in his hands, he's sure it's a missive from Hamal. A blob of wax seals the paper closed.

Except on this card, the wax is a dark pink and the indented seal isn't the same, semi-round shape. It's a small, clear outline of a diamond shape; the four sharp lines are just big enough to engulf the tip of his pinkie.

"Now what's your weird beef?" he asks the letter while he tears off the side of the envelope. He pulls free a card printed on off-white, recycled paper. The front of the card is a print lifted from what he imagines to be a larger piece of art rendered in pastels. It's the earth from space, a swirl of blue, white, green and brown set upon a starry background.

Inside the card is a simple message: It's the only one we have. Love her! Happy Earth Day!

And below that is a hand-printed message. But instead of the loopy, curly writing of Hamal, this card's font is squat, the lines heavy with ink and all the letters are written in caps:

We're that much closer to Lucky Number 8 and so much has already changed for the better. Am I the bull in the china shop? Or is that bullshit? Don't judge me for being heavy-handed with the idioms. I think I'll swap roles around this time. Sometimes

bull. Sometimes matador. Always fun.
   Love,
   Aldebaran

When he reads the name he frowns. Riley is confused about the signature. Aldebaran instead of Hamal? And the handwriting is inked in a vastly dissimilar style than the messages written in the other cards. He doesn't know if this is a new tormentor, or the same one using a different name and a different technique. Regardless, his reaction is the same. He notes a tight squeeze where his left foot struggles to heal and an odd scratchiness in his throat. A familiar and welcome friend arrives. Anger.

"Fuck you," he says to the card, lifts it up to his face and screams into its open seam. "Fuck you! No, check that. When I find you, I'll be doing all the fucking. And you'll deserve everything I give."

13 PEACH

It's just after nine at night but Peach is already in a dusky rose-colored fleece robe. It's early for her to shimmy out of her street clothes and get comfortable, but the weariness she feels mentally and physically demands it. She feels a poke at her inner arm and puts her hand up the sleeve to find the plastic price tag toggle still clinging to the soft fabric after going through the wash. She grabs hold of it and yanks it free from the sleeve and lets the plastic fall to the floor. The next time she vacuums she'll suck it up. But for now, her attention is consumed by something else.

A lump of sepia clay sits in front of her. She plopped it down in the middle of a large square of wax paper minutes ago, sat at her chrome-body dining room table to stare at it. She lets her eyes assess the soft earth, take in the bulges and divots. It's no more than a handful of material, just enough to play around with and get a feel for how she might work the clay. She's not sure what she wants it to become just yet. She's heard artist-types talk about the raw material speaking to them, telling them what it wants to be.

Peach listens, but all she hears is Roman under the dining table, chewing on the metal legs with new, blunt teeth. It sounds painful, a piercing squeak, but the animal is blasé about his actions. She is no artist; she's always struggled to draw a passable stick figure. But she's already had the notion to paint the figure of Saint Roman, in thanks and reverence for his sacrifice, at some later date. Now she wants to manipulate this material into something special. Never an artist before, she thinks of her pelvis, the way she was bombarded with the energy at the time of Roman's death straight into her core. Could part of his artistic spark have been passed on to her?

She cautiously reaches out to the damp clay and pushes her index finger through the middle of the lump. When she pulls it free, the orange-tinted clay is underneath her nail and her skin is coated with a bit of the slimy muck. She brings it to her nose and sniffs. It smells lightly sour, but there is also a soothing richness to the scent.

"So what do you want to be?" she asks the clay.

The sound of Peach's voice causes the lamb to bleat under the table and bump her shins with his forehead. She picks up the entire lump of clay then and closes her eyes. She smashes the wet mound between her fingers and lets pieces of it bud off and drop back to the table and the wax paper. She imagines herself swollen to epic proportions, like a titan in Greek mythology, but larger still. So massive she floats outside of the world, only space big enough to contain her, and she crumbles the earth with powerful hands.

Peach knows the clay is like her. They are made of the same stuff. It could become anything, in theory. But ultimately there is only one thing it can be. Just like there is only one Perfect Peach for her to become. The clay, the bits of crushed planet, seems to sink into her skin, communicate with her cells its intended form and purpose. She opens her eyes and tells the clay thank you. Peach pulls at a length of it, puts it in her palm, and rolls it with the flat of her other hand. It flips about like a fish flung to a dry embankment, until it evolves into an elongated cylinder. Peach sets the tube up vertically on the paper, smashing the tip of the thing into the table so it stands upright for a moment before pitching over.

"No stability yet," she nods at the clay and then dips her head underneath the table to whisper at Roman the Lamb. He looks at her with dark eyes, lips wet with saliva. He halts his teeth from grinding on the metal and cocks his head. He listens.

"But earth can be hardened. And then what it is meant to be can come into unyielding, tangible existence. Clay or human or sheep."

14 RILEY

He waits at his front window, watching for Walker to pull up in his little Miata. Riley greets his friend at the door with the four cards, three from Hamal and one from the new Aldebaran tucked between his fingers. He flaps them in front of Walker's tan face. He looks like he's scalping tickets or showing off a new card trick.

"Not another one, brother," Walker says when he comes inside. He's still wearing his work clothes and his collared shirt is smudged with a bit of pen ink. His hair is smoothed back, his side part deep and defined, and he keeps on his leather loafers even though Riley removes his shoes inside his own home. Riley knows Walker is pulling late hours at the law firm. That had once been Riley's life as well.

"Not just another one," Riley says and hands them all to his friend. "But one delivered sometime this morning or afternoon, maybe even late last night. By hand, apparently, and with a new signature after the message inside."

Walker slips off his suit coat, uses his hand as a hook, and meanders to the living room before letting it slip from his fingers to the couch. He opens each card, rereads the contents and then moves the newest card to the top. Walker takes a fresh look.

"I don't know if it's the same person, Rye. Probably? The handwriting is pretty different, but the voice isn't that off. Same references made to a "lucky number 8" in two of the cards. Could be two people working together. Or it's one person who takes the time and effort to alter their handwriting enough to really mess with you. It's odd, for sure."

"Oh, you mean that you aren't getting these cards? It's not common for people to receive letters from strangers with bizarre, borderline threatening messages and really bad animal-related idioms?"

Walker smirks and hands the cards back to Riley. "Don't be an ass. I told you to do something about them after you got the Easter card. Call the police or something."

Riley shakes his head and speaks without thinking. "I don't know if that's the best option right now. Not with what they think of me."

"Who thinks of you? Not ladies. No way."

He's upfront with Walker only because he's the only person he can be upfront with. "The police. I got escorted down to the station yesterday. You remember that tattoo parlor you took me to when I was drunk awhile back?"

Walker's face tightens but he nods assent. Riley continues.

"The tattooist, a guy named Roman, he was murdered the other night. And I don't think I'm a suspect, but they asked me some questions. So I'm not sure coming into the station with some perplexing greeting cards is going to make me look super normal."

Walker holds his index finger in the air, a habit Riley noticed about him years ago. It means that he's weighing options, considering information. The finger in the air begs all other people in the room to shut up and pause so that thinking can smoothly and succinctly remedy the situation.

"Could the person writing these cards to you be involved in the tattooist's death?"

Riley doesn't suppress his laughter. "Well, sure. But that's a mighty big stretch, Walker. I like to think I'm the center of the universe, but no matter how much I like the thought, I'm aware that I'm not, in fact, even He-Man. And he's at least Master of the Universe."

"Cute. Anything else happen?" Walker asks Riley. "I saw the news about the sheep downtown on Easter morning. You never said whether or not you went to breakfast on the Basque Block but I assumed you did. You're shit at resisting challenges, even from strangers. Anything else?"

He hasn't yet told his friend about the truck fire or him bedding Nell while he was in a drunken stupor and she was worse off. It's all too much to push on Walker at the moment. Riley prefers to work with the concrete elements. What's in front of him and solid. The cards.

"Forget the murder for a second. Look at these names. Hamal and Aldebaran. They both sound foreign. Maybe Arabic?"

Walker shakes his head. "Did you just tell me to forget about a murder? A murder you've been questioned about? Rye, do you hear yourself? The cards are weird, but a man was killed. What the hell is going on with you? You've had some low points recently, but after you lost your toes, these past few weeks have been epically strange."

"Don't say 'epically' or 'epic.' It's overused. And yes," Riley agrees, his voice taking on a serious, quiet tone, "I want to know who the hell is sending me these cards. At least that's one thing I can figure out. I can't bring that dude back to life. I'm thinking of my own torment right now. And working out a way to stop it."

Walker snatches back the cards and steps close to Riley's face. He locks eyes with his friend and takes Riley's face between his two hands. The hard cardstock cuts into Riley's chin while Walker holds him steady. His friend has had garlic for lunch.

"Rye, you've been in the hospital, obsessing about having sex with a stripper, refusing to work for Double Al and now a murder pops up with you on the police's radar for some reason. I get why you want to figure out who's sending the cards. But I'm worried you're losing it. Just a little. Maybe it was the trauma of the accident. Maybe you should see someone."

He does not believe he needs psychiatric help or the attention of some simpering counselor. Riley shakes free of Walker's fingers and grabs the cards. "These are *real*, Walker. I'm not hallucinating them. And they're signed with names. Hamal and Aldebaran. What does it mean? Who the hell are they or him or whatever?"

Walker sighs, pulls out his phone and touches an application, bringing it to life. Then he shoves the screen into Riley's hands and plucks up Riley's wrists to bring them level with his face. It's an open internet browser.

"Have you even Googled the damn names?" he asks Riley.

Riley's mouth widens into a grin as he eyes the search bar, blinking line at the ready.

"Man, it hadn't occurred."

"Maybe all the blood in your body has been slow to move back up to your brain."

"Touché."

"No thanks," says Walker. "I've touched you enough tonight."

THURSDAY,
THE 23RD OF APRIL,
2015

15   PEACH

The iron in the bloody steak makes her body feel energized
and hearty. She wonders at how a metal can do such a thing.
Something that, when in larger amounts and form, is a heavy
element of dark, earthen nature used to make swords suited to
antiquity, Dutch ovens, or brands to sink onto the hides of cattle.
And the iron makes her think of lead, the two metals and her
ideas of them interchangeable in her mind for some baffling
reason, excepting the fact that she knows lead is poisonous.

She puts down her steak knife and sniffs the Merlot in front
of her, having it with dinner for looks only. Some of her timidity
had returned when the waitress had asked her what she wanted to
drink. She didn't want to let the woman down with an order of
tap water, panicked a bit, and then grasped for a specific name of
wine. The smell of booze makes her gag a little, think of her
wounded knees, pitted and bloodied when she was a child. Peach
reorients her mind away from her own past and into another. She
recalls reading that the Romans were keen on putting powdered

lead into their wine. It supposedly tastes as sweet as sugar.

"Do you need anything else?" the cute waitress sporting pigtails asks Peach. She has wrinkles radiating out from the sides of her eye sockets, betraying her true, older age. The lines remind Peach of cracked frost. "Another glass of Merlot?"

Peach puts her hand over the untouched glass of alcohol and smiles. "No, my stomach is a bit off tonight. But the steak is wonderful. Compliment whoever grilled it for me, would you?"

The woman swishes away, a flouncy skirt just covering her butt brushing past the side of Peach's seat. She takes a look around the old joint well outside of downtown Boise, a dive that serves good meat and cold drinks. It's rough around the edges, vinyl peeling away from cushions, and the air is scented by the deep fryer. The place is known for its finger steaks, but Peach goes with the hunk of cow, unaltered, thick.

She finishes the steak and the side of fries she ordered with it, drowning the crisp potatoes in streams of ketchup. She's the only one sitting alone in the restaurant. All the other tables are either empty or occupied by bikers in their leathers for riding. A family of six is seated near the entrance. Three of the four children hover around adolescence, their cell phones more interesting than the recriminating tsks of their parents.

Peach dabs at her lips with a soft napkin that feels more like fabric than paper. She pulls it back to look at the light blush of watery blood it absorbs from the corner of her mouth. The pink wash flows into the weave of pulp and makes a peculiar design. She holds the napkin under the light hanging over her table and can make out a curvy shape, like that of a goddess, perhaps Venus. She folds up the napkin and tucks it away in her purse. Then she pushes her plate away and waits for her bill.

Once she's paid, she moves to the part of the building where most of the bikers sit. A chipped, well-worn bar top likely put in during the seventies runs down the east corner of the room. And on a wall near the passage to the kitchen is a dart board. Peach puts her bag and rose-colored sweater down on a bar stool and asks the man behind the counter for the darts.

With one of the darts in her palm, she stands as far away from the board as she can get without running into one of the bikers; she feels the weight of the sharp metal and the flared fins in her hand. She grasps the length of the dart in her fingers, eyes the board, and lets it sail.

It clinks off the rim of the target and spirals to the floor. Instead of retrieving it, she lets another one sail and then another. Out of five, she sinks only one; it holds loosely, at an upward angle at the very top of the dart board. Her waitress exits the kitchen, a tray loaded with cheeseburgers high over her shoulder. She steps over the fallen darts and winks at Peach before Peach trots over to retrieve them.

The song "Dream Weaver" plays over the speakers in the bar. Peach moves her shoulders to the tune and thinks of sharp projectiles and hunting with lances. She sings along with some of the chorus, looks to a dart and melodically croons about the night. Then she lets it loose with a flick of her wrist and forearm. Then she lets the rest of them loose. Two stick this time. So Peach gathers them up again and stands back from the dart board farther this time. She sends the darts toward the board for hours. When the bar empties out and the man behind the counter knocks on the old laminate each time she hazards a throw, she can't guess at how many times she's sent the sharp metal points through the air. She's already better. And she plans on practicing more.

But for now she hands over the darts to the barkeep, who takes them with a frown and nods his head to the exit. As if Peach cannot find her own way out.

FRIDAY, THE 24TH OF APRIL, 2015

16 RILEY

The book he wants the most is eighty dollars with a glossy dust jacket and a sturdy, threaded binding. It has a complete listing of humanity's most-favored stars from ancient times to modern-day and detailed directions for locating stars with a telescope. Riley thinks the book weighs a good five pounds as he drops the hard-covered tome on the desk at the bookstore's checkout.

Hamal and Aldebaran turn out to be far-flung gaseous balls occupying space. So says Google. Both enormously bigger than the Earth's sun, Riley is determined to figure out why distant stars are sending him strange cards in the mail. Rather, why an admirer of distant stars is harrying him.

"You'll get a workout with that one," the cashier says and heaves up the book to scan it under his red laser.

Riley nods and digs his wallet out of his jeans, anxious to pay and get the book home so he can read about each of the stars in detail. He's hungry for vetted, academic information about the stars. He wants to be sure of what he reads. He believes too much of the information available on the internet to be misleading. It's a rule he picked up in law school; the belief that knowledge accurate enough to be printed on a page will always beat that of someone's subjective, first-person blog post.

The cashier points to the card reader at the edge of the counter. "Swipe your card when you're ready."

Riley runs one of his credit cards through the machine and waits to accept the total and sign his name. But the machine locks up and the cashier squints at his screen, invites Riley to try again. Another swipe, nothing happens, and the cashier shrugs.

"It's not like the computer is rejecting your card. It's not reading it at all. Do you have another you could try?"

His debit card runs clean and a long, glossy receipt slides out of a gray box near the cashier's computer screen. The man folds it in half and hands it to Riley. He takes it and slides his purchase off the counter.

Walking out of the large bookstore, Riley is curious to know why his card didn't work. He stops at his homegrown, Idaho credit union and gets his favorite teller—a woman with sleek black hair and several knotted chains in gold, silver and gun metal around her throat. There are cups of lollipops on the counter, little circles mimicking the vividness of stained glass.

"Hi, Mr. Wanner," she greets him. "What can I help you with?"

He checks out the name placard in front of her teller window to remind himself of her name. "Lori, I was out shopping and this credit card wouldn't read when I swiped it. Could you check it out for me?"

She takes the card he pulled from his wallet and runs it through a card reader near her elbow. Twice, then swipes again for a bit of third time charm. She hands it back to Riley with a blank face.

"Did you put it on something heavily magnetized? Because

it's toast. The strip on it is desensitized."

He turns the card over in his hand and tries to think of how the card could have been compromised. But he comes up with nothing.

"Hmm, could have been my magnetic personality. Fried it with my ego. My nickname used to be Chickneto in high school. Like Magneto from the X-Men, but stellar at pulling women instead of metals. Get it?"

She doesn't brush back her hair or lean closer to him across the wooden barrier which keeps customers from employees. Instead she licks one of her incisors and waves at a coworker ending his shift.

Riley plucks up one of the candies in bright green and unwraps it. He gets back to business. "No idea on what desensitized it. Can you look at my account and just let me see the recent activity on it? Not that the strip getting messed up means anything sinister, but maybe someone had it at some point? Without me knowing?"

He gives the teller his account number and wonders if someone could have taken the card while he was drugged up and healing in the hospital. Shoving the lollipop onto his tongue, his taste buds come to life and he experiences momentary pain with their puckering. His mouth is inundated with the tang of lime.

"Oh," is all she says when she pulls up his number.

He cranes his head around to see the screen and she turns it toward him so he can take a look. "Maybe someone did get a hold of your card. There are an awful lot of charges in liquor stores. And some place with the processing acronym BLZ LNGE?"

His eyes slip over the numbers. Nothing unusual though he's not anxious to tell her Blaze Lounge is justified in its charges. But then he follows the teller's finger, where it sits on the screen, capped in a curved, white tip of nail.

"You've hit your credit limit. See?"

"What do you like to do for fun, Lori?"

"Fine dining and trips to Paris," she smiles.

"Point taken."

And he can see he really is at his limit.

He thanks her for her help, orders a new card and sits in the parking lot outside the bank long enough to make a call to his financial advisor and set up a meeting. He crunches through the last of the candy and shoves the soggy, white stick out his cracked window. Then he pushes the gas hard all the way home, anxious to get the thought of money out of his mind and turn his attention to the brilliant burning of faraway stars.

17 PEACH

The men play Ultimate Frisbee in an area of sod and greenery unsuited to the game. There are wide, thick-trunked oak trees scattered around Municipal Park, their limbs covered with verdant growth. Peach watches the men try and keep the flat, blue disc in the open area, away from the sentinels that have been growing in the park near the east end of Boise for over a century. She sits at the base of one of the trees—its roots snaking through the earth for yards, their topmost skin lifting up the soil. The exposed roots look like fat, desiccated worms. She touches the scaly bark of the bulging tree roots under her bottom while she watches the group of six men run the length of the open grass, bare-chested, shirts tucked in the backs of their shorts though the temperature is just past sixty degrees.

She's brought a roast beef sandwich and a bag of jalapeño chips with her, but she doesn't touch either of them. Her attention is on the skill of the men as they leap for the disc. Once they catch the plastic, they plant themselves, pivot in the

66

direction of a teammate and send it flying again.

The cobalt-colored disc slips from a set of outstretched fingers, happens to fly at Peach, and she sees it coming before she hears one of the men yell a heads up. She brings her hands up to her face to shield her nose and eyes, but the Frisbee catches the wide trunk of the oak instead and sends a shower of flaky bark into her hair.

Peach stands and picks up the disc. A man, ripped and tanned despite the lack of sun they've had all winter and early spring, walks slowly in her direction to retrieve the toy. But Peach moves toward the men instead, to a man a few years older than her. He's turned away from her approach, taking the stop in play as an opportunity to stretch out his calves.

The well-built man gives her a shrug as she moves past him and toward her intended. She's got the attention of the other players as well, excepting the one she seeks out. One of them mutters something to one of his friends and she hears a laugh in response as she closes in on her mark. Once she's a few feet away, she can see the expanse of his back. It's dotted with brown moles that look like a scattering of little seeds. And at the top of his right shoulder blade is a birthmark in tawny brown. Her breath catches a bit at the sight of it.

The man is still oblivious to her approach and she holds her hand out in front of her, covering the sight of the birthmark. It's similar to the outline of her palm and splayed fingers. It could be the wing of a raptor, detached and pinned to the back of a human.

She drops her hand when he turns and his eyes widen. Peach holds the blue Frisbee out to the man and smiles.

"I don't think the tree was playing," she says as he takes it from her.

"Oh yeah?" he flirts back and wipes at a trickle of sweat coursing down his forehead.

Peach notices the sharp widow's peak of his hairline. His

hair is deep brown aside from some of the hairs that grow at the point of the V. Those few locks are light gray. His eyes are a brown to match his hair and his smile is crooked, his front teeth separated by a little gap.

"Yes," she goes on, her focus on the arrow of light hair that points to his soft eyes. "You seem to be the most competent player out here. I know you'll keep the trees out of it from now on. So I thought I'd bring the disc back to you."

One of the man's friends stands close enough to hear and Peach can hear him object to their chitchat, but she doesn't catch exactly what he grumbles.

"Don't want to incur the wrath of the Ents, right? Weren't those the tree people in the Tolkien books? Now I've done it. I've labeled myself a dork. However, I am pretty amazing at tossing pieces of plastic around in the air. And I have a rare day off. So I'm outside to exercise. Good for the soul." He smiles wider.

Peach smiles back and finally drops her gaze away from his forehead. "You boys are like maids in a meadow."

"Excuse me?" he asks, "I'm not sure I follow."

"I just mean you're at play. That's all," then she smoothes down her blouse with the lacey-bits of pink at the hem and backs away. "You guys have fun."

When she turns, she blinks heavily and walks slowly back to her food and bag, doing her best to act indifferent to the exchange. And when he yells at her to wait, she stops her feet quickly and watches him run past her to a pile of car keys and discarded jackets on a weathered picnic table. He jogs back, his muscles not as developed as the man's who aimed to get the disc back from Peach. But this man, covered in signs, possesses a torso lean and fit.

He stops in front of her and hands her a little square of stiff paper.

"A business card?" she says and waves it at him. "Are you

trying to sell me something?"

"No," he inhales heavily to catch his breath. "But it has my name and number on there. In case you ever need help or anything."

"In case my rain gutters need cleaning? Or my imaginary kitten gets stuck in a sycamore tree?"

"I was thinking of being helpful in other ways."

She takes a second to read his job title and laughs. "A pillar of society then. All right, thanks. I might just give you a call."

He doesn't respond, but smiles his gapped grin and runs back to the game, tossing the disc to one of his friends. Peach doesn't look back but instead looks down at the card. She flicks it with her index finger and thinks of the man's birthmark and his distinguished hairline.

"Lars Apitz," she whispers to herself, "I'm so pleased to finally meet you."

SUMMER, 1991

18 RILEY

The coins are spread out on the brown rug, a ragged line of metal between Riley and his mother. They've been staring at the bits of money for what Riley believes are hours, hours that should have been spent at the Natatorium on the waterslide or playing tee-ball with the neighborhood kids. Instead Riley's mother practices a stoic patience he's become used to, even though he doesn't understand how she can sit so still and be so quiet while he works out what she wants him to learn. Yesterday they talked about insects. He learned spiders have eight legs. He likes spiders more than money so today is a hard day to focus.

He considers whining, kicking at the metal with his feet. Her pointer finger is on one of the copper-colored circles. She waits for him to answer. He puffs his cheeks full of air first, imagines he's a monkey and pulls his ears away from his head by tugging out on his earlobes. She doesn't give him a smile. So he drops the act.

"Penny," he says, "and a penny is one cents of money."

"Cent," she corrects.

Then she puts her fingertip on three different coins and he names them: nickel, dime and quarter. Most new words sound weird to Riley, but these words are some of the silliest.

"All right, Riley," she says and groups the coins into little piles. She makes sure all the circles can still be clearly seen, so she doesn't stack them. "Tell me how many pennies are in this pile."

It takes him a moment and he has to count out loud, but when he's sure of the number he responds with twenty-five. She doesn't say anything, which tells Riley he's right. She usually only says something when he is wrong. Then she motions to another pile. This one has a mix of dimes and nickels. "How many of each?"

"Two dimes, one nickel."

And lastly, she picks up a solitary coin. This one is a quarter, the biggest and shiniest of all the pieces of money. "And what is this worth?"

"Twenty-five cent. No, cents," he says, his eyes locked on the gleam of the silver. He thinks of what the round coin with a man's head on one side and a bird on the other could buy him. There is a whole wall of candy and toy dispensers at Albertsons, just waiting for a quarter to be put in, the knob turned and a treasure dispensed. Slimy balls made of blue goo and squat plastic ninjas, jawbreakers dappled pink and white and small packs of baseball cards.

"I like the man-bird coin," he says, reaches for it.

"It's an eagle and George Washington," she tells him while holding the coin away from his fingers smudged with the remains of strawberry wafer cookies.

"So," she says and puts the quarter back down on the carpet. Her eyes look tired; he knows she probably has a headache because she squeezes her nose under her big, round glasses. "Which pile is worth the most? The pennies, the dimes and nickel or the lone quarter?"

His response is instant. "The quarter, Mom."

She drops her hand to her lap in surprise and frowns. Her wavy brown hair slips out from behind her ears. "Riley, you know that's not right. They all have the same worth. They're all twenty-five cents."

"Okay, they count up the same, but they're not worth the same."

"Explain," she demands.

Riley picks up the quarter and puts it in the middle of his small hand. It feels heavy. It's full of possibilities. He thinks of the candy and toy machines. None of them can take pennies or nickels or dimes. Only quarters.

"It's best, Mom, because the quarter is prettier with the man and the bird. And it's bigger. And the quarter coin can get me what I want."

She tries to get the quarter back from Riley but he closes his fist around it and giggles.

"You're being silly, Riley. Take this seriously. We're learning before we play for the day. Now tell me why the quarter is worth more?"

He giggles until he can pause long enough to get the words out, bits of water escaping his eyes from all the mirth. One of his laughing fits is starting. He loves when his body shakes because it's so full of funny thoughts.

"It's worth more because I *want* it, Mom."

And he rolls about on the chocolate-colored carpet with the quarter enveloped by his fingers. His chest heaves with laughter while his mom plucks up all the meaningless bits of metal in silence.

FALL, 1996

19   PEACH

She does her best to explain it to her, but the woman is stern and smells of Pall Malls. Inflexibility and cigarette smoke: two things Peach hasn't ever liked. Patti's arms and legs are sharp angles of thin flesh and obvious bone and though the woman isn't that old, to Peach it's like the woman has been pickled and preserved in something especially sour. She believes the woman will always look this gaunt and annoyed.

"Nobody is going to give a twelve-year-old a job, Patti."

"I told you to call me Mom, Peach. And you're almost thirteen, right?" The woman takes a sip of a flat Diet Coke in a glass tumbler and smirks.

Peach counts the months to her birthday. She's not that close to changing age. And she's not too keen on the arrival of her birthday after the sad lack of presents when she turned twelve. It was just after Patti had adopted her and Peach had been expecting more of a fuss in her honor. After all, she'd been adopted by the woman, hand-picked from all the available foster children in Boise. Before Peach had met her, she had envisioned being spoiled and coddled by the woman. Her case manager had told her tales of Patti Lewsky, the career woman who was a vice president of sales for a local potato chip manufacturer. She told Peach she came in with a new manicure for every adoption meeting. When she and Peach were slated to meet, Peach would be in awe. She would be impressed with the single woman who wanted her above all others.

But that was all before Peach met Patti.

Now she was in the position of having to convince her new mother she wasn't old enough to be applying for after-school jobs. She knew this to be true. She'd looked into it already, knowing she'd have to fend for herself even though her papers said she had a parental guardian now. Perhaps she could pick up a paper route, or do some babysitting, but she didn't like riding bikes and she wasn't too fond of children.

"You'll need pocket money soon. I'm not going to just give you money to spend on things you don't need. That'll be your responsibility. I expect you to know it and live it."

Peach nods. "I understand. But I still don't think that I can get a real job yet. Not in some store or anything."

The thin woman's left eye twitches. Peach learned quickly that it wasn't a sign of annoyance or anger. It just moved of its own accord no matter the situation. Instead, Patti clenches the tip of her nose between thumb and index finger when she feels put out. As she does now.

Patti exhales. "Well, then you'll just need to make do until you can get a job. I don't believe in allowances. Children have a responsibility to do chores and shouldn't expect money for it. I don't ask you to reimburse me for giving you a roof over your head, do I? I hope you understand I'm doing this to help build character. It's not that I don't want to share my money with you. Heavens, what would people think of me?"

"I don't know what they'd think of you," Peach echoes. She

is not being sarcastic; she truly feels bad for the woman even though she is unkind to Peach. She never has friends over to the house, no men asking her out on dates. Peach pities her yet hopes she can someday feel confident enough to be better than Patti at whatever work she chooses. She looks to the floor of Patti's kitchen in Patti's condominium. It is not her home at all. Just Patti's. Peach only looks up when the woman says nothing in response.

The woman is staring at Peach's chest.

"You'll be big-chested. My sister was. I can tell already. You're not too developed yet, but you'll be popular with the boys. I can see it now. And when they come calling, you'll have no more time for me, will you?"

Peach folds her arms in front of her and walks out of the room, mumbling about the math homework she has yet to complete.

Patti calls after her. "We'll take you bra shopping this weekend. Get you something that's expandable. So you can wear it once your breasts fill in. No need to spend money wastefully."

Peach doesn't respond, closes the door to her small bedroom and tries to pray away her impending job and her impending womanhood while seated on the comforter of her bed. Her folded hands crumple into fists and her silent prayer changes to a lament. She tucks her feet under her thighs, clutches a pillow shaped like bowed lips to her belly and tries not to cry. She tries to stop thinking about the woman who chose her for her own. Despite the fact she has little love to spare for Peach.

MONDAY, THE 27TH OF APRIL, 2015

20   RILEY

The receptionist with the kind eyes gives him two options
for a drink: iced coffee or cranberry-apple juice in a little box
with a tiny, bendable straw.

"We're trying to mix it up. Do something different than the
usual hot coffee and water," she explains to him, and likely to
everyone who looks at her with a lifted eyebrow.

"I'm fine with nothing," Riley says and takes a seat to wait.
He's a few minutes ahead of schedule, which is unusual for him,
but he figured he'd rather head downtown early then stew at
home. He'd already read the sections about the stars Hamal and
Aldebaran in his astronomy text. He has their details memorized.
Hamal is known by several names, including Alpha Arietis and it
burns 65.8 light-years away from Earth. Aldebaran is a bit
farther away from Earth, but as a red giant, its mass eclipses that
of the Sun by thousands of times.

But the information is useless to him when it comes to the
greeting cards. He isn't sure what he'd expected to find in the

book pertinent to his situation, but he did expect to find something. Riley decides to take a break from the speculations and research into the letters and deal with an issue concrete and immediate in annoyance: finances.

The older woman behind the tall desk smiles at Riley and he picks up an outdated copy of *National Geographic*. The cover is a picture of a computer-rendered bit of a DNA spiral. The tagline asks: *Can We Be Anything Other Than Our Genes?* He flips through the pages, looking at a picture of a zebra facing down a winded, slathering cheetah. He reads the picture caption and learns the zebra, healthy and swift, outpaced the cheetah and its ability to sprint. But instead of just running away once the predator had given up the chase, the striped animal had turned and stared into the eyes of the big cat for a moment before rejoining its herd.

"Like a big 'fuck you,'" Riley says out loud and the receptionist looks up from her own reading material and gives him a cautious smile. He doesn't apologize, but looks down again at the picture. The intensity of the situation comes through in the photograph but the font used in the picture's description is what captures Riley's attention. It's blocky and bold. And it makes him think of the lettering in his latest card delivered from Aldebaran. A thought sticks in the folds of his brain and he's sure he's seen the handwriting in the newest message before.

A quiet buzzer goes off at the receptionist's desk and she punches at a button on the phone to silence the summons. She wheels out her chair and stands. She waves Riley to the bright hallway that snakes from the open waiting room to a length of offices punctuated with stretches of glass walls in the interior hallway. Their insides are replete with wide windows overlooking downtown Boise outside.

"Head on back, Mr. Wanner," she says while Riley puts the magazine down and tries to hold onto the idea of the familiar writing. She peers over the desk at the magazine he was reading and then regains her seat. Her voice is lightly muffled by the high shelf of the desk as he walks toward his meeting.

"Lars will see you now."

21   PEACH

She readies herself outside a glass door with a white, opaque bull logo centered at eye level. The bull's horns are thin but sharp at the tips and it has a thick tail which curls up around its seated hindquarters. She studies the figure for a moment and then pulls the door open. She's greeted with the smell of new carpeting and recycled air.

A woman in her fifties with a tight bun and small, yellow-orange amber earrings smiles at Peach and asks how she can help her. The receptionist's eyes are a bit red and she squints through droopy eyelids. Peach wonders if allergies are to blame.

"I'm here to see Lars Apitz," Peach responds. "Do I need to sign in or anything?"

"No," the woman says as she stands from her rolling desk chair. "Just let me know your name and when he's done with his current meeting he'll be ready for you. Are you his one o'clock?"

"Yes," Peach says. "I'm Lisa."

"Okay," the woman says as she looks down at an old-fashioned appointment book. She takes a highlighter to the one o'clock time box and clicks the cap back on the pink fluorescent marker. "It shouldn't be too long. Would you like some iced coffee or a cranberry-apple juice?"

Peach opts for the juice and the receptionist leaves for a moment and returns with a malleable rectangle and a wrapped bendy straw. She unwraps the white straw for Peach and hands over the little waxed, cardboard box. Peach punches the sharp point of the straw into the juice and takes a sip of the tangy liquid.

Instead of taking a seat and looking through magazines, Peach wanders around the waiting room and checks out the framed art on the walls. At first she can't discern a theme from the artwork. There are Italian coastal villas in watercolor, salmon-colored bougainvilleas creeping up the sides of crumbling plaster walls. There are photographs of swimming pools without definable edges, their boundaries plunging off into gray oceans or placid lakes or city skylines. Then there are her favorites, the oil paintings of still life fruit, sugary desserts and succulent meats. She studies the way the artist was able to capture the shine of greasy fat pooling beneath a raw-cut rib-eye steak.

And then the premise of all the images comes to her: opulence, the luxuries of wealth. She takes another sip of juice and sees the varied artwork dot the spaces of solid wall leading down the corridor to the financial advisors' offices. She points a finger down the hallway and gets the attention of the receptionist with a little whistle.

"Can I wander back there and see the pictures?"

The woman waves her permission and Peach takes in the rest of the miniature gallery. She stops in front of an office and eyes a piece hanging on a wall space between glass panels. The art is nestled in the confines of a faux, gold-gilded frame. It's of a king; a long, fur-lined cape drips down the raised dais upon which he sits, scepter in hand. His face is passive, almost a mask of boredom. A jester in a belled cap and shoes with an up-curling toe does a bow-legged jig in front of his liege. Peach wonders why an artist decided to freeze the action with the jester's left leg high in the air, his left elbow coming down to meet the tip of his foot. Judging from the look on the royal's face, even wealth can lead to boredom.

But Peach thinks this painting is about power. And not the sort of power that's appreciated or wielded effectively against others. It's a picture of power without power ever being earned. And it's a picture of the effects of power. Peach can see her face on both the jester and the king as she turns away from the print and realizes she's standing outside Lars's office.

She steps away from the name placard on his door and peers through the glass wall of his office. He's talking, waving his hands in the air, using his fingers to trace out a square for his client. His client sits with his back to Peach. But she recognizes his blond, shaggy hair and the wide, sharp line of his shoulder.

Lars notices her then through the glass door, stops talking and makes to stand. His client grabs the side of his chair and turns his body to look at what has caught his advisor's attention, but by then Peach is already down the hallway, passing the desk and the receptionist.

"Tell Lars I'll be back. I just need to get something from my car. I'll be back," she repeats without stopping.

She pushes open the heavy entrance door to the suite of offices and walks swiftly to the elevators. She hits the button and it lights up, signaling down, and then she hits it five more times. When the doors to the elevator open, she sees it's already occupied. She slips in past a man in a tailored suit colored a deep russet and rests her back against the far side of the elevator box. He looks over his shoulder at Peach.

She squeezes the last of the cranberry-apple juice out of the box, compressing the weak container by sucking the air out of it. It folds in and she crushes it with her fingers tight around its middle.

The man continues to stare and Peach nods down at the juice box.

"Too much sugar. My parents never let me have it when I was young so now I go to town whenever I get the chance," she lies. "Makes me feel on edge, then I need to get air and get out of enclosed spaces. I should know better. Does it every time."

22

RILEY

Lars takes his seat and his eyes flip over the pamphlet he was about to pass to Riley. Riley can tell he's lost his train of thought.

"Who was out there?" he asks.

"Oh, just my next client. New woman," and then he breaks into a wide smile. Riley thinks he should ask if the woman might become more than a client, but he and Lars aren't exactly close friends.

"Right," Riley taps on the pamphlet and asks a question. "So you're trying to get me to do some investing in your hedge funds, but you seem to be missing the point of why I'm here. I have no money, Lars. I'm out of work and while I might be looking at getting a disability check at some point, it might be some time in coming."

Lars lays down the glossy tri-fold decorated with pictures of happy, retired couples riding bikes together or playing golf. "Riley, you received the initial lump sum and monthly allowance from your parents' trust that was outlined in their will."

"But there's more money in their trust," Riley pushes. He looks around the office. All the furniture is light oak or beech, Scandinavian in design. He wonders if the man had his office furniture shipped from some northern European country covered in snow nine months out of the year. He hates him for his comfortable lifestyle and neglects to admit that he, once, was just as well-off.

"Where are you from?" Riley asks just as Lars is about to answer him. The financial advisor pulls in his chin and the flesh there crinkles into a mess of lines.

"Madison, Wisconsin," he answers and then immediately goes back to Riley's initial inquiry. "And yes, there is more money. But you're forgetting the stipulations that were explained to you when you came in here last year. Explained by me and explained again by your parents' estate lawyers."

Riley remembers the parameters for gaining more money from his parents' trust. It's just that he doesn't think the parameters need apply to him. As much as he loved his parents, they were controlling and prone to meddling in his life. And with them dead, why would it matter to Lars or lawyers or the law as to whether or not Riley performed to their exacting expectations in order to pull from his inheritance?

"Remind me," Riley says and crosses his arms. He puts his feet up on the crossbar underneath Lars's desk and leans his head back. "Tell me why I can't just put on a red bowtie and play at being Richie Rich? I have the blond hair for it. Needs a cut but it'll do."

The financial advisor logs into his computer and clicks open a folder where he enters a different password. They spend a moment together in silence as Lars re-familiarizes himself with the Wanner trust and digests the information.

"I'm not even suited to discuss this with you. Hit up the estate lawyers. That being said, there are two big things I can remind you of," he begins, eyes still on the screen. "First, marriage. If you marry and stay married for five years, you receive one half of the remaining funds in the Wanner trust."

"Five years? I need to have a wife for five years?" Riley rolls his neck around the back of the chair and sighs. "Were they high when they had this thing written up? It's like they'd never met me."

Lars goes on without comment. "The other stipulation was parentage. If you have a child, then you receive the other half of their estate." Lars reads a bit more and then nods at the screen. "Except you've also got to prove parentage of the child with a paternity test."

Riley pops his head up and he stands, walks around the desk and leans his body in front of Lars to read the stipulation for himself. Then he walks to the wide, clean window that looks out over the small city center of Boise and cracks his back. A woman strides across a cobblestone sidewalk, a toddler trailing from both hands.

"I might be able to do something about that one," he says to the glass and the trees outside and below him—spots of lacy, dappled green splaying out over an expanse of brick and concrete. He thinks of Tate Marchesi or rather the idea of Tate, living in another town with his mother Kristin. He can't call to mind the five-year-old boy's face. It's been too long since he's seen him.

But Riley admits to himself the boy has yet to show any physical characteristics of Riley's or any of the Wanners for that matter. He doesn't have Riley's mother's eyes or the big ears of his grandfather. His skin is olive, unlike Riley's pale coloring. He doesn't walk like Riley or laugh like him. What he does remember of his face are his hazel eyes, changing tone from green to light brown depending on his clothing or the intensity of daylight.

"Or maybe not," he turns and says to Lars. "Know any

THE BULL

ladies looking for a baby maker? One who refuses to change
diapers, make artisan baby food or care about the next generation
of puppets on Sesame Street?"

Lars laughs, offers a suggestion. "Well, there's the marriage
ultimatum. You could make an honest woman out of someone."

"Wouldn't I have to be honest first? For it to rub off of me
and onto her?"

"I don't know, man," Lars says, his status as Riley's
financial advisor crumbling under his desire to commiserate with
another man around his age. "Most women out there have their
fair share of honesty problems. I hate to sound like a borderline
misogynist, but most women are crazy. Hard to find good ones."

Riley nods his head in agreement and thanks Lars for
looking into the estate for him. If he wants to access his parents'
funds, he'll need to speak further with their estate lawyers. He
thinks of calling Kristin, his ex-girlfriend and Tate's mother,
asking her to submit a swab from the boy's mouth for paternity
testing. As much as he wants the money, he's not sure yet if he
wants the responsibility of the boy. With the verdict still out on
his biological connection, he can continue to ignore the
occasional feelings of attachment and concern over missing
Tate's childhood which always hit him on bad days and
hangover days.

Riley turns to leave and notices something new hanging
over the few feet of solid wall running above the glass door
opening out into the hallway. It's the head of a boar. Its fur is a
light black, bristly and two tusks the width of Riley's thumb jut
out the animal's open mouth. The eyes are glass, the lips pulled
back in a frozen snarl.

Lars follows Riley's gaze and stands, circles back from
around his desk and walks over to pause next to Riley.

"I took him down last fall. In Texas. Pigs get out of their
pens down there and within a generation they're producing feral
piglets and growing as big as a few hundred pounds. He almost

had me. But I outran him. Would have been able to put more distance between the two of us before pulling back my bow, but it was hill country. I got surprisingly winded from the little hillocks."

"I've never killed anything on purpose before," Riley says.

"There's nothing like it," Lars sighs, shakes out his hands. Riley watches as the man's face flushes with blood and his eyes grow wide. "Especially taking down an animal designed by God to be a challenge to weaker beings. I started out with deer and elk. But then I moved on to predators. Now I only hunt predators. I only kill things that can potentially kill back."

"I suppose that's fair," Riley says, opening the office door and moving under the lintel capped with the taxidermy head of the boar. He takes quick steps, irrationally afraid the severed head will fall, tusks embedding in the mended crack of what used to be his soft fontanel.

23   PEACH

"Let's have our meeting outside," Peach says into the
device cupped by her hand. She's not used to the outmoded flip
phone. But it was the cheapest pre-pay option she could afford.
She didn't need anything with a screen or data. She needed
numbers she could press to dial up Lars and get him out of his
office and out of the building. Out to her.

"Susan said you were in the waiting room and that you
forgot something in your car? I thought I saw you look through
my office door. You're wearing a light pink cardigan, aren't
you?" Lars's voice raises in question.

"Yes," she goes on, "and then I got outside into the sun and
the heat. Wow, Lars, you need to be outside in this weather. I
think it's the first perfect day of spring and you can't miss it
sitting around looking at spreadsheets or whatever it is you do.
Those office buildings will slowly kill you. Come down. I'm
waiting on a bench at 9th and Bannock. You'll be able to
recognize me at a distance by that pink sweater you mentioned."

He laughs into the phone and says he'll come to her and he'll be bringing some pamphlets. She pushes a red button to end the call and settles back onto the wooden slats of the bench. A small songbird, gray and white feathers on his chest, attempts to pick up a burdensome twig in his petite beak. He holds the middle of the stick in his mouth and tries to lift off the ground again and again without success, letting high-pitched chirrups sound out his frustration. Peach reaches out to the bird and he drops the stick and flies away. She plucks up the brittle twig, breaks it into three parts and waits for the bird to return.

She hears a voice calling to her but it takes her a moment to respond to the name he's shouting.

"Lisa," Lars calls out when Peach turns her head. "You're right. Beautiful day." And then he holds up his hand to reveal a cluster of colorful pamphlets about personal finance just as a cumulous cloud rolls across the path of the sun.

Peach gets up and offers her hand in greeting. He takes it and then steps in for a hug. They bump cheeks briefly but Lars laughs off the awkwardness and hands over the papers to Peach.

"Brought these for you. Thought they could trigger some talking points. I wasn't sure if we were discussing 401Ks or real estate or generals today."

Peach looks down at the folded papers. One of them is entitled *Retirement and You*. Some of the others discuss the basics of the stock market or Roth IRAs.

"Right," she says and feigns interest in them. "I think I'd be more excited about Sloth IRAs. Just a whole bucket full of the furry guys." She opens one of the brochures and glances at the pictures of white people smiling in big houses before folding it back up.

Lars watches her with a goofy smile. She notes the gap in his teeth and finds it makes him more attractive instead of marring his looks. "So what's got you interested in your financial situation?"

"Oh," Peach says, "I think there's just something in the air. Just the season for it. I'm guessing a few weeks from now I won't even care about it anymore." Then she laughs and smiles back.

"Right. Let's walk and stretch our hammies a bit, okay?" he says and starts strolling east, Peach falling in next to him. "I thought you were going to say you weren't interested in bonds, that you were just trying to get to know me. I guess I'm vain or my radar is off. I thought you might have taken an interest in me."

Surprised by his candid speech, Peach is about to say he is right, that it is all about him. But as she's about to respond, Lars opens his mouth to yawn or start back up with his flirtatious honesty and a beetle as big as a grape, with a translucent sheen of blues and blacks on his carapace, flies directly into his open mouth.

The man sticks out his tongue and gags, fingers waggling at his neck like he's an orchestra conductor urging on instrumentalists who won't play. Peach believes he's likely just afraid of insects.

"Don't bite down," Peach warns and then steps in front of him to peer into his mouth. She puts her fingers onto his tongue without asking permission and delicately extricates the insect from the back of his throat. He closes his mouth and coughs, then spits. Peach holds her hand steady, the beetle perched on the fleshy mound connecting her thumb to her wrist.

"It's beautiful," she says and takes in its legs covered with fluffy feelers, its antennae moist with Lars's saliva. She tilts the bug up to the returning sunlight to see the spectrum of colors swirl about on the casing over its wings.

"It was in my mouth," Lars says, spits again. "I hate big bugs. Give me the creeps."

As the beetle flies off, she starts to cough herself. Her coughing is due to alarm instead of a bug tickling her uvula. She realizes the beetle was indeed inside the man's open mouth, at the back of his tongue. She looks at the man still hacking, his eyes squinting and focuses on his prematurely graying widow's peak. She thinks of that disembodied bird-wing birthmark spanning his upper back. Peach impulsively pulls him into her chest and hugs him tight. His body goes rigid, arms stiff at the sides of his torso.

"It has got to be you," she whispers into his chest.

"What?" he asks. "I didn't catch that."

"Retirement at sixty-two," she says, letting the man go and holding up the pamphlets, a beaming grin of lips stretched tight over teeth.

24   RILEY

He can't sleep. The idea of going back to work at the High Desert Trommel, into that smelly, hot fabrication shop keeps him from drifting off. Even though he'd be pushing papers for Double Al—a desk jockey until he learned to get by with half his toes and still wield a sledge with vigor—the oppressive heat of the shop floor is what sticks in his mind.

That and the omnipresent annoyance of the cards. Then the idea of the dead tattooist, a man he only met once while highly intoxicated, enters his mind. He laughs away the notion Walker proposed about his cards and the death of Roman Saucedo being linked. He cannot recall the details of the man's face as he crooks an arm under his neck. He gives up on calling it to mind. Once the moon is bright overhead, its light peeking through the blinds covering his bedroom window, Riley tosses off his covers and shuffles downstairs to his kitchen where he left the cards and their strange messages near the aluminum kettle on his stove.

He opens the latest letter, the one with well wishes about

Earth Day and a bunch of bull-themed lines. Carefully, he inspects the writing again. That spark, that inkling hits again and he wanders into his den. He flips on the light and illuminates piles of old papers and a seldom-used elliptical machine near a pre-fab desk of dark metal and blond wood.

Riley rummages around on the desk top and finds what he's hunting for. It's the square, white napkin embroidered with a poem, parts of its center dotted with holes from a pen pressing too hard into the pulp.

Dark waste blooming, sinews snapped. We are monsters.

He doesn't concern himself with the possible meaning or interpretation of the poem. Instead he eyes the letters. He brought the cards with him from the kitchen and opens up the Earth Day letter from Aldebaran and smoothes it flat with his hand. Riley takes a look at the M in "blooming" and the Ms used throughout the message in the card, especially the one in "matador". The similarities are clear; the legs of the Ms are all thicker at the bottom than the top and the lines that angle toward one another in the middle look to be drawn inward—their points not always matching up, as if the author drew each line individually, lifting his pen up from the paper four times with each M he wrote.

Then he takes the time to reread all the cards. His attention stops on the first card, the one he got as a belated birthday present. He reads the sentence to himself over and over. *Don't you just feel like a wolf in sheep's clothing sometimes?*

He knows Sev considers him to be a sly, opportunistic hunter. A wolf. He can't be sure the man has ever said so to his face, but most of their interactions have been under the haze of alcohol. Riley recalls referring to himself as a wolf in sheep's clothing on many occasions and he wonders if he could have labeled himself so in the poet's presence. Was the man echoing back the sentiment? He feels he's growing closer to uncovering the identity of his stalker. He puts the poem into the birthday card and piles the cards into a stack on his desk.

Then he peels off his white t-shirt he got for doing a fun run in college and pulls off his boxers. He gets onto his elliptical machine, the piece of equipment Walker joked about being only for women, and fumbles with turning it on. He lifts his legs to move the pedals forward. His left foot flares with ardent pain each time he presses down. But he doesn't quit his stride. He works off the anger and suspicion. He plots and fumes about his fist connecting solidly and rapidly with Sev's face.

WEDNESDAY, THE 29TH OF APRIL, 2015

25   PEACH

She looks for Aldebaran in the dim sky just after sunset, but gives up after an hour of hopeless searching. The star was visible earlier in the month but it is gone now, tracking the Pleiades across the sky like a beaten bull with a leash through its nose ring.

"*The follower*," she says to the sun millions of light-years away, the brightest star in the Taurus constellation. "That's what your name means. And that's what I'm trying to do."

She watches the lamb at the end of his tether. They're both out in the grassy common area between apartment buildings, the other residents inside with their television shows or late dinners. At first the animal wouldn't accept the loose collar around his neck, attached to the leash set into the ground with a spike. But once he realized he could ramble somewhat freely over the cool grass, he no longer would sound a plaintive bleat at the pressure around his neck. Peach pats him on his head but he doesn't pull his attention away from the earth and the smells and flavors against his flat lips.

She searches the black for a glimpse of another friend but it has left with the season as well. "And Hamal, my friend, the *head of the ram*, I miss you, too."

And then Peach recalls reading somewhere that the human eye, taking in the expanse of the night sky, can't see millions of stars. The eye only takes in about four thousand glimmering balls of gas. Peach thinks this number is more than enough. If there were many more, she'd truly go mad from their singing and questions and commands and opinions.

She holds her pink sapphire ring up to the universe, barely able to make out its shape in the black night. "What do you think of it?" she asks the stars.

"I needed it, sure, but rent will be hard to make this month. Money matters seem so asinine. But I must remind myself what cycle I'm in. Taurus. Governed by the House of Material Wealth. I'll relax into it. It's all part of my path and your instruction. I'm sure of it."

After a time of silence, so she can listen for the suggestions and advice of the stars, she pulls the camping stake used to secure Roman to the ground and leads him back to her apartment. She's careful to be on the lookout for her building manager and any questions he'd pose about the small sheep.

At her front door, she runs into Linx leaving her concrete-slab patio. He's sullen, his hair a mess from brittle, old gel and body oils. He sniffs hard to gather up a bit of phlegm and then leans over to the bark-covered planting bed near the sidewalk and shoots it out his mouth. Peach smiles at his bad habit and is acutely aware she hasn't seen him since making her first sacrifice days ago. She wonders if he'll be able to see how much she's changed in so little time.

"I knocked on your door and called your cell phone. No answer," he says.

Peach hands him the green and silver leash attached to the

lamb and unlocks her door. Then she steps aside and Linx shuffles in, the lamb trotting behind him. She takes a moment to appreciate her favorite males entering her home.

"And I haven't seen you in days. What's going on?"

There is a sulky presence in his tone and she notes it, understanding his frustration. Peach knows his question is self-referential. She's used to Linx thinking all things in Peach's purview relate somehow to him.

"I've just been a little stressed over money lately. Patti's been bugging me about my debt payments. And then there's the rent," she covers. Money isn't at the forefront of her mind, but she knows Linx will buy it and find sympathy for her. A sympathy he would not, could not, express during a recounting of the way she planted the sharp needle of a tattoo gun inside the ear canal of a man.

His face animates then and he puts his arms around her. They are slim but his hold is firm. Their eyes lock, pairs level to one another. She matches his gaze for longer than she would have in the past. She wonders if he's just come from his job managing a Vietnamese eatery because he smells of fry oil and ginger.

"It'll be fine," he announces. "What's up with your rent? Did they increase it? You don't usually have problems paying it."

"Just an added expense this month. Nothing to worry about."

"You know," he says and pulls away from her to study her face. His smile has gone soft and Peach squirms a little in his grasp. "I have plenty of room at my house. That spare bedroom is just a place for junk. We wouldn't have to share a room. It could be all yours. It's just an idea. Like two peas in a pod."

"Like two bees in a fog," she teases, knowing Linx is prone to mucking up idioms though he's managed this one just fine.

"Like two knees on a cod," he plays.

She relaxes a bit, forces out a giggle until her laughter becomes natural. Then she unlatches his fingers from her back and steps into the kitchen. She pulls a bag of beef jerky from her cupboard pantry and opens it with her teeth. She offers the open bag to Linx and he crinkles his nose at the smell of animal flesh.

"Just checking," she says and then pulls a length of rough meat, with dry white connective tissue running lengthwise down the center, from the bag. She puts the end of it in her mouth and sucks at it to soften the texture. Linx holds his stare and she knows he waits for an answer to his proposal. His face has returned to its slack somberness.

"I'm going to go putter around with my clay," she says. "Have you had dinner?"

26   RILEY

Instead of going into the strip club, Riley leans against the side of his Nissan and watches the door of Blaze Lounge through the driver's side mirror. He's forgone a jacket and he keeps his arms wrapped around his middle. The night is pleasantly warm but his nerves have him shaking, peculiarly, because he has never been flummoxed by confrontation before. He waits for nearly an hour, his eyes focused on the mirror until his mark comes out the front door, his hands cupped around his leather duster, a ratty t-shirt framing his muscles.

It's Sev, the Australian boyfriend of Nell Hyde. He's the poet, the control freak, the cuckold, the man who sends Riley disturbing greeting cards.

Riley counts out three deep breaths to center himself. His antsy shaking begins to abate as he walks toward the Aussie. Sev doesn't see Riley approach. He gets right up to the man before Sev stops and blinks quickly in response to Riley materializing in front of him.

"It's my favorite chum," Sev says to Riley and the word play is not lost on him. He's aware the man would gladly throw him into the ocean as bloody bait or consider him little more than the finale of a hand job. Riley's not sure he deserves a nicer moniker, but he's certain he doesn't deserve the written harassment.

Sev pulls at one of the gold hoops in his ears and then tries to walk around Riley, to the sidewalk bordering the main thoroughfare next to Blaze Lounge.

"I want to talk to you," Riley says but Sev doesn't stop. The bulky Australian keeps his eyes forward and calls back to Riley.

"Chummy chummers chumming with chum. My, how they chum their lives away."

"Did you get a BA in English or just an Associate? Just enough schooling to feel clever using your words?" Riley shouts back at him.

Sev keeps walking and leaves off his baiting. "I've got to get my Kung Pao Chicken before Twin Lotus closes. And I have no interest in talking to you, asshole."

Riley bristles at the word "asshole." He's used to being called that by women, but when men use the term, he can feel the muscles in his calves tighten and the sweat quicken on the back of his neck. He steps quickly, careful about how he strides with his left foot, and places himself in front of Sev. The man stops short and they stare at one another. Riley's feet are nearly off the curb of the sidewalk and Sev is backed by a row of gnarly, half-dead juniper bushes like the ones directly in front of the strip club.

"What?" Sev asks him. "You're always mucking around here with me and with Nell. Are you tired of trying to get her starkers and now you're moving on to me? Want me to be your sheila?" The poet smiles, drops his duster to the ground, and steps into Riley's personal space. He smells like cut limes and unwashed denim.

Now Riley knows for sure Nell hasn't told him about their sleeping together. He gives the girl more credit than he used to; she might be smart enough to know when to shut her mouth. Or, Riley considers, she really was too wasted to remember the night. In either case, he's glad Sev doesn't know. He can't imagine what the man would do if he knew his girlfriend had been screwed by Riley. It could prompt the poet to do more than send weird cards in the mail.

"Chubby, OCD Aussies don't give me boners. So no, you're in the clear when it comes to my affections, dick hole. But you do know why I'm here," Riley says and resists stepping away from Sev. The man towers over him by a good several inches.

"I have an idea why you're here, little guy, but I'd think you'd be inside the club instead of outside preventing me from getting Chinese food before the restaurant shutters."

Riley hasn't been insulted about his svelte frame and middling, five-foot-nine height in years. After the taunting he received in junior high for being unusually short, he developed a thick skin. The rough veneer still holds strong.

He does his best not to blink, his eyes tilted upward to look at Sev's nose. It's bulbous and slightly askew, no doubt the product of several fist fights. Riley has been in a fair number of scrapes as well. Luckily, he didn't wear their effects on his face.

"It's about what you've written. To me," Riley pauses to let Sev's brain soak in what he's said. He folds his fingers into his palms but keeps his hands at his sides.

Sev snickers and a fleck of spit escapes his lips. He steps closer into Riley's chest. His breath is hot and hits Riley on his forehead. At this range, Riley can see specks of black in the man's brown eyes, oblong like wild rice.

"I know what I've written, you entitled prick. Question is, do you know what any of it means?"

The contents of the cards flash across Riley's mind. He

doesn't, in fact, know what they mean. All he knows of is their effects: anger, anxiety, paranoia. And it's the feelings which cause Riley to bring his right fist up, fast, and hook the poet square in the soft flesh under his chin.

Sev's head snaps backward but his legs remain planted on the sidewalk and his body shows no signs of losing balance. He shakes his head from side to side, looks down at the crown of Riley's head and pushes him off the curb, into the nearest lane of traffic.

Riley keeps his ass from hitting the asphalt by shooting out his arms wide and centering his weight. He's lucky enough to keep his injured foot from taking too much of the abrupt impact from the descent off the walkway, but he has little time to recover completely before a minivan trundles around the gentle curve of the street. Riley hops forward to the gutter to avoid the car as it passes by, the driver making no attempt to slow his speed.

Sev snatches at Riley's cotton button-down shirt with both hands and lifts him back onto the sidewalk before tossing him toward the bank of spiky junipers behind him. His torso sinks into the hedge of the prickly-limbed, waist-high conifers and he gets long scratches down his hands and his lower back where his shirt has ridden up to expose his pasty skin.

The poet watches him flounder to escape the needles, his lips tight together. He keeps his eyes on Riley but bends down to his duster, pulls his fingerless gloves from a pocket and slips them over his palms. Riley doesn't make the mistake of standing back up completely. He uses the time Sev gives him to gain his footing to pitch up quickly and tackle the man's knees. He hits the poet with his full weight, collapsing his knee joints while Sev tries to pivot away from the assault, only to land on the edge of the curb. His ribcage thwacks on the concrete.

Riley's hands are bruised and bloodied, pinched under the poet's weight. He tugs them sharply out from under the man, bits of dirt and a small piece of plastic imbedded in the flesh of his left palm. He stands up. Sev remains on the ground, his arms outstretched, his mouth open and gasping for air.

Riley takes the opportunity to gain the upper hand. He's not above fighting dirty. In fact, he's always been for it. He considers a fight won a fight won, regardless of tactics. He picks up his right leg and brings it down on the small of Sev's back and his efforts are greeted with the sound of popping bone.

"You piece of shit," he says to the man, kicking at his exposed ribs. "You don't own people. You're not on this planet just to watch people and terrorize them and possess them."

And then Riley forgets himself, his right foot aching from the repeated impacts with Sev's torso. He reels back his wounded left foot and plants it directly under Sev's armpit. The intense shock of smashed, newly-forming flesh and nerves battered against bone makes his testicles tighten. He pisses himself a little before crumpling to the sidewalk next to Sev.

Both men lie prone on the white concrete, a streetlight casting a ray on their tiny war. Riley notices the slim-necked outline of a mourning dove hunkering down on the lamp. It does not coo or fly away but simply watches them, spent after their fight. Sev doesn't make a sound but Riley lets fly a slew of swear words until the bouncer of Blaze Lounge sticks his head out of the door of the club and tells him to calm the fuck down.

FRIDAY, THE 1ST OF MAY, 2015

27 PEACH

There is no way she will get the smell off of her hands, so she asks the cashier at the garden center for a squirt of sanitizing alcohol before loading up her small pushcart with more gardening supplies. Lifting the heavy bags has caused her to pull something in the middle of her back next to her spinal column. She vows to start exercising but she knows she won't. She's never played sports, never lifted weights or punched a heavy bag. The most exercise she gets is from occasional sex with Linx.

She pushes her cart into a small greenhouse at the end of a parking lot—the store protecting their annuals from the last frost of the season that typically comes in early May, before all the snow has left the summit of Bogus Basin. She ditches her shopping cart for a moment and walks the short rows of shelved plants. The little plastic tent is warm and the air smells of peat moss and peppery nasturtiums. A flat of bright fuchsia impatiens catches her eye and she slides two of the best looking specimens off the wooden planking and places them softly into the bottom of her cart.

Next, she locates a light-weight, bowl-shaped pot and a small bag of potting soil. She runs through her shopping list in her mind and then takes her items through checkout. After a man rings her up, he eyes her cart and pushes a number on a phone hanging from a tall pillar in the middle of the checkout stand. He holds the receiver away from his mouth and yells into it for help, his voice infiltrating the store over the loudspeaker. A teenage boy with bangs swept to the side of his forehead appears in seconds and ferries the cart to Peach's car, despite her protests. She tells him she can do it herself but then her back spasms and she shuts up.

"You having a nice day?" the kid asks, likely something he's been trained to do.

"Yes," Peach answers. "I'm just getting some things for some projects. It's the warm weather. Makes me want to work with the earth."

"Okay," is all he says in response and waits for Peach to open the trunk of her Honda. He loads the heavy, glossy plastic sacks first, then sets the sage-green pot and impatiens on top of the bulging bags.

"Anything else I can do for you?"

"No," she says and closes the hatch. "Happy Beltane!"

"My what?"

"Happy Beltane. Merry May Day," she tries.

He stares at her blankly and she thinks to let him go, but decides instead to give him a little education.

"It's a pagan celebration, to usher in the summer season. It welcomes the warm days with dancing and bonfires. Herders would move their cattle from winter pastures to their summer pastures." She waits for a light of interest to play on the boy's face. But he gives her nothing.

"Sometimes," she continues before opening up her car door

and flinging her purse into the back seat, "modern-day pagans will celebrate by going skyclad. Do you know what that means?"

"I have to get back to work," the boy says, looking over his shoulder to the garden center.

"It means they dance about in the nude. Men, women, all sweaty and wild, writhing around roaring fires. It's animalistic and powerful and a big middle-finger to polite society."

His eyes snap back to Peach and he shakes the hair from his eyes. "Cool," he quips.

"The things they don't teach you in school," she answers back.

28   RILEY

"You've severely compacted the stitches into the mending tissue at the end of your amputation. What were you doing, Mr. Wanner?"

The doctor at the immediate care facility shows Riley a stern brown and frowning mouth. While Riley should have gone to see the doctor who observed him while he convalesced in the hospital, he didn't feel like explaining his stupidity to a person who tried his best to properly manage his wounded foot.

"I completely forgot myself. I was playing soccer. And I hit the PVC piping around the net."

The doctor laughs and sets Riley's foot down on the white paper covering the examination table. "You're telling me that your balance is good enough a few weeks after major surgery for you to play soccer? And you're telling me that you kicked a piece of plastic and that's what drove your stitches deep into your flesh? And all those abrasions and bruises you've cleaned up on your knuckles and wrists are what, from falling on the field?"

"Yes?" Riley responds and only realizes after the word has left his mouth that it came out as a question.

"No matter what you did and how you might have done it," the doctor answers and picks up a tablet to make notes on, "it will require us cleaning out the wound and pulling those stitches. And putting new ones back in. I can't do much for the pain. You've already received a prescription for a pain killer like oxycodone, correct?"

"Is that what you call those white, round pills? I've just been referring to them as my La-La Nummers," Riley jokes. Then he wonders if he should act as though he knows something about soccer and playing it, even though he despises the sport. "But yeah, do what you need to do. It was worth it. Playing soccer, I mean. It felt good to kick...balls?"

The doctor doesn't respond to his levity but flicks his eyes up to Riley's unfinished tattoo. He doesn't ask what the black ink is supposed to be, whether or not the line is complete or if there was supposed to be more drawn there. And Riley doesn't offer an explanation.

Riley leans back and tucks his arms under his head while the doctor applies a topical anesthetic to his foot. He feels strong, resilient and victorious, despite the stabbing sensation in his wound. Riley is certain his display of aggression will cause Sev to back off. The Earth Day card will be the last he receives. And while that means he'll have more time to focus on other problems— like his finances and whether or not he should go back to work for Double Al or worry over Detectives Mallory and Sewell prodding him for more information about the dead tattooist—for now, in this moment, Riley rests in a miasma of smugness and self-righteousness he hasn't felt since bagging Nell.

The doctor pulls a black piece of stiff threading out of Riley's foot and holds it up for him to see. It's caked in scabby blood. It looks like a lure a fisherman might toss into running water in hopes of catching a fat trout.

"Say goodbye to your old bindings," he says and tosses the stitch onto a folded paper towel.

"Done," Riley replies.

29   PEACH

She looks away from her laptop screen perched on the old, wooden desk in her living room. Now that Roman roams the entire apartment, she's been able to clear out the kennel fencing and use her desk again. She has more cleaning to do, careful to check for urine or worse left around the place by her wooly companion. She used a staple gun to tack lengths of plastic wrap over her carpets and it helps a bit to control the filth. She's drained, though, by the tasks she's created for herself all because she ran away with a helpless lamb slick with afterbirth.

Her eyes are seeing double and she can't do any more research for the night. The room is dimly lit and the glow of the screen sticks in her retinas as she cups her hands over her eyes and gives them a rest. These are all the things she sees in her mind: triggers, fuses, timers, incendiary devices. Too many elements to consider after a long week of activities. Yet she knows she is capable. Blueprints and tutorials abound online. When she is fresh, she will be able to craft and create.

She pulls the drapes open that cover her front window and looks to the slab patio out her front door. The bright pink impatiens she has planted seem to have their own inner source of light and their vibrancy makes Peach smile. The days are growing longer and the sun sticks around tonight, despite the smattering of wispy clouds lit lavender in the evening sky.

She thinks to pick up the book she purchased by Fredrik Pohl. It's about underground tunnels and chambers honeycombing Venus, tucked full of alien artifacts humans have discovered and uncovered from the planet. But then Peach hears a shout, a high-pitched yell which reminds her of the baying of a stressed hound. Then another shout and a giggle follow and she realizes some of the kids who live in the apartment complex are out playing, scampering about before the impending dusk.

She decides she could use some air and a stretch of her legs. She checks on Roman before going outside. He's found a piece of junk mail on the floor of the kitchen and he gums at a corner of the envelope. A runny line of mucous escapes his nose. A streak of blue soy ink stains the wool at his chin.

"Good boy," she says to him and then she lets go of her thoughts and machinations. She replaces them with the smell of lilac and the hum of the first crickets of the warming season.

Out of curiosity, she follows the sound of the children and finds them behind her apartment building, busy with their amusement in the grassy common area she frequents in the middle of the night with Roman in tow. There are four children, two boys and two girls, tossing darts into circles lain upon the grass. The biggest circle is a hula hoop and the smallest circle is a well-used jump rope looped on the ground in a close approximation of an oval.

When the children see Peach walking toward them, one of the boys demands the others hide the large darts behind their backs. They stay silent and look up at Peach with heavy-lidded eyes.

"You're playing with lawn darts," Peach smiles. "Do your parents know?"

The biggest boy—his belly hanging over his low-riding pants, his chest full with all the chubbiness of an overfed eight-year-old—does his best to bluff Peach.

"They play with these darts all the time. They said it was okay."

Peach sticks out her hand and one of the girls steps forward and turns over the two darts she holds. Their oversized, plastic fins are burnt orange or yolk yellow and brittle. The metal on the darts is rusty where they meet the long, plastic shafts. Peach assumes they're from the seventies, old and worn and were likely hidden away in a garage or storage bin for years. Until the children found them.

"Do you know the United States government banned lawn darts years ago? You can't even ship them into the country. And do you know why?"

The girl who handed over her darts without prompting shakes her head no. There's a smear of something purple near her lower lip. The others keep silent.

"Because thousands of children were getting skewered by the metal points of the darts. And some were killed. I think I heard of a little girl dying. She was what, seven?" And she poses the question to the girl who gave away the darts, with a grass-stained dress, stoic with shame, as if she'll know the answer.

"Nuh-uh," the thick boy speaks up.

"It's true. Go ask your parents," Peach says. "Unless they don't really know you've found these and are tossing them around."

The other girl, thin with a pinched face, tilts her chin up and smirks. "So what are you going to do? Tell on us?"

Peach tosses one of the large lawn darts at the smaller target from six feet away. It lands dead center in the piece of twine. The kids break out into smiles and the smallest boy claps his hands together.

"Stars no," Peach says. "It's a holiday. No reason why we can't all have some fun together."

"What holiday? We didn't get off school," the outspoken boy asks but Peach does not answer.

And then she takes her other dart, the one with the ugly, chipped yellow fins, rust smudging off on her fingers, and she throws it. But instead of sending it sailing toward the target, she pitches it upward, into the air, as hard as she can, knowing it could come down on any of their heads.

"Scatter!" she screams, and they scream back gibberish and giggle and all go running amok into the gloaming.

SATURDAY, THE 2ND OF MAY, 2015

30   RILEY

He looks at the bottle of Maker's Mark. It sits on his deck railing, the amber liquid catching the new sun of a weekend morning. He hasn't taken a sip yet, and while part of him wants to get hammered in a celebratory sort of way, he doesn't feel safe to do so. Riley is concerned about retribution from Sev, no longer certain his show of strength will keep him at bay. If the man was bold and strange enough to send him the cards and unafraid to fight him when provoked, then Riley figures he'll have no problem coming at him for kicking him while he was down. Literally.

So he chooses to enjoy the day sans alcohol and the choice isn't too hard to live with once he's firm on staying alert. There are already two oxycodone dissolving in his belly to help with the pain in his foot and the lesser pain lancing the skin of his hands. He tells himself he can drink again, someday soon, once the danger has passed. Then he can toast himself, be it alone or with Walker, for screwing Nell *and* Sev, albeit in different ways.

He looks down at the decking underneath his propped up foot. He had it installed in his backyard last year, had it stained a deep auburn and explained away the cost for the value it added to his home and social life. The decking could accommodate a large table, a cluster of sofas covered in durable, all-weather material, and a grill. Except it stood nearly unused, tasked only with holding up Riley's weight. Never that of twenty or forty people in revelry, drunk and garrulous.

A horsefly lands on his wrapped foot. In an effort to give the wound some air and keep off of it, he'd taken it out of a stiff, foam wrap the doctor had insisted he wear to avoid any more imaginary soccer accidents. Now it rests draped in gauze, and the fly does its best to stab its leg tips around the weaving, looking for some sort of purchase for its eggs.

He pitches up and waves the fly away from his wound but it comes back in seconds, lands and goes about its poking.

He turns his body to a little glass table next to his chair, cloudy with water stains, and picks up his heavy tome about the stars. He has torn an old business card from his lawyer days down the middle and marked the passages about the stars Hamal and Aldebaran. He puts the book in his lap and wonders why Sev had a thing for stars. Riley wasn't much for literature or poetry in school. He couldn't call to mind any references to stories or characters Sev might be drawing upon. If he was referencing literature at all.

Then Riley considers there might be very little meaning in Sev's writings. They could be bizarre missives meant to scare without an ounce of allusion or metaphor within them. But then he wonders how a writer could possibly write without meaning, hidden or plain, driving his pen.

Just in case some new connection comes to mind, Riley reads each passage again and this time he notes the constellations where Hamal and Aldebaran spin. Hamal belongs to Aries and Aldebaran belongs to Taurus. Both constellations represent the bodies of animals, specifically the heads of a male sheep and a male cow.

"What's with the head fixation?" he asks out loud and thinks back to the boar over the door of his financial advisor's office. "I look at the stars and don't see any shapes. Let alone heads."

But the words Aries and Taurus stick with him. They stay in his mind as he fights a war with the fat, black fly. Until he finally loses his temper and smacks the fly dead with a lucky swat, at the same time pummeling his already throbbing foot. The pain sears and to keep his mind from it, the words slip past his lips over and over, as he considers whether or not he's made the right choice by forgoing the booze.

"Aries, Taurus, Aries, Taurus…," he picks up speed with the new mantra.

He fetches the bottle, holds it up in the mid-morning light, swirls it, shakes it about, and does his best to make out the shapes of beasts in the bubbling foam.

PEACH

"It's a Pyrrhic victory," Peach tells Linx, the hamburger between her wheat buns sliding away from her lettuce and tomato. She tucks the flesh back in place and takes another bite.

"A what?" he asks. "Remember I went to public school in California. Lived with my Thai-speaking mom. I don't know all your fancy terms."

She dips her ears from shoulder to shoulder as she chews and when she's done she puts the meat down and takes a sip of iced tea. "What happened at your work. When your boss was a giant prick over the phone to the owner of the company that comes in at night to clean. They both lost, in the end, even though your manager gave their work to another cleaning crew. He might have had a Pyrrhic victory. He may have won, but he might end up worse off than the losers of the battle. Time will tell. Maybe these new guys will be really bad at Cloroxing toilet bowls."

"Okay," Linx starts and leans back in his metal chair. He's

done with his salad and picks at his teeth with a toothpick. Then he hacks up phlegm and spits it into a planter of pansies at his back. Peach swallows in disgust instead of smiling this time. It's a cultural trait of Linx's she's never gotten used to seeing while she's eating.

A cell phone starts ringing, a set of mimicked cow bells going off, and Linx looks around at the other people lunching on the outdoor patio. Peach stuffs a fry into her mouth before she realizes it's her phone. She wipes her greasy fingers on her napkin and hurriedly digs the flip phone out of her purse.

Linx cocks his head when he sees the handset. "New phone? You going retro or something? I don't think it'll be cool again until several decades have gone by."

Peach answers the call instead of answering her friend. She already knows who's on the other end of the line. Only one man has this number.

"Lisa?" the voice asks. "This is Lars Apitz."

"Yeah, hi," Peach says and then brings her other hand up to muffle the conversation. Linx watches her intently as she speaks. He thumps on his slender ribcage with his fingertips and then abandons that move to play with a plaid scarf wrapped around his neck.

"You said you were going to call my workplace and schedule another meeting. You know, one where we could sit down in my office so you could look at my materials, other than those few crappy pamphlets I brought to you? But the receptionist said you haven't scheduled anything yet. So I thought, why not call and get you in the appointment book?"

Peach keeps her eyes on the remains of her burger, aware of the attention coming her way from Linx. "Okay, sure. I just don't know what will work for my schedule yet." She picks up her drink and takes a sip.

There is a short silence on the other end of the phone and then Lars sniffs and begins talking again. "Right. So I might be totally wrong about this, but I get the feeling you really don't care about your retirement portfolio. And I could be misreading that awkward hug the other day, but Lisa, would you rather date me or just listen to my money market account suggestions?"

She hadn't expected him to be so dryly funny and she nearly expels the mouthful of iced tea onto Linx sitting opposite of her. She coughs in order to get the liquid down and then tries to answer as slyly as possible.

"I think you might be right about that."

Lars laughs, too, and continues. "So that means you'll go out with me tonight?"

"Tonight?" she says a little too loudly into the phone.

"I know it's last minute, but the warming weather makes me want to get out. I've got some serious cabin fever. Can you believe I'm actually in my office right now, doing work? On a Saturday?"

"I guess I can?" she answers and then when he doesn't say anything back, she has to clarify. "I mean about your doing work."

"And what about some drinks and maybe *tapas* tonight?"

"I guess I can?" she says again and Linx narrows his eyes at her. They are deep brown crescents, no distinguishing between iris and pupil.

"Great," Lars says, "I'll text you later when I come up with details and time. I hadn't thought it all through before my mouth started running. I thought you'd say you had a boyfriend or a jealous lover."

Peach finally lets her eyes drift up to Linx's glare and she's met with a cool stoicism.

"Sure, okay," Peach pushes. "I'll let you get back to work then."

After they end the conversation and Peach flips down the casing on the outdated phone, Linx doesn't waste time in asking questions.

"Who was that?"

"Ah, no one, really," and then she tries to change the subject. "How was your salad? I see there were pecans in there with the Fuji apple. Good pairing."

Linx taps out a little beat of nervousness on the brick pavers at his feet. His upper thigh rubs along the leg of the wrought-iron table and the entire dining set vibrates.

"I think you just agreed to a date with some guy. While I'm sitting here. Eating. With you."

"What? No, Linx," Peach tries to explain but he's already in the process of standing and he tosses his napkin on the tabletop with the flourish of a victorious bullfighter.

"Sometimes I wonder if your heart is made of fucking rock, Peach."

And then Linx is moving away from the patio. The other patrons of the restaurant do their best not to stare, but all of their conversations are hushed to catch the drama happening around them.

Peach decides not to go after him, to let him have time to cool off. She looks at her hamburger and suddenly doesn't have the stomach to finish it. A family the next table over sits in silence until she can't take their muted embarrassment for her anymore. She speaks to the mother, her hair in a messy updo, a ten-month-old pulling at her blouse.

"He's a vegetarian," Peach says and points to her burger. Then the family smiles, starts talking to one another again and Peach waits in her own silence for the arrival of the check.

32   RILEY

With the help of his laptop, he spends forty-five minutes looking into the sign of Aries. Once he finishes with that sign, he spends the same amount of time looking into the sign of Taurus. Then he spends the rest of the afternoon looking into the sign of Pisces, the double fish, his own birth sign.

He's overwhelmed by the amount of information available about astrology. He'd only ever given thought to his own sign once or twice in his life, preferring to think the entire horoscope thing was complete nonsense, a thing for spiritual ninnies and those who believed they were governed by fate. And he isn't ready to change his mind on the matter. Because while some traits of a Pisces fit him, he doesn't feel that the zodiac sign is any more in tune with his personality than some of the traits he's read about associated with Aries and Taurus. He has the authority of a ram and the stubbornness of a bull.

And then he finds a link to an article written about Pisces people and money. He clicks on it and a garishly bright green font pops off the page. He turns his eyes away for a moment but there is an after-burn of lines in his vision.

"This better be worth the headache," he says and turns back to the webpage with its black background. The site is antiquated; the color-scheme something reminiscent of basic HTML homepages in the late nineties. There are no ads popping up on the side panels of the page and it's just one long scroll of blocky paragraphs talking about North Nodes and Houses and other astrological terms Riley doesn't understand.

A few paragraphs in, his eyes catch something of interest. He reads that Pisces folk usually have good ideas on how to make money, but because they're a dualistic sign, they might have problems with flipping back and forth on projects instead of sticking with any one idea.

Riley thinks of his own work experience, moving from the life of a white-collar, well-paid contract lawyer to damaging his toes to the point of amputation as a laborer in a metal fabrication shop. He thinks of other times he radically switched direction in career, and thus, ability to make money.

Even now, he feels like work is an untenable reality and living off the rest of his bank account coupled with disability checks is better than perhaps taking up his law practice once again.

"And what's this gem?" he speaks to his empty house and brings his finger up to the computer to trace a new bit of information. He reads it out loud.

"Pisces are often times good at marrying into money or starting partnerships with people who either make a good deal of money or are inheritors of money."

And then Riley immediately thinks back to his conversation with Lars Apitz, the man reminding Riley about the stipulations he'd need to meet in order for Riley to receive more of his parents' estate. True, if he were to marry, he'd have to wait five years for the first money to trickle in, but instead of that being a deterrent, he was beginning to think of it as a reason to get serious about finding an eligible match.

Instead of asking Kristin to be amiable to a paternity test, one he's certain would prove his hypothesis that Tate is not related to Riley in any way, he chooses to consider marriage and marriage only. He thinks about being thirty-one, old enough to settle down. He thinks of meals shared in Italian restaurants while wearing cuff links and rocking a pocket square. He thinks of routine sex without condoms. He thinks of hundreds of thousands of dollars and a prenuptial agreement.

And then he thinks of the one woman he'd ever consider marrying. The other living soul he considered calling to talk to about his recent amputation aside from the five-year-old Tate. The woman he chose not to call on Easter for fear he would hear the deep timbre of a new man speaking of Catholic mass or family or her hips from somewhere in the background.

"Mayra," he says out loud to no one. "Mayra Vega Pena, the one I didn't ask to leave my bed at two am after fucking. The one who would wear my old charity fun run shirts as nightgowns. The woman who smelled like cinnamon and citrus."

"If only she didn't hate me," he mumbles. Then he closes his eyes and can see rows of white angles, after-burn from the screen, brilliant and enduring on the backs of his eyelids.

"Maybe it's been enough time. Maybe that hate has mellowed."

33 PEACH

"You have a methodical way of drinking margaritas. Makes me wonder if you ritualize everything. Like lining up your silverware before you eat or stacking your bras just so," Lars teases Peach. His body is turned toward hers at the rooftop patio of a Brazilian restaurant in southeast Boise.

Peach licks the rocky salt off the rim of the glass and then immediately takes a swig of the virgin strawberry margarita. Lars had ordered the drink for her and then she had gotten up, feigning the need to walk downstairs and use the restroom, to track down the waiter and tell him to change her drink to a non-alcoholic mocktail. So far, Lars hadn't been able to tell. And Peach didn't plan on letting him close enough to her to smell her breath, which would be absent of the smell of liquor, only tart and sweet from the pink-red berries blended with the ice.

"I like the salt and then I like the drink," she says and shrugs her shoulders.

"It's cute," he says and then follows with, "and you, too."

You're cute."

Peach accidently dips her nose in the wide-mouthed glass when she takes another swallow of the drink and then does her best to wipe the crushed ice and juice off with the back of her hand. She looks out over the side of the low walls encasing the bar. The sun is nearly down in the west and it casts the Boise foothills in shades of plum and rose. The shadows of the gullies between peaks are runs of black on an otherwise ruddy pallet.

He doesn't wait for a response to his compliment but nods at the spring asparagus, grilled and coated in parmesan, sitting untouched in front of her. "You aren't into spears?"

"Excuse me?" she says and Peach can feel her face grow red. She hopes Lars will think it's the slight chill carried in by the wind. The wide umbrellas tucked into the corners of the rooftop patio billow in its embrace.

"Your asparagus," he says and picks up a length of green vegetable and folds it into his open mouth.

She feels relief and reaches down, plucks up one of the spears and puts the forked top of it between her teeth, sucking off the cheese before biting down. "No," she says as she swallows, "they're great."

"So Lisa," he says, wiping his hands on his tan trousers, "do you like tattoos?"

And again she can feel the blood in her cheeks. "Sure. But I don't think I'd ever get one. I'm too noncommittal."

"I have three total," and then he looks into Peach's eyes and she does her best to hold his gaze for a second before looking down at her drink.

"Most people ask me where they are."

"Oh, okay," she says. "Where are they?"

"I have two on my ankle and the other one is on my ass. It was a phase I was going through, back when I thought I might want to do something especially hippie-esque. Like organic farming or commune management, if there is such a thing. I thought there was such a future for me. Back before student loans were due."

Peach keeps playing along. "What's the tattoo on your behind?"

Lars stands and unbuckles the braided, leather belt at his hips. Peach looks around at the other tables and people with their happy hour cocktails but none of them look their way. He unzips his pants and pulls them down to reveal a pair of boxer-briefs in navy blue. He looks over his shoulder and tugs the elastic of his underwear down his left butt cheek. Peach sees nothing but white skin and the suggestion of a crack still hidden by fabric. And then her eyes lock onto the faded ink.

A moon, in curved crescent, with the shading of dark and light on the sliver in line with the perspective of someone in the Northern Hemisphere, is displayed on his skin.

"No," she says as he pulls up his pants and regains his seat. "No way."

She thinks of all the symbols: the bird's wing birthmark, the widow's peak, the beetle diving into his mouth and now, the moon on his backside. They are all signs. They all have rich, cavernous meanings.

"Hey," Lars defends, "at least it isn't Road Runner or a lover's name."

"Right," she says. "No, I mean it's special. It's beautiful."

"Thanks," he says and they both sip their drinks and take in the hills awash in dimming light. Then his voice lowers and his spine straightens.

"I have to tell you, Lisa, that I'm actually separated. From my wife."

Peach puts down the virgin margarita and tries to smooth out the line she knows cracks along her forehead. "I didn't know you were married."

He looks at her, lines of puzzlement on his face as well. "How would you know that I'm married if I didn't tell you?"

"Right, I wouldn't," she covers and as he tries to explain, she waves away his attempts with the palm of her hand.

"You don't need to explain anything, Lars. It's not my business. It should be left between you and your wife, as odd as it sounds for me to say out loud. I'm just out to have some fun tonight. Let's not get too serious about anything too soon, okay?"

Peach looks up at mountains and then cranes her body around to check out Bogus Basin, the peak many Boiseans ski each winter. She motions for Lars to turn around and look at the hilltop as well. It's still capped in a dollop of snow, soon to be gone with the warming days.

"Do you know how Bogus Basin got its name?"

He shakes his head and so Peach goes on.

"Back in days of the gold rush, when Idaho City was the biggest town in the Northwest and thousands of gold miners were flooding into the mountains around Boise, they had their fair share of conmen come out West, too. And those who were dishonest to begin with or more likely, had no luck in finding a rich strike of gold ore, would turn to counterfeiting."

She holds up her right hand, finger encircled by the pink sapphire, dull in the evening light. The band isn't made of solid gold, but plated in white gold. She taps the ring with one of her fingernails and smiles.

"They wouldn't make fake coins or bills. They'd make fake gold. Each area of the Boise front would bring in different kinds of gold, with different karat levels into the assay office in Idaho City. And the gold that came from that peak would more often times than not be fake. No one would take it in exchange for goods. It was bogus. Hence, Bogus Basin."

"Huh," Lars says and settles his arm on the table, stretched out to be closer to Peach. "So it wasn't real wealth. Only something made to look like it had value."

"Right."

"I guess that would have been me, then," Lars says and pulls the skewered olives out of his martini. "Back in the mining days."

"Well, now I'm not going to let you handle my money," Peach says, tries her hand at a joke.

And Lars laughs so hard he shoots martini up into his nose and pinches at his nostrils, coughs a bit at the stinging pain.

34 RILEY

It isn't until he's halfway down the side street in Boise's east end that he considers Mayra could have moved from her house long ago. He can't remember the last time he actually visited her at her little bungalow with its brick terrace in the front yard and stands of giant, feather-like grasses bordering the front walk. But he's already made the effort to pull a shoe over his foot and drive to find her, or at least check out her house, so he decides not to turn around.

Locust Street is lined with old growth sycamores and oak and maple, but absent any locust trees. A woman walks a small Yorkshire terrier on a harness, a light attached to the leash, casting wobbly rays onto the sidewalk. Riley slows as he approaches the house and turns his head to the right to see if a light is on or her old Bureau of Land Management pickup she takes into the field is in the driveway.

What he gets instead is a view of Mayra entertaining a handful of friends on her front patio. He turns away, tries to speed up, but she's already seen him. He can see her stand up sharply from her plastic folding chair and put her hand to her eyebrows like she's looking out to sea or into a bright expanse of sky.

He turns the next corner and puts his car into park. Riley drops his forehead onto his steering wheel and recalls how perceptive she always was. Of course she would sense him if he were in her vicinity. He wonders if she's trained her nose to scent him out, to catch warning of his approach. To her, he likely reeks of rotten vapors, sour notes.

"Shit," he says and knows that since he's been seen, he'll have to say something to her. He's not one to run. He thinks it makes him look less masculine and less self-assured. So he takes a minute to debate whether he should get out of his car and walk back to her house or drive by again and idle the engine—lean across the seat, his arm over the passenger headrest, a mix of boredom and mild intrigue on his face.

But his plotting is needless because suddenly there is a light tapping of fingers on his window. Riley looks up and finds Mayra standing outside his car, waving at him, no smile on her lips.

He opens his car door and shuffles out of his seat to stand on the asphalt. Mayra moves back a few steps. She points at his forehead and he reaches up to feel the indent of the steering wheel left on his face.

"You've aged. That's a big wrinkle, Riley."

He rubs at it, willing the flesh to give up its redness and fill back in. He'd forgotten her ability to point out what was wrong with him at any given moment, mixing her criticisms with dry humor. It had been an especially inconvenient trait in the bedroom.

"I'm on my way to a party. At some guy's house. I think we're tasting wines. Real upscale crap. I dunno," Riley lies and then plunges his hands into his pockets. He can feel the longer hair around his face fall down over the indent and hide it from view.

"Well, I just saw you drive by and I thought I heard your engine shut off. So I thought I would be polite and say hello."

Mayra still doesn't smile and begins to walk away. Riley steps forward with his left foot to stop her, leans in her direction, and the pressure is too much on his wound. He winces audibly and she pivots to look.

"What?" she stops and asks.

"Oh," he grimaces and does his best to act blasé. "It just looks like you're having a nice night with your friends."

"I am," she replies. "Just a couples thing."

He stutters out his response, aware she's the only woman who ever makes him nervous. "As in you are a couple. I mean, you're part of a couple?"

She scratches at her bare forearms, her skin light brown. She flips her hair off her shoulders, thick black locks clinging to the fabric of her knit shirt. Riley watches the movements of her body with interest. He's noticed she's put on a little weight, her hips a bit wider on her short frame. But the effect makes her even curvier, more sensual, and inherently feminine.

"What do you want, Riley?"

And he takes a moment to convince himself of what he wants. And he can't think of the reason he and Mayra ever broke up.

"We should get coffee or something. No pressure. Just to catch up. How about next weekend?"

She bites her lower lip and looks in the direction of her house. Riley notices the way her body is square with his own. He can't think of the last time they had sex, but he remembers that she would go silent and still before an orgasm.

"I don't think so, Riley," she says, not a bit of hesitation in her voice. "And it's Mother's Day next weekend. You know my family. We have, like, twelve mothers to toast with tequila shots."

"Right," Riley says and then he notices her face softens a little, her shoulders drop.

"Oh, I'm sorry," she mumbles, "I forgot about your mom. That was horrible. I should have called you. I didn't and I'm sorry."

Riley does his best to casually slide into his car, the need to escape the situation paramount in his mind. He's aware he has lost control, been rejected and now she wants to talk about his dead mother.

She stands away from him, but the windy night carries her scent to his nose. She smells of gardenia, a new scent for her. He imagines she mists on a perfume each morning after showering, the drops of oil and alcohol clinging to her warm skin like collecting dew.

"You changed your perfume. You used to smell like spice cake," he says. Then he slams shut his car door and drives away from the only woman he's ever loved.

SUNDAY, THE 3RD OF MAY, 2015

35   PEACH

She waits for the basement bar to open, pacing outside the stairwell plunging downward, the stairs swept clean of the dried vomit and discarded beer cans of last night's patrons. No one else waits for the bar to open on this early Sunday evening.

Peach wears a light pink dress, a draping of gauzy pleats she's belted with a second-hand find of braided, golden nylon. She spent an hour getting her hair ready for the outing, taking the wig from her head and placing it on an overturned colander Linx left at her place a year ago and never reclaimed. It made it easy to twist the locks into a low bun to ride just at the back of her head, over her tattoo, and secure it with a handful of bobby pins. Now, she wears a cowboy hat of soft brown leather on top of her wig. The entire outfit is Aphrodite meets Calamity Jane and the doorman gives her a strange look once the open sign illuminates in the window and she brushes past him into the spacious, darkened room.

She's the first one in the bar and she takes her time to look around the place. There is a raised dance floor—the colored lights and disco ball turned off—taking up a fourth of the entire nightclub. The bar itself is forgettable; the bottles of liquor are lined up against a plain, mirrored wall. And then Peach allows herself to look at what she came for.

In a back corner of the nightclub is a mechanical bull. The body of the machine is a cylinder of padded vinyl. Its front end is painted with a large snout, a *trompe l'oeil* ring through the nose. There are no horns to grasp onto, but a pommel covered in duct tape emerges from the top of the mechanical form. Surrounding the thing is a padded enclosure, like an especially cushioned boxing ring.

A few more people wander into the nightclub; a cluster of fraternity boys yell something about gravity bongs. Peach doesn't know whom to talk to about riding the bull, but she sees the DJ setting up near the vacant dance floor. He's a young kid with smooth cheeks and spiked hair and Peach stands in front of him for a minute before he looks up and notices her there.

"I don't play for an hour. And I don't accept requests for eighties music. Fuck Madonna," and then he looks back down at his deck.

"No, I was actually wondering whom I talk to about riding the mechanical bull?"

He shakes his head down at his turntables. "They only do that on Saturday nights when the place is full of women. But maybe they'd switch it on for a few bucks. Don't know. Want me to get the manager?"

Peach tells him yes and then he clicks on a microphone off to the side of his little cubby near the dance floor and pages the manager over the loudspeaker. While Peach waits for the boss, the DJ checks out her hat, its front brim dipping low over her hazel eyes.

"I usually announce a name when a chick is riding that thing. Makes them feel even more badass to get a shout-out. It's not like anyone is here, but if you get on it, want me to say something?"

Peach asks him for a piece of paper and he pulls a discarded receipt from McDonald's out of his baggy jeans and hands it to her. She pulls a pen from her purse and writes out a name, spelling the last word phonetically so that the DJ pronounces it correctly.

He eyes it in the spotty lighting, tilting it around to better read the letters when the manager arrives at Peach's side. She's a middle-aged woman with collagen-injected lips and a miniskirt showing off her tanned legs.

"How can I help you, sweetie?"

"The bull," Peach says. "I was wondering if I could ride it. I'd be willing to pay if it costs to operate it."

The woman tosses her head back when she laughs and then reaches out and runs Peach's dress through her fingers. "Boy problems? I get the sense you want to feel in control tonight, am I right?"

And though the woman isn't exactly correct in her assessment of Peach, she notes the attention given to her by the manager. Peach feels there is a good chance the woman might be going through her own relationship woes. "That's right," Peach lies. "Men. All assholes."

The manager smacks her inflated lips together and smirks. "I'll turn it on for you. Lift your hand in the air and wave it in a circle when you want the beast to kick on."

Peach walks back to the mechanical bull and steps onto the foam padding around the cylinder. It crinkles under her leather cowboy boots with the white embroidery. She pulls herself up onto the vinyl amalgamation of a bucking animal and centers her weight just above the middle, the pleated skirt of the dress riding high up her legs. She grips the thing with her inner thighs and puts one hand on the pommel. Peach uses her other hand to tighten the leather thong at her throat, to keep the cowboy hat in place and hopefully, the wig on her head.

Then she punches her hand into the air and waves it around like she's a rodeo queen who's ditched her horse and the parade and taken to the bull riding arena.

At first she feels nothing, and then the cylinder spins and dips on the length of metal bar beneath the false beast. She puts both hands on the pommel and smiles despite the fact this is all part of her sacred ritual, a purposeful nod to the mascot of Taurus, and it's not for her personal enjoyment. It's for the stars and their procession. It's for her eventual ascension.

The bull bucks and torques faster, until her focus is dedicated to holding on and not losing her seat. And it's then she hears the loudspeaker of the nightclub click on once more and the voice of the DJ speak to the room inhabited by Peach, the thick-lipped woman, the fraternity boys and the record-spinner alone.

"Riding the night away is Venus Kay-less-tis," he says the last name carefully, Peach's phonetic spelling helping him with the job. "Let's give her a round of applause, cowpokes."

The room stays silent except for the manager, whom Peach spies when the bull swings its painted nose to the bar. She leans against a cluster of stools, champagne flute in hand, slapping her free hand against her thigh and screaming at the top of her lungs for Peach to "ride him until he breaks."

36   RILEY

He does his best not to think of Mayra. The first time he met her she'd been helping one of her younger cousins at an ethnic food festival in order to raise funds for international student scholarships at Boise State University. She'd smelled of fried corn tortillas. Her hair kept falling into her mouth and she would angrily flip it away with a greasy pinkie. Later he learned she was no cook. All their meals together had been takeout or previously frozen and she disliked corn except for when it was popped and buttered.

Instead he conjures up images of Nell. For wanting someone as badly as he did, he's having problems seeing her pierced belly button or the shape of her eyes in his mind. All those evenings watching her dance, he realizes now most of his focus had been on pissing off Sev instead of actually seeing the stripper as a whole person. All he can call to mind are her tiny, dark nipples, tall and pliant to his touch.

None of it is enough to get his dick hard.

He cradles his member in his palm and is finally resigned to letting images of Mayra pass through his head. Blood flows south when he thinks of how she used to shave her legs with her foot perched upon the high counter of the bathroom sink, her forehead swaddled in a wrapped towel. He can hear her speaking loudly to her mother over the phone, Spanish slipping so quickly from her lips Riley has no hope of catching a word. And then he can smell her. Not the new smell of heavy, sweet gardenia. But her old smell of light citrus mixed with a spicy cinnamon.

It's the mundane, familiar thoughts that get him aroused. Nothing sexual or flirtatious. And it's a reminder to him, as he grasps and pulls at himself, that he really feels something for the woman. When it came to Mayra, the most exciting thing about their past was her willingness to be so intimate in her normalcy with him.

Just as he feels his balls suck upward and his mind go blank, his doorbell rings. Riley swears, fumbles for Kleenex and lifts himself off his bed.

Instead of putting on his pants, he goes to his bathroom and swings on a fluffy yellow bathrobe and belts it tightly. The doorbell sounds again and he screams out that he's coming as he uses the handrail to descend the stairs. His left foot is especially tender today and he's tempted to take another oxy.

He does not expect to open the door to Sev.

The poet stands hunched over. He wears his leather coat but the shirt underneath is disheveled to the side, clings to something at his waist. Riley figures it might be bandages and then looks at Sev's face. He has a black bruise ambling from his chin to his sternum along the underside of his throat.

"What the fuck?" Riley asks. He briefly considers the man is now ringing his doorbell to pass off his cards.

"Hell, you misplace your knickers?" he asks as he eyes Riley's bathrobe. "Don't freak out." Sev takes his hands out of his pockets so they're visible to Riley. "I'm not here to fight you.

I'm here for money."

Riley holds the doorknob firmly in his hand and squints at his enemy. "Excuse me? You want money for what? Being a really stellar piece of shit?"

"My ribs, asshole. I'm pretty sure a few of them are cracked and I have no insurance so I can't pay to see a doctor."

Riley wonders if Sev even has a job and figures the man is too romantic about his ego and so possessed with Nell he can't likely work. And then he realizes he's not too far off from the same description and bites his tongue.

"Why don't you just report me to the police?" Riley taunts but hopes the man hasn't done such a thing. He has no desire to end up in that cold room again, fielding questions about his brawling along with a new Q&A session concerning the dead tattooist.

Sev looks away from Riley then. And Riley peers out past the poet's shoulder to a truck parked alongside his front curb. A passenger sits in it, waiting, but he can't be sure it's Nell. The form slumps low against the seat, head tilted down.

"Oh," Riley says then, "unless you have a record or some problem with your visa and you don't want to get officials involved. Is that it?"

Sev doesn't confirm the suspicion. Riley can see he's acting tough but he must be in significant pain. His chest rises shallowly for breath, Sev's mouth slightly open, dark circles under his eyes. If he were altruistic, if he were certain Sev wasn't tormenting him, he'd offer him a few tabs of oxycodone.

"How much do you want?" Riley asks. "And if I give it to you, will you leave me alone for good?"

"A few hundred, yobbo. I'm asking for just a little."

Riley doesn't have a few hundred dollars in cash lying around. All of it is earmarked for his mortgage or groceries and booze. If Sev had come knocking a year and a half back, he could have easily paid him off with the contents of his wallet.

That was before he burned through money like it was kindling coated in pitch. But now, he would have to scrounge for it.

He decides to stay noncommittal and change the topic. "Why the hell did you have to harass me like that?"

Sev does his best to keep his face calm, but by the way he clenches his jaw, Riley is ready for him to throw a punch at any moment. "Me? You're the one trying to bag my Nell."

"And that made you feel justified in sending me strange messages? Justified in threatening me?"

A honk sounds loudly from the truck. Sev turns around and waves his hand at his companion before looking back to Riley. "I don't know what you're talking about, mate," and he says the last word with barely controlled anger, his voice slipping out past teeth held tightly together.

"Fine. Play dumb, Lord Byron. And oh, do you want your poems and your cards back, in case you're ever famous enough for that bizarre shit to be worth anything?"

Sev shakes his head and the horn sounds again. "Look, I just need some money to see a doctor. You're the dick who kicked me in the ribs over and over so you can pay for it. Get me some cash. I'm not mucking around."

And then he backs away, keeping his eyes on Riley. Sev turns only when he reaches the driveway and strides off, his hands just below his pectorals to hold in the pain. Riley watches him go, eyes the truck again and thinks he can see dark red hair on the passenger's head.

"Come to my house again and I'll meet you at the door with a bucketful of rocks. I'll throw them at you, one at a time."

He slams the front door and leans against it. He's angry at Sev and even angrier that he'll have to build back up his drive to orgasm. All the blood that should be in his dick dallies in his cheeks.

LATE WINTER, 2014

37   PEACH

She nearly ran her Honda off the side of the road. An ice storm—a weather anomaly that used to be unheard of in Boise but occurring more frequently during the last few winters—had coated all surfaces in the Treasure Valley with a crust of opaque ice a half inch thick. It had taken her fifteen minutes of pouring cool water over her windshield to get it to the point of clarity for driving. And though the roads were precarious and her tires nearly bald, she was determined to make it to the estate sale on a freezing, dark January morning. A patch of ice on a back road had other plans for her hatchback until she remembered to turn into the slide.

Peach had intended on being one of the earliest lined up in the bracing weather to get first pick of the items on sale. But five others had beaten her to the doorstep. She stands behind them all, the line snaking up the front walk, her chin pushed deep into a twisting bit of knit scarf around her neck. One elderly man has an open mug of steaming coffee in his hands and Peach wonders how early the people had all set out from their warm beds to make it to the estate sale.

The outside of the residence is brown siding and a shingle roof. It's a sprawling ranch house, well-kept but outdated. She has no doubt it was a coveted home in the eighties. The yard, shellacked in ice, would have been lovely in the middle of summer with little Japanese maples and pruned spruces dotting the front lawn. The people who had lived here took pride in their home and that effort was obvious to Peach.

At exactly eight, the front door opens and a woman wearing Isotoner gloves waves all the outsiders in from the cold. Once Peach passes through double doors of auburn wood, she's overwhelmed with choices of what to look at first. She decides there is unlikely to be anything important in the kitchen, and so she veers off down a hallway dotted with skylights casting a gray light on the passage.

The first bedroom she comes across is the master suite. All the woodwork is dark brown, a stamp of the Regan era. But the bedroom furniture, all dotted with paper price tags, is a mix of new modern and well-worn antiques. She pokes around a bit, picks up a few small things off a long bureau and digs around in a glass jewelry box. She fingers a pewter broach inlayed with a cluster of aquamarine gems and decides to hang on to it. She tucks her findings into her folded arms, unsure of what she will actually buy.

Then she moves on to the next room down the hallway. It's a child's room, the den of a boy, or at least the posters on the walls would label it so. It, too, is a mishmash of frozen time and an attempt to modernize. Next to a large poster of Tupac is a flat-screen television no more than a few years old.

Peach looks at each item in the room, tries on a little sailor's cap and touches a grouping of stuffed lions and bears that send up poufs of dust at her pressing fingers. She pulls out drawers and shuffles around their contents. In a bottom drawer of an old, fiberboard dresser she finds a lone sock with a knot in it. She sits down on the bed. Another woman comes into the room, lifting up the price tags of two lamps, while Peach unknots the sock and spills the contents of the white tube into her lap.

It's treasure, of a sort. Nestled amongst the cache is a little piece of lined paper folded into a square, tan with age. She carefully unfolds the paper and reads it. Her eyes widen at the find. Then she refolds it, tucks all the contents of the athletic sock back into the knit and adds it to her pile.

When she's finally explored the entire house an hour later, she dumps her chosen items onto a buffet table set up in the front room. Waiting behind the table is the woman in tight gloves, armed and ready with a metal cash box and a credit card swiper on her phone.

"Everything is for sale, right?" she asks the woman. "Because I found something without a price tag on it."

Peach pushes the fabric toward her. The lady pulls open the mouth of the long sock, once meant for a runner or some type of athlete. She jangles about the treasure inside with her hand cupped on the outside of the sock's arch.

The woman tosses the bundle onto the table and the contents clunk loudly against the thin wood.

"You can just take it, dear," she tells Peach and then begins to ring up the other items by keying the numbers on their tags into her cell phone.

"Are you sure? I'd be glad to pay for it."

"It wouldn't feel right," the woman explains, "taking money for something that's worthless."

SPRING, 1998

38   RILEY

When junior high ends for the year and yearbooks are passed around, Riley makes sure he collects all the offered adolescent well wishes. He wants those lines about having a great summer or 2Cute 2B 4Gotten scrawled in purple from the cute girls in his grade and the grade below. He counts the number of girls who signed his book. Fifty-seven.

He thinks about the deal he made with his dad, how he must go to work as a grunt laborer for a local landscaping business. This is all due to his face breaking out in painful, blind pimples which never come to a head but leave purple splotches on his skin after their pus is absorbed back into his body. This is part of the deal. His paycheck will pay for his antibiotic pills and acidic face creams. His father had said he would have to pay, literally, for his vanity. His mother had nodded in agreement and then told him to start putting his dirty clothes in the hamper.

The man who runs the landscaping crew and insists on Riley never operating a lawnmower is named Mr. Hannigan. He only responds to this name if Riley has a question. The other, older members of the maintenance crew call him by his first name, Herb. But Riley isn't afforded that same right. He's something of an apprentice landscaper, relegated to weeding and occasionally schlepping around the leaf blower and clearing off sidewalks.

"Missed a leaf, pitface," Mr. Hannigan heckles him and motions with his outstretched foot to the errant leaf. Riley moves up the sidewalk, picks it up by hand and then sets the blower down, arches his back.

"No time for a rest. We've got two more houses to get to this afternoon. Hey, maybe we'll trim those barberries outside your bedroom window when we reach your fancy neighborhood," Mr. Hannigan smiles at Riley and waves his hand in front of the boy's face. "You'd think with your parents' money they'd be able to get you treated for all that acne? Don't they love you?"

Riley picks up the blower and draws the straps over his shoulders. "They think I should pay for my pimple treatment. Like with this job. They think it all builds character. But I think it just makes me sneeze a lot and causes me to eat five Hot Pockets every day after I get home from working."

"Ham and cheese?"

"Pepperoni, actually."

"Does it build your character? Will you be a good citizen when you grow up?" Mr. Hannigan stands with his hands on his hips while the rest of the crew runs hand rakes over the surface of the flower beds behind him.

"I don't know," Riley says. "I'll just be happy to have my own pocket money. If anything is left over after I get these pimples off of me, I'll get something good with it."

"What, like a new bike or something?"

"Nah," Riley answers and then decides, because he's fourteen, to speak with the man as his equal instead of his superior. "I'm not into BMX anymore. I have different tastes. Maybe get some Cool Water and a Hilfiger shirt."

"I get it, rich boy," he says and then turns away from Riley.

Possessed to do so, but not sure why, Riley pulls the hose of the leaf blower around to the level of his crotch and lifts up the black piping, an exaggerated representation of a boner. He has no fear about the man reporting his behavior to his parents. He's certain he'll understand his sense of humor. Man to man.

"Mr. Hannigan, check it out. It's probably the only thing worth spending money on."

And when his boss turns to see, Riley clicks on the leaf blower. A plume of dust and ground leaves shoots from the tubing held flush against his groin. The man laughs so hard he wipes at his eyes with a ratty red handkerchief, cussing at a blade of grass that gets under his eyelid. He tells Riley, once he regains his composure, that Riley can start to call him Herb.

WEDNESDAY, THE 6TH OF MAY, 2015

39   PEACH

There are no lights on the dirt road next to the expanse of pasture, so Peach lets her eyes adjust to the dark before getting out of her car. She knows switching on a flashlight could draw attention and the last thing she wants is a farmer or rancher coming out of his house and disturbing her work. A coyote lets out a strange yelping howl in the distance. She scans the bushes around her for other predators but soon realizes she's the only predator on the earthen path.

She walks up to a wide gate set into the fencing surrounding the paddock. Its width allows one cow through at a time and she figures it's that size in order to control the herd's movement when swapping them from barn to open land. A large metal lock loops through a link of chain securing the gate to the thick post where the rest of the fence begins. She has bolt cutters in her car, but she decides to leave them there for a moment and walk the perimeter of the pastureland to get a visual on her mark.

All is silent and motionless on the plot of open, slightly

rolling land just outside of town. She knows that there should be only one animal in the field, in the enclosure. And then she hears him before seeing him, a hard exhalation of air escaping his nose.

The bull is only ten feet away from where she stands outside the fence. From what she can see in the lack of light, he's a young creature, thin with small horns. The bull swings his head in her direction when he hears her feet crunching on a plane of gravel underfoot. It's as if he acknowledges a lady's presence, bidding her good evening.

Peach thinks about how easy it had been to gather up the flock of sheep. A snap, loading them into the trailer which had been left just outside their grazing area in the foothills. They'd been foraging on public lands, the owners paying a small fee to nourish their flock on the sagebrush and grass mounds belonging to the government. Mace in hand, she thought she'd run across a guard dog, some shaggy Newfoundland or Bernese. But there was no canine with ears pricked in alarm to threaten off her thievery. So she took them all with some patient coaxing, painted numbers on their sides in red and hung pictures of stunning ingénues and sexy pinup girls around their necks.

The numbers and the pictures of women on the sheep had meaning. Everything she did and would do had meaning.

She thought dancing with the bull would be the same easy matter. Even though he would be a more dangerous tool, he was a tool all the same. Her charmed fate would be enough to carry her through releasing the animal safely and successfully. Besides, the bull wouldn't be fated for a trip downtown. She didn't have access to a trailer and truck like she had with the sheep, left untended with a key under the visor. The bull would just trot about the little community outside Boise once freed. Maybe getting into a pasture full of willing cows, maybe making the news as a quirky local bit.

Peach watches the shadowy form of the bull, his tall legs

solid on the earth, his head dipping low. And though he could charge her and the fence, she doesn't move. And as she watches, waits, she can see he's not aggressive. He's sleeping.

"Aldebaran," she says up to the sky, "don't you want me to release him?"

And the response she gets surprises her. Perhaps her time on the mechanical bull was enough of a gesture to the mascot of Taurus. But she does what she's told and moves away from the bull. Farther away from her car, she follows the line of the fence until she comes to a patch of blackberry brambles. The mound of prickly whips is little more than a dark blob to her but she uses her feet, protected in their leather boots, to feel around under the thicket.

Her toes touch down on something hard. She drops to her knees and pats around with her hands. From under the leaves and thorns and tiny buds just forming along the flexible limbs, she pulls out five metal stakes. She stands and they reach to her waist, notches of metal running perpendicular up them. She doesn't know what they're used for, whether they're part of discarded fencing or meant to secure rope or twine to plants.

She doesn't care what their intended use is. Because she knows how she is going to use them. She lifts them up and balances them on her shoulder. Walking her find back to her car, the feel of dusty dirt beneath her nails keeps her present.

Peach passes the bull. He slumbers still. She wonders if he dreams of mating or chewing cud or goring an adversary. She smiles at the strong beast, and then looks up at the stars, her friends.

"You keep me guessing," she says. "Thank you for the proper tools."

THURSDAY, THE 7TH OF MAY, 2015

40   RILEY

"I could give you my state track trophy as collateral. You know I'm good to pay you back."

Walker balances the shot glass of vodka on his knee and shakes his head. He'd arrived at Riley's place just after getting off work; the tie at his neck is loosened and his sports jacket is off of him and on the back of the deck chair. He smears a stick of honey-flavored lip balm on his thicker lower lip and mashes his chops together.

"I don't want that weird, metal statue. The dude on it looks like he's lifting his leg to try and give himself a blow job. I know you're good for it, Rye. But you haven't told me what you need it for."

Riley, half a bottle of Jameson in his gut, almost tells Walker everything. How he banged Nell and decided to attack Sev for sending the weird cards. And how the poet has asked for money to cover a medical visit and Riley's rising suspicions that he kicked the shit out of an innocent man. He keeps replaying the look on Sev's face when he said he didn't know what Riley was talking about. There had been no dishonesty in his eyes. But the whiskey sides with his self-delusion and he slurs out a lie he thinks his best friend will believe.

"It's for Kristin and Tate. I mean, for Tate. She said they need to get him new shoes and Brian's been having problems with finances."

"They need to get a five-year-old new shoes so they want three hundred dollars?" Walker shakes his head. "Since you've left the firm, your skills at lying have really gone to hell."

Riley stomps around on his deck and plucks up a handful of Cheetos, stuffing them all in his mouth at once. The orange powder stains his fingers.

"Come on, Walker. Just lend me the money."

"Just get a job, Riley. You show me you give a crap about your life and I'll give you as much money as you want."

Walker stands, too, and goes into the house to take a leak. He comes back with a rolled up piece of newspaper in his hand. He smoothes it out in front of him on the little glass table and sets his drink on one corner to anchor it down. Riley never questions his friend's love of partying but when it's time for business, logic, focus and serious effort rule the day.

"I'm trying something old school. They're called the classifieds. They post jobs in these things. They're not just found on the computer. Come here. Look at it," he says to Riley and then moves away from the table so Riley can see.

Through hazy eyes, Riley picks out the words line cook immediately.

"Oh! I have the perfect reference to list for this position. Typhoid Mary and I go way back. We've been making people sick by hanging around kitchens for ages." And then Riley rips the newspaper away from the table. The motion sends Walker's vodka sailing for a second before the glass lands on the deck and shatters.

"Nice, Rye," Walker smirks and Riley can see how his shoulders slump. He'll leave off the job stuff for now. "Do we clean it up or leave it and go to the strip club? I can only hang there for an hour, though. I need to get in my ladders. Weighted squats. Chiseled hams and quads grow for no man sitting on a stool holding up two-dollar bills."

"Blaze? Nah, I'm done with that place."

"Since when?" Walker asks, eyeing the pieces of glass but not moving to pick them up.

"Since I'd done everything in there I ever needed to do," Riley slurs and his mouth turns upward.

"You shit," Walker says. "You fucked her and didn't tell me. I should have guessed it. You've been decidedly less crippled from the effects of blue balls recently."

"I'm a proper gentleman. And a gentleman never tells."

"If you're a gentleman," Walker laughs, "then I'm the Pope."

Riley drops to his knees, doing his best to avoid the sharp shards on the deck and folds his hands in prayer. "Then give me the money, Pope Walker the Kind, and I'll confess my sins."

Walker reaches down, dips his thumb into the vodka evaporating on the deck, and anoints Riley with his own version of holy liquid.

"All your sins? Like I said, I've only got an hour for bullshitting."

41 PEACH

Michel Rothschild strokes his goatee. The cigarette he puts into his mouth and takes out without ever smoking, again and again, peeks out of the pocket of his thrift store shirt. Michel stares at Peach, at the empty space between her breasts and neck. He frowns.

"Where did your pretty necklace go, *ma chérie*?"

"That has nothing to do with our talk, Michel. Eyes up top," and then she points two fingers splayed out in a V at her face. This is the client with the romantic notions directed at her. This is the man who, in numerous sessions, reminds Peach he has never hurt a female human being because he considers them breakable, delicate souls in need of soft handling.

"It looked so good on you, Perfect Peach. That's what I want to talk about now. You. Maybe you and me."

Peach sighs and gets ready to discuss his inappropriate behavior yet again, but he holds up a hand to muss with his chestnut hair and steeples his thin hands into the point of an arrow.

"I'm joking. But I've talked enough. Now it's your turn."

"I'm not here for a session, Michel. In this room, you're working to get better. Not me. I have my own methods."

"Ah," Michel says, as though he's uncovered a bit of secret hidden from him. "You do have faults, though they don't appear on your skin or your chest." His eyes alight on her cleavage this time and widen slightly.

"Tell me a story, *ma chérie*, and then I'll get out of your hair for the day. Your hair you say you haven't dyed. That's one lie you've told me, but it's okay. Just tell me a story and I'll go. It doesn't even have to be about you."

She knows he's observant enough to notice some of her flaws, paranoid enough to catch her lies. Peach can only hope he doesn't dig out all her deceptions, like a truffle pig turning over black dirt in his search for worthwhile prizes.

Peach leans back in her chair and searches her mind for a tidbit of information. Anything to satiate Michel and get him out of her office, so she can get home to feed herself and Roman. She thinks she may try and call Linx as well, having heard nothing from him since he stormed off during their lunch together.

And then the information presents itself. And though she knows Michel has violent tendencies and it's not, perhaps, a proper story to tell him, she tells it anyway.

"Did you know in Spain, in the bullfighting arenas, the matador wasn't always the star of the show? There were, are, other men on horseback who send lances into the bull to pierce his muscles. Especially to cut the muscles of the neck, with the intent to get the bull to lower his head. It is a service done for the matador. They're called picadors. And they need to possess great skill, because the bull could come around and lift them off their mounts with his horns and gore them. Most of the time, before they started padding the sides of the horses, the mounts would be disemboweled or their innards crushed by the constant trauma inflicted by the bull."

Michel fondles the same soapstone obelisk he always pulls from Peach's shelves, his hands trembling slightly. "So they were the main attraction, *ma chérie*? But then something happened and everyone started to cheer louder for the matador?"

"Yes," Peach says and then instantly regrets sharing the information with her patient. She feels exposed but heady with her revelatory snippet of history. "And that's your story."

"But the story you're telling me is yours, Perfect Peach." Michel stands from the upholstered client chair and puts his hands on her desk. He dips his head low and faces Peach down. She can see the jet-black lace of his thick lashes. "Why does the matador get all the attention when the picadors are the ones wearing the bull down, zapping his reserves, making him bleed out? Why aren't they the ones the crowd is cheering on?"

Peach does her best not to laugh at the man's assessment, because she thinks her laughter would only encourage him to believe he's right. Because he is right, and that awareness of correctness, she doesn't want to encourage. Instead, she asks him a question she knows he can't answer.

"If I'm the picador, then who's the matador, Michel? Who do you think is besting me and getting all the energy from the crowd?"

"I don't know," he says and pushes off the desk. He retrieves the little obelisk and puts it down on the paper-strewn plane in front of Peach. Its surface is nicked and scratched from Michel's handling of it each session. There are half moons from his nails festooning the statue.

"But I don't think you really care about bulls or Spanish men who lance them. I think you've told me your story and you didn't realize it."

"I don't care about bulls or Spanish men with lances. You're right on that count, Michel."

"And about your story. I know I'm right. Someone has taken away your glory, Perfect Peach. I wonder what you will do to get it back?"

Michel smiles, pulls his well-worn cigarette from his pocket and places it in his mouth.

Peach closes her eyes for a moment and then grins at her patient. "Whatever you want to believe, Michel." And she's happy the man can't see how her legs under her desk shake a little, how sweat begins to dampen her underarms.

"I would fight the matador for you, *ma chérie*. I would be your perfect bull."

"That's sort of sweet, Michel, but inappropriate," she tells him. Then her mind slips away from her office and her patient and she sees her perfect bull in her mind. She envisions the way in which he'll ultimately lead to the matador's demise.

FRIDAY, THE 8TH OF MAY, 2015

42   RILEY

Riley catches Double Al in the showroom full of examples of the dry mining equipment his company produces and ships around the world. He's talking to a customer about different sizes of trommels, and how the metal cylinders shake the gold loose from the rocks as they spin about the open grating. He flips off the motor on one model with a strong, callused hand and stands back up with his barrel chest pushed forward.

"And since gold is one of the heaviest materials you're going to come by in the field, it'll drop down here," and he points out the flume that runs underneath the yellow cylinder. "And then you'll do your final panning and maybe another method, like a Gold Cube or acid to get your flour."

Double Al notices Riley and winks at him. The customer, a man who looks to have never spent a day in the mountains let alone out of a suit, is a greenhorn to mining and doesn't understand how black sand helps a miner or how to get gold flakes into miniscule glass vials. The patience inherent in Double

Al will come into use here. Riley hopes he can find some of that same patience to wait out the flurry of questions the man will surely spit at his boss.

Riley does wait him out, pokes around the shelves of plastic pans and little suction tubes for lifting flecks of gold out of pan divots. Though he'd worked at making the equipment, he'd had little experience actually mining. The only time he'd put a pan in the water and pulled out anything other than rocks and little, dark purple garnets, was when Double Al convinced him to come to work for him. They'd spent the day up on one of his mining claim sites by Idaho City panning and chatting.

Riley still had the delicate, pounded gold he'd pulled from Elk Creek. He kept it in a cup in his kitchen, one stacked between a tower of others. Once in a great while, he'd take out the little glass vial with its black screw-on cap and hold the water and gold up to the light—imagining finding a vein of gold, as long as his cul-de-sac, as big as his house, and then never having to work again in his life.

The customer eventually leaves, but not before making the promise he'll be back to buy something once he finds a claim to purchase and mine. Double Al holds open the heavy front door for him as he exits and waves him away.

"Doesn't it bother you to spend so much time on someone who will never be back?" Riley asks and lifts up a magnet used to sort black sand. He runs it around his wrist and pretends he can feel its pull.

"Some might think you fall into that category, son," he says and lets the door go so it can latch shut. "You just here to socialize or to get back to work?"

Riley puts the circular magnet down and folds his arms. "I came by to see what's going on about your truck. Anything new? Have they found anyone?"

"Not yet," Double Al says and shuffles over to stand next to Riley. "Detective Dauchaun says the lab tests on the residue near the truck will take a good while yet. They're in queue with all the other bits of crime scenes that need to be analyzed by men in white coats. He keeps telling me testing takes time. Says police work isn't like CSI but I have no idea what a CSI is."

The older man switches topics. "How's your foot doing? It getting healed?" Double Al bends down to hover his hand over Riley's mangled left foot.

"I banged it up a few days back. It was an accident. But I'm healing. I'll eventually just be the guy your staff gossips about. Like, 'hey, remember Old Five Toes?' and you'll laugh along with them."

Double Al reaches a hand up for Riley to take as he struggles to move his bulk upward from his squatting position. Riley can see the man is starting to go bald at the crown of his head and there is more white in his short, tight curls than black.

He pulls up on his pants and his belt and huffs. "Son, I would never laugh at a line like that."

"You people with taste and morals," Riley says and then gets to his real reason for visiting. "I was wondering how those insurance EOBs are looking. And whether or not there's been any say on disability going through?"

Double Al squints, sniffs and leans his right arm against the counter with the register and piles of outdated mining journals for customers to look through. Then he launches into a story instead of answering Riley's question.

"There was a miner up in the Owyhee range back in the 1880s or so. He would set camp at Ruby City and for the longest time he'd only work the hard rock mines with the other boys. Spend fourteen hours a day under the earth, crawling on his belly like a terrier, looking for which way the vein was going. One day there was a cave-in and his legs were completely crushed, but his fellow miners got him out of the hole and to a doctor. And the doctor took off his legs, probably some ex-field surgeon from the Civil War come west to look for new excitement."

"All right," Riley says and waits for Double Al to finish. But the man goes silent for a moment and looks to be dredging up the last bit of story from some back room in his brain. That or he's about to move on to some other subject likes he's prone to do.

He sums it up eventually, his face solemn. "And that man, that miner, he did indeed lose both his legs. But he'd have the boys who lived in some of the mining company barracks carry him out of his little pup tent each morning. They'd set him down on the banks of Jordan Creek so he could pan out enough to buy fatback, hardtack and coffee. And do you know what?"

"Um, he got stupid rich finding a nugget and married the madam over at the local cathouse?" Riley guesses, positive the amputee made out great in the end.

"No," Double Al responds with a clipped voice. "He made barely enough to survive. Until one day, when he'd been panning all day and his arms were like jelly, a hard wind pitched him over into the creek. He couldn't get any purchase to get out of the current and he drowned."

Riley scrunches up his nose and frowns. "What the hell kind of story is that? Was it supposed to be inspirational? Thank God no one ever paid you to write a mining episode for *Schoolhouse Rock*."

"One, nobody owes you a living. Two, it was supposed to remind you you're not a cripple. You can work, son, and you work well when you choose to put effort into it."

"And the part where he dies, drowns in the little river?"

"That's just the end of the story," Double Al says innocently. "We all work at something until we die."

Riley picks up the magnet again and runs it over the counter this time. He tries at lifting a penny from an old ashtray that acts as a change receptacle.

"Copper ain't magnetic, son."

Riley tosses the magnet into the ashtray and pouts. He

knows Double Al won't appreciate his face so he straightens his spine.

"So maybe I just want a little break from the work? Or maybe I'm working at getting the government to pay my bills while I learn how to live with only five toes?"

Double Al puts a hand on Riley's upper back and escorts him to the only window near the front door, looking out onto the dirt and gravel parking lot. The expanse is canopied by an old sycamore chartreuse with fresh leaves. He points to a little economy-sized car parked between two lines farthest from the building. Its paint job is light blue and it has a little speed fin above the rear window.

"See the outfit same color as the sky? That's what the auto insurance company gave me to drive around until they can rule on my truck. It's a piece of crap. I can't fit any of my prototype equipment in the trunk and the roof clearance is so low I'm going to have to start doing squats and lose about fifteen pounds just to make it into that tin can each morning. But at least I have something to drive. And it gets me where I want to go."

Riley watches as a crow dives from the sycamore tree with its multi-pastel trunk and lands on the hood of the little foreign car. It caws loudly toward the building and bobs its head.

"You're full of stories today, Double Al," Riley says, his eyes locked on the carrion eater.

"Next time you show up here, bring your work suit and your boots. Or a pocket calculator and a tie and you'll get less stories and a paycheck instead."

Then Double Al wanders off to his back office and leaves Riley alone with his view of the bird. But instead of thinking of work, he thinks of the sad replacement for the man's old Dodge Ram and wonders if Sev could have blown the vehicle up and knows, deep down in his bowels, that the answer is no.

43   PEACH

She shuts the door to her bedroom and lifts the wig off of her head. The tattoo is healing nicely, but coupled with her growing hair, it takes extreme willpower for her not to scratch at her scalp all day long. Taking a tube of antibiotic cream, she smoothes a layer over the little tattoo she can't see, her fingers gently seeking out the slightly raised skin. Soon the puffiness will be gone completely and eventually her hair will be full again, long, and the tattoo will be unnoticeable by all who look at her.

For now, as she tends to the sore skin at the back of her skull, memories of the night she killed Roman visit her and she wills them away. Though it had to be done, she didn't revel in the act. Excepting for a moment when she was high on adrenaline and reclaimed energy from the tattooist. Then she'd been enraptured, her skin prickling, her mind clear and calm.

She didn't completely latch the door to her bedroom and Roman the Lamb butts it open with his forehead and trots over to

Peach. His blunt strike against the wood makes her think of the tattooist again and she promises herself she will complete his beatific portrait one day.

"At least you're his namesake," she says to the lamb and runs one of his ears between her fingers. It feels just like the leaves of the wild plant which grows low to the ground, silver hairs on leaves shaped like spades with the eponymous name of lamb's ear. The lamb is putting on weight and his wool is getting wiry. He doesn't show any signs of aggression yet, and Peach enjoys the way he follows her about and insists on rubbing up against her legs.

The lamb's attention reminds her of Linx and she's not sure it's a good comparison to make of her best friend and casual lover. She wonders if she should call him but decides against it. She'd only ever been clear with him about the limits of their relationship. Linx choosing to ignore her words was on him. And besides, Lars wasn't a real threat at all. Linx would understand that someday.

In her bathroom, she tries on various scarves around her neck. There's a wide white one with tassels and a red and brown thick knitted one with scalloped edges. They're all beautiful but warm, and with the spring fully established, she won't be able to wear any of them without sweating and receiving questioning looks from strangers. She makes a note to go shopping if she has the time, to find a square of light silk to loop in a bow around the collars of her shirts.

She closes her eyes and touches her throat, where the hollow of her esophagus and larynx plummet down to her chest. The skin there is smooth but the muscles running from her chin to her collarbone are tight. She rubs at them and picks gently at a small mole that's come, new and unnoticed, the same white shade as her skin.

Peach thinks there are better things than scarves to wear. Like a golden torc. It could be so wide it would need a hinge at the back to wrap around her neck. The metal could be slightly pounded so the texture would catch the light.

She can almost feel it there, if she concentrates hard enough. The cool wrap of precious metal against a vulnerable part of her body, protecting her from harm. She feels like a Celtic princess astride a war chariot. She feels like a bedazzled goddess, expecting those in her thrall to fall at her feet.

SATURDAY, THE 9TH OF MAY, 2015

44   RILEY

Riley checks one of the sprinkler heads that doesn't hit the right spot in his yard. The grass is yellow and dry in a round, sizable patch. A UPS man pulls his brown truck alongside the driveway, parks, and walks back into its depths. Riley keeps fiddling with the plastic head until something snaps in his grip. A torrential plume of water skyrockets from the sprinkler pipe, arcs high in the air, and then smacks down to earth on Riley's driveway.

"God damn it," Riley cries and tries to push the head of the sprinkler back over the stiff PVC to no avail. He grabs at a medium-sized rock near his foot and jams it in the black piping. It stops the water for a second but then he rethinks his fix. He wonders if the water pressure would be significant enough to send the rock up into his face. He pulls out the rock quickly, steps away from his mistake and wonders if he'll have to find a water valve to twist shut.

"This is for you, man."

Riley turns to see the delivery man standing to the side of where the geyser of water pummels the brickwork of his driveway.

"Just need a signature," the man urges.

Riley takes the cardboard box the size of a large dictionary and cradles it in his arms while signing his name on the man's clipboard.

"Any suggestions on how to stop the water?" he asks the man with a laugh.

"No idea. I try to stay away from mechanical things," he says. Then he takes the clipboard back, waves it at Riley, climbs back into his behemoth of a van and takes off.

A trip into the garage yields results; Riley finds the water shutoff valve and pulls it tight. He'll have to go to Home Depot for a new sprinkler head before it gets too warm and all his grass begins to yellow and dry. But for now, he takes the package inside and puts it on his kitchen table. He eyes it, notes the address label is typed on a square of white stick-on paper. The return address is smeared and illegible, as if a wet sponge was taken to the ink. The box begs to be opened, its mysterious contents uncovered.

He slices the side of the box with a steak knife he'd used to pierce a potato last night, the metal gummy from the starch. Looking inside, he can see a smaller container, white and waxed, along with a letter. He pulls the letter out first, the envelope blank. Except for the wax seal on the back of the flap.

"Unbelievable," he mutters.

And it's in this moment Riley concludes Sev was not the one sending him the letters. No way would he risk sending them again, not after the fight and the plea for money, if the cards and gifts were Sev's doing. He wouldn't push back at Riley. Passionate about his poems and his woman, yes. But Riley doesn't have evidence to label the man a certifiable lunatic.

He slits the side of the envelope and knows deep down in

his lower gut that Sev is innocent of sending the communications.

The card is on heavy stock with a glossy picture of a mother holding a newborn infant in her arms, a blue swaddling blanket keeping the child's face from view. The mother looks down on her progeny with a soft gaze and wide smile. There is a warm light at her back, casting her body in a golden halo. The text reads: To You on Mother's Day.

Upon opening the card, the printed message continues with: You're the healer of all wounds, the one who chases away bad dreams. I wouldn't be where I am today without you, Mom. Nothing can express how much you mean to me. Wishing you the best of days today and always. Happy Mother's Day.

Riley notes the line through the word "Mom" in the text with his name written out beneath it in the same bold, all caps lettering he'd seen in the last letter. And there is one other substitution, a strange one at that. Instead of the "you" after "wishing", it has been slashed through. "Me" is written there instead.

There is no additional message. But it is signed with the name of a star. Aldebaran.

Riley tosses the card back on the table, as if it could burn him or possess him or stab him. Then he reaches into the larger box and pulls out the smaller one, anxious to check out what could be inside. It has a slight smell to it so he keeps it away from his face. He immediately thinks of ricin or anthrax but then considers those poisons probably don't smell. Then he comes up with the idea of documenting himself opening the box.

He fishes his phone from his pocket and flips on the video component, touches the screen to begin filming. It's only then he realizes the top of the white box is like any other takeout or leftover container to be found in any old restaurant. He uses one hand to peel back the little tab that keeps the box closed while trying to keep his hand doing the filming from jerking out of nervousness.

Pulling back the four flaps, he tilts his head to the side and his forehead wrinkles. The smell of deep-fried meat wafts upward and he holds his hand over the little ovals of battered something. They're cold and grease is halted from seeping out of the container by a plastic tray fitted into the bottom of the box.

Riley clicks off the camera on his phone and picks up one of the fried items. He's not about to eat it, but he's confused about what could be encased inside the batter.

"What are you?" he questions the gift sent from Aldebaran.

With the strange turns in his life as of late, he half expects it to answer.

SUNDAY, THE 10TH OF MAY, 2015

45 PEACH

"They're bull testicles," Peach tells Patti, trying to explain the concept of Rocky Mountain Oysters. "And some people really like them."

"I don't know why anyone would put a testicle in their mouth," Patti answers and Peach does her best not to laugh out loud. If she makes the slightest guffaw, Patti will accuse her of teasing, mocking or plain meanness. And Peach doesn't want to upset her today. Not on Mother's Day.

"You're the one who asked me about it," Peach explains into the phone, her spare hand trailing through a bowl of whipping cream and delivering the white emulsion into her mouth. "You're an Idahoan like me. Shouldn't you know what they are?"

"My sister didn't know and I wanted to be sure. To give her the right information. Let's talk about something else, Peach, before you get inspired to tease me over my honest question."

Patti inserts one of her lengthy silences to control the

conversation and give pause before steering it in a new direction.

"Now, you know I'll be back in Boise soon. And I'll expect a ride home from the airport."

Peach turns the phone away from her mouth and allows herself a sigh. Her adoptive mother refuses to take taxis, convinced the foreigners who drive many of them will bilk her of more money than what's due, even though meters are always in use. After years of this behavior, Peach is used to the woman's casual bigotry.

"I'm planning to pick you up as usual. Send me your arrival info so I can schedule time off work and come get you. Unless you're arriving at night?"

"Of course I'm not arriving at night," Patti says, her voice higher and firm. "That would be unsafe. Waiting outside an airport in the evening. Who knows what kinds of degenerates prey on confused travelers and then hop a plane away from the scene of the crime?"

Peach puts more of the heavy cream into her mouth and holds it on the middle of her tongue. The subtle flavor is what interests her the most, how it tastes of nothing more than a scant bit of milk.

"Like I say, just let me know what you need from me."

"And one other thing we need to talk about when I get back to town, Peach. Your payments. I haven't had a check from you in a few months. And when I loaned you that money years ago you promised me paying would never become an issue. Unless you mean to drain my bank account dry with your inconsiderate actions?"

Peach swallows the dairy. She hadn't had much of a choice in borrowing the money. It hadn't been for some extravagant trip or new car. It had been a necessity of sorts. At least it had seemed that way at the time. Still, Peach made the choice to ask for and accept the money. The fact her adoptive mother couldn't simply give her the money from her substantial nest egg was wound enough, reopened and salted each time Patti jabbed at her lapses in pay. Patti insisted the thousands had to be a loan, interest charged, monthly due date set.

"Yes," Peach says and then forces herself to say the word, "Mother. Why don't we talk about it when you're back in Boise?"

Patti exhales into the phone. "I just wanted to warn you I'm not forgetting your debts. If I did, you'd never learn your lessons. Do not test me on this point, Peach."

"I understand," and then Peach lies, because it's Mother's Day and her mood is high. "I'll be glad to have you back home."

But Patti misunderstands the attempt at affection and tsks loudly. "Don't be foolish, Peach. Orlando is now my home. I just come back to Boise to make sure the condo is well tended."

Peach can hear a clinking sound over the phone. She knows Patti must be playing with her silver cigarette case. The one etched with an outline of a lake. Perhaps she taps it against the rim of a glass full of Diet Coke. Tab maybe, if she can find it in Florida.

"I know that's why you come back," Peach says.

She's fully aware Patti does not return to Boise for her. The older woman does not miss her. Not one iota. In this, they are akin.

MONDAY,
THE 11TH OF MAY,
2015

46 RILEY

The smell of the library calls up memories of his childhood.
That's when his father would schlep him along on Sunday
afternoons to the third floor of the Boise Public Library to read
the periodicals never delivered to their house. Psychology Today
was his father's favorite but he didn't believe in spending money
on sheaves of paper held together with staples. That frugality
was part of the reason for their family's wealth. But only part.

The smell is consistent: of aging paper and unwashed
homeless men. He looks at the woman sitting behind the
reference desk on the second floor, her nametag on a lariat
around her neck. She's heavy but her breasts are small, her face
delicate except for the rolling of a double chin. She wears a shirt
in hideous, shiny polyester and her black hair ends along the
sides of her jaw. He can just make out a name on the little piece
of white plastic.

"Amelia," he says, "I could use your help."

The woman looks up from her typing at a computer and

tells him to take a seat. "I'll give you my best. What do you need, sir?"

Riley has brought the cards with him in the old satchel he'd lug about as a lawyer, but he doesn't pull them out. He doesn't know how much he wants to share with a stranger. But he does think Sev wasn't the author of the notes. And that revelation means someone is still hassling him. So he decides he needs to start with what he knows.

"Astronomy and astrology, I think. I was wondering if there were good resources which combine the two. Science and New Age stuff."

She types something into the computer and stares at the screen. "You know there are a lot of excellent resources on the internet for that sort of thing. I could direct you to a few sites."

"No," Riley says and resists leaning over her to look at the screen as well. "I'm sure there are, but I'm old-fashioned in some ways. I'd like a book or periodical."

She clicks on something with the mouse and pulls up a new set of information. Amelia eyes the list and shakes her head. "There are some books, but they're all checked out. I can put you on hold for them, but it might be a while. You're not the only one who's been in here asking for books on astrology."

And she laughs at her statement, nods her head like it's a personal joke she agrees with and Riley doesn't follow.

"More people than usual interested in the heavens and zodiac-themed personality tests? Is there a reason for it?"

Amelia pulls in her chin and her face seems to sink backward. Her eyes go big and she laughs again at Riley. "Is there a reason? Yes, there's a reason. I have conspiracy nuts in here once a week over what's been going on in town."

And then she composes herself but her head takes up nodding again, as if she jams out to the minute sound of people flipping the pages of books. "I'm sorry if you're one of them. I didn't mean being into conspiracy theories is a bad thing. Please don't take offense."

"What are you talking about?" Riley asks her, leaning his body across the expanse of desk.

"Uh," Amelia starts, "you did hear about the graffiti last month at the intersections, right? Maybe you drove over some of it? That was the astrological sign for Aries."

Riley recalls the red painted Vs all over Boise that he'd seen when leaving the hospital. But it wasn't until now that he remembered them and understood that they were, indeed, the head and horns of a ram. When he'd been looking into the sign of Aries, the link hadn't even occurred to him.

"And people just figured this out?"

Amelia shakes her head. "Not until April 22nd. Otherwise it would have just been dismissed as some random tag."

"And what happened April 22nd?" Riley can tell the woman enjoys drawing out the story, keeping Riley enraptured.

She laughs again, her giggle high-pitched and staggered as if her hilarity fires from a small pistol. "Another astrological symbol. For Taurus. On Simplot Hill. Don't you watch the local news?"

Riley stands up sharply. "I guess I'll start," he says.

He tells her he'll be back to get his name on the list for the books, though she tells him she can add it now if he has his library card. But there is no time to pull out his wallet and hand over the flimsy piece of white plastic. Riley is possessed, ready to set off across downtown and northern Boise to seek out another sign.

47 PEACH

As Lars is walking out of his building to leave on his lunch break, Peach can tell he doesn't notice it's her arm holding open his door, waiting for him to pass through. He absently tells her thank you before doing a double-take and realizing Peach has her fingers wrapped around the handle.

"You're welcome," she smiles.

"Were you coming to see me? I didn't think we had anything scheduled," he questions and then lifts his phone from his pocket to check his calendar. He's wearing a pair of sunglasses Peach would expect to see on a fly fisherman or an outdoorsman of some sort. Squishy-looking, fabric-covered toggles trail from the frames, wrap around his head and disappear behind his ears.

"No," Peach says and pushes the phone down. "I just thought I would surprise you on your lunch break. I have something to ask you."

He looks up at her and smiles and she focuses on the little

gap in his front teeth. She tells herself he's the one, though there might be other options on paper, all the signs are pointing to Lars. Literal signs. Peach feels her stomach flip, aware that while it had been hard to maneuver close to Nell, the stripper had ultimately come out of the whole thing intact and well. Her attempts at befriending the woman hadn't ended in bloodshed and she wasn't saddled with the weight of taking a life she'd already had relation to in the past. The sacrifice had been carried out with a relative stranger, the tattooist. Lars Apitz was becoming less of a stranger every time they exchanged words.

She takes a breath and reminds herself this is all necessary work at the behest of universal elements much bigger than she is. This is the path to becoming Perfect Peach.

Lars is waiting for Peach to speak and he pushes his reflective glasses up onto his graying widow's peak. Then he cracks his lower back by placing his hands on his hips and twisting. "What is it?" he prompts.

"I never ask men out," Peach says and leaves it at that.

"So you're not asking me out? Or you are, and it's just you don't typically ask men out?" Lars punches Peach lightly on the shoulder, a bit of awkward contact to add to the awkward situation and the light tap hits a sore muscle on Peach. But she doesn't reach up to rub at it. She musters up courage instead.

"The latter, actually. I was wondering what you were doing this Saturday?" and as soon as Peach says it she wishes she could take it back. Because as much as she desires Perfect Peach to emerge completely, she also likes this man. Perhaps not as a romantic partner, but as a person.

Lars's smile drops away. "I've actually got plans. With my wife. She's wanting to talk about our financial arrangement and I said I'd see her." And then he gets quiet.

"No, oh, of course. You need to communicate with her. And we're not even really seeing one another. Just hanging out as friends. That's great. Really," Peach stutters and rambles until she conjures up an excuse to leave the conversation.

"I've got to get back to work. I've got a client in forty-five minutes." Then she begins to walk away, a mixture of happiness and frustration flowing through her due to his resistance. Perhaps the signs on his body are wrong. Perhaps there is another she can take instead and leave Lars to his failing marriage and his hedge funds and his Frisbee games.

But Lars grabs her under her elbow before she's out of reach and holds her steady. He steps his body closer to her and as he does so, he reaches a hand to his lumbar and frowns. Looking over his shoulder, he releases Peach and fingers the black, braided leather belt encircling his waist. Its leather softened from years of wear, the strap has frayed and come apart. Two dark tails grow out of the back of his work slacks. The ends are capped in unwoven fringe reminding Peach of thick, coarse hair.

Peach now understands there is no other for Taurus. There is only Lars. She can't remove her gaze from the broken, supple dyed bits of hide. They are heavy with portent. They mark the bull she means to use. The bull to wound her matador.

"The last of them!"

"The last of what?" Lars asks and then smiles. "It doesn't have to be Saturday, you know. For us to go out again."

"It does," she says.

But Peach will set plans with him later. For now she walks away, the noon sun bright on her face. Her eyes water and she convinces herself it's because of the stark power of the light and not because she knows Lars is good and nice and will still have to die.

48   RILEY

    Since the leaves of trees around town have burst forth with the warm courtesy of late April, Riley can't quite make out what's etched into the side of Simplot Hill as he drives up Harrison Boulevard. The street is lined with grand old houses, the architectural spoils of Boiseans who transformed the community from a military fort and mining post to a proper city in the late 1800s. He ducks his head up under his windshield while driving, trying to peer around the full canopy. No peek of the sign of Taurus yet. Then he's free of the trees and cruising up Bogus Basin Road. He finds a spot near the base of the hill to leave his Nissan, parks, and starts to climb the green incline.

    But he's stopped by a security guard in a blue uniform with a reflective orange vest across his ample torso. It's a curious getup for a man plainly visible, working in the light of midday. He catches Riley as he stretches his legs up the hill, careful how he steps with his left foot. The paid security waves a baton in his direction.

"I can't let you up there right now," the man explains. He has a wad of chew in his mouth, causing his lower lip to puff out in the middle. "Since the vandalism."

"But there is a sign up there, right? An astrological sign. How did they put it up on the hill?"

The guard spits into the manicured grass and Riley spies little flecks of tobacco nestled in the cracks between the man's teeth. "Could have been vinegar. Maybe a sludge of herbicide. They just killed the grass to make the shape. It's a bunch of dead sod. Not worth seeing."

Riley nods but knows he needs to see the symbol with his own eyes. "Are you sure I can't go take a look at it? You could come with me."

Riley hopes the guard will capitulate. Part of him thinks there might be some message or gift up on the hill just for him. It's unlikely, but the cards were never expected, the truck bombing a shock, the package of deep-fried flesh confounding. There was murder, paramount in ethical concern, though not as detrimental to Riley's life. He's not sure all these bizarre occurrences share causation but there is some link here he can't yet see.

"I can't help you there, bud. I have to walk the base of the hill and make sure no one is climbing up the sucker. But if you walk with me around the path, there's a place where you can see right up to it and get a good look."

He doesn't want to anger the paid security so he accompanies the man instead. They walk past a hedge of wild roses, pink blossoms reaching out over the little worn footpath around the hill. The guard speaks as they walk, fulfilling the role of a tour guide as well as a watchful eye.

"Did you know that the big house up on the hill was built by Joe Simplot? He was the one who made potatoes big business for Idaho. Sold tubers to McDonald's. And then it became the Governor's Mansion. Except Governor Otter won't live in it. He was married to Simplot's daughter for years. I suppose he didn't want to take up living in his ex-father-in-law's digs. The Governor has his own ranch somewhere. So it sits vacant. No one was up there to see who was dumping acid on the grass."

Riley keeps his head turned toward the rise, expecting the symbol to come into his line of vision at any moment. "Yea, I've heard all of that. I grew up in Boise. I used to sled down this hill during Christmas break."

"Right," the guard goes on, stepping high over a piece of fresh dog shit. "Now the muckety mucks don't want kids coasting down it and busting their bones. Mansion belongs to the state but the Simplots still own the land. It's my job to keep lookie loos from tramping about on private property."

"If I were chief I'd live in that big son of a bitch. I'd raise and lower the giant American flag flying over the house everyday and thank my Danish parents for coming to Idaho." The guard sniffs and stares up the grassy hillside.

"There are plenty of rich people out there who could live in the house. The state should off-load it. Sell it to a Kardashian or a Hilton. They could spend their monthly allowance to buy it," and Riley looks up and can just barely make out one of the sides of the house high up ahead. The roof is deep auburn, the trim on the house a tone of clay. It looks like a Mediterranean-style villa transported to an irrigated desert mountain.

The guard sticks his lip out and spits again. "I heard a rumor they plan on demolishing it later this year. But who the hell knows."

Then the path widens out and the men pass a little curve in the dirt walk. The guard points upward. Riley follows the path of his finger to the side of the hill. There, in vivid relief against the deep green of the sod, is a circle mounted with another half-circle in dead, yellow grass. The circle is wide enough to encompass a very large swimming pool and the lines above it stretch out, the killed-off grass ending at tapering points.

"I think it looks like a pig. The circle is his snout," the man explains. "But they tell me it's an astrological sign. Taurus, I think they said."

Riley gazes up at the looming symbol. "They're right," he confirms with the man and stays there long after the security guard walks on, promising he won't climb the hill. And the guard shakes his baton at him, not as a threat, but to wave goodbye.

49 PEACH

She knocks on the door and doesn't expect Linx to answer. Peach rarely visits her friend's house. It smells of fish sauce from his cooking and his neighbors work on a junker outside on their driveway each afternoon. Their stares are lewd and heavy. But she braves them now, one of the men scratching at his stomach while sipping on a can of light beer. She knocks louder and faster until Linx answers, apron around his waist, his hands coated in flour.

"Okay," he says to her but doesn't invite her in. "You must be sorry if you're here."

Peach doesn't believe she has anything to be sorry about, but she's missing the attention and comfort she's accustomed to receiving from Linx. As much as she doesn't want to be in a relationship with her friend and sex buddy, she still loves him as much as she can, as much as her soul and personality allow. He's perhaps the person whom she loves the most. And why she can't convey that fact to him confuses and taxes her.

"I don't want you to be mad at me," she says and looks at the white powder on his hands. "What are you cooking?"

Linx dusts the flour onto his front porch and the light breeze takes up the granules of wheat and sends them floating. "That's not the same as being sorry. It's like some murderer saying he's sorry he was caught after killing a bunch of people. You're just thinking about yourself."

"I'm trying to apologize for hurting your feelings, Linx." And then she uses his full name for effect. "Tuksin Lincoln, I was rude and insensitive the other day and I'm sorry for it. Now can I please come inside?"

Linx tries to hide his smile but as quick as he is to get upset, he's even quicker to warm when Peach admits wrongdoing. "You can't come inside right now. I've got to get cleaned up and get down to work. I've got a sous-chef saying he's sick with tinnitus. I'll have to call someone into the restaurant."

"A person can't be sick with tinnitus. It's ringing in the ears. A pain, but not like the mumps."

"The guy is a theatre major, I think," Linx explains it.

Peach tells him to wait and then walks quickly to her car parked behind his blue vintage Vespa scooter. "Now that you don't hate me, I have a favor to ask you," she hollers back over her shoulder.

"I never could hate you, Peach," he yells back. The men tinkering with the car snort in reply.

She pulls open one of the back doors of her car and takes hold of a woven dog leash. Roman the Lamb unfolds his legs and stands up. He's nervous about stepping down out of the car. Peach gives his leash a little tug, speaks softly to him and soon he's hopping down on the concrete, his tail waving in anticipation.

Linx's smile disappears as Peach leads the lamb to his door. She hears one of the lurkers next door call out "nice sheep!" and the other men back him up with laughter.

"No way," he says. "I didn't steal the lamb from its mother. Why would I raise it?"

"I'm not asking you to raise him, Linx. The fencing can't contain him anymore and it's not helping the possibility of me getting my deposit back on my apartment with him gumming on the cabinetry in the kitchen. Besides, you have a backyard. He needs air and grass all day instead of only in the middle of the night. Show some of that Buddhist compassion your mother forced you to practice."

Linx says something under his breath in Thai and Peach knows better than to ask for a translation. She tries to sweeten the deal.

"Besides, if he's here, I'll have to come over all the time and tend to him. You'll see even more of me. And you can name him. Whatever you'd like."

Linx looks down at the lamb and his shoulders drop. "You still haven't named Harry?"

"Harry? Really? I haven't thought of any good names and apparently neither have you," Peach lies. Then she takes Linx's flour-coated hands in her own and pries open his fingers. She slips the end of the leash into one of his palms and pushes his fingers around it.

Roman bleats, his light pink tongue shooting out of his mouth. It's nearly the same pink of the delicate, wispy scarf around Peach's neck.

"See, he likes you," Peach pushes. "And so do I. Do this for me and when I get my finances under control, I'll throw money at your church as payback."

"It's called a sangha," he corrects.

Then she grabs Linx's face, smearing his cheeks with the flour transferred onto her hands, and kisses him hard on the lips. She holds her lips there until she can feel the muscles around his mouth relax and yield to her pressure. There is more heckling of their exchange from next door, but Peach tries to tune out the catcalling.

When she releases him, Linx puts a hand on the lamb's head. "Why do I always let you get your way, Peach?"

"Because," Peach says, "no one else ever does."

SUMMER, 2012

50 RILEY

"It's not like I was showing off, Mayra," Riley tries to explain to his girlfriend. The woman's tan skin is a deep red and she pulls at her cuticles with her teeth. "I just showed your family my motorcycle. They liked it. Screw me for earning their praise."

She stomps around the large, covered patio at her parent's house in rural Caldwell, Idaho. The screening keeps the mosquitoes out as the day slips to night. Bright, warm colored lights cling to the gutters outside the patio, illuminating the fight between Riley and Mayra.

"They're just being polite to you. But now when you leave, they'll be asking me all these questions. Like how much money you have and if you plan on marrying me. You don't think of these things or the situations you put me in."

"But you have a nice house and a government job, Mayra," Riley paces behind her but doesn't dare reach out for her. She's been known to slap when she's angry and he's borne the red welts of her rage three times in the past. "You can take care of yourself."

She puts her hands in the air and tries to manage her voice, wrangle it back to a whisper. Her immediate family, father, mother and five siblings, along with their children, play a game of charades in the living room. "My parents are Mexican-Americans from a conservative generation. They were immigrant farm workers. They think the man needs to take care of the woman, no matter her paycheck. And you bringing that BMW bike here tonight will make them think you're wealthy."

"But I'm not wealthy. My parents are, but I'm not. What I am is a lawyer though, and I make good money. And I deserve to spend it any way I want."

Mayra lets her hands fall and she goes quiet. She looks around for a place to sit before slipping her hourglass figure into a chair with a metal frame and translucent blue and white plastic rungs. She puts her chin in her palms and stares out at the decorative lights, a border of luminescence marking where the yard begins. The rest of the expanse is swallowed in darkness.

"Sometimes I think you forget I was a migrant farm worker as well. That I had to miss school in the late summer and late spring to work the onion fields and the old cherry orchards they had in Emmet before they all burned down. How do you think it makes me feel to hear you speak like a titled rich boy?"

"It's entitled," he corrects.

"Jesus, Riley."

Riley stays on his feet in front of Mayra, her father's stiff tumbler of proffered tequila and soda rallying in his stomach. "What way am I speaking? Honestly? I'm enjoying myself."

"You're living to excess and then showing it off. I understand it's the American way. But it's not attractive, Riley. I hope you know I don't find it cute or sexy or something I'd want in a partner."

Riley scowls. "It's not about you, Mayra. What I do with

my finances. You've got zero say in how I live."

She dips her face completely into her hands and Riley can just make out her muffled words. Even in the dim light he can see she's bitten one of her cuticles down to the quick and a little trickle of blood winds down her right thumb.

"And maybe that's a problem."

He doesn't reply and instead makes for the rickety, wooden-framed door that leads from the screened-in porch out into the black. He aims to disappear into the sound of spraying water from sprinklers and the shouts of amusement and resonating bass drum emanating from a house party a block away.

FALL,
2008

51   PEACH

    Sick of eating ramen noodles every other day, Peach breaks down and begins to treat herself to weekly visits to a Vietnamese restaurant in an outdated, rambling series of storefronts in West Boise. Subsisting on the meager amount of money she saved while she was with her ex-husband Adam and the lump sum he gave her when she agreed to an annulment has been a challenge for Peach. Though he agreed to pay her tuition for Boise State University, her credit load is massive and she's unable to work on the side to bring in a paycheck. She eats when she's stressed. In this tough time, the bright cilantro and slivers of mango used as garnish in the restaurant meals are not just vibrant accoutrements to her entrée but a reminder, a promise of life and growth.

    Even when she does treat herself, the meal is still modest. She sits alone, her blond hair pulled into a ponytail at the top of her head so she doesn't dip any of her hair into the broth of her *pho*. She slides a smattering of bean sprouts from another bowl into her soup and stirs them around. Peach adds a small ladle of hot sauce, the little yellow discus seeds of the spicy peppers chunky in the red liquid. She smells it all before dipping in her Chinese-style spoon with the elongated head and short handle.

She's aware of the man looking at her from behind the host podium. Peach has seen him each time she's come to eat at the restaurant. It wasn't until a week or two ago he started staring at her openly while she dined. She never smiled his way, never encouraged his attention. After her spent marriage and the stress of trying to fit in at BSU, she had little interest in rallying the energy it would take to make a new friend.

But the man clearly feels differently. Peach can see him coming toward her, even with her face looking down into the brown broth.

"How is your *pho*?" he asks. Peach glances at him quickly and goes back to eating. He's small-boned, Asian, with short, black hair managed with gel. He's what some would call a hipster, sporting straight jeans and a cardigan in mustard yellow. He's attractive, but not her type.

"It's fine. Thanks," she says and doesn't continue the conversation.

"If there is anything else you need, let me know. I'm the manager."

And then the man points to his nametag to validate what he's just said. The name Tuksin is etched into the small, rectangular pin above his work title.

"Great," she says. But her aloofness doesn't deter him. He pulls out the seat opposite her, sits, and puts his elbows on the table.

"You should get some spring rolls or something with your *pho*. That's not enough to eat."

Peach does her best to remain polite and pushes away the desire to put down her spoon and excuse herself to the bathroom. "I'm sort of on a tight budget," she tells him.

"Ah," he exclaims, "I got you." He puts his hand up in the air and waves down a waitress. She rushes over and he orders a side of crispy, shrimp-filled rolls for Peach.

"On the house," he says and smiles.

She smiles back and says something stupid before she can stop herself, wanting to repay his kindness with a compliment. "Thank you. You know, your English is very good. I can't hear a Vietnamese accent at all."

He reaches over and places a handful of slender basil leaves directly into her bowl of *pho*, unbidden and unasked. "That's because I'm first gen American. And I'm not Vietnamese. I'm Thai. Well, half Thai anyway."

Peach watches him stir the fragrant, purple-hued vegetation into the soup with a chopstick, smiling all the while.

"There, try that. It's better with more basil."

Peach obeys, takes a cautionary sip of the broth and nods in appreciation.

The waitress is already back, a little plate of fried food and a vinegary sauce plopped down at the table. Peach wonders if it came out tout suite because the manager had asked for it.

She looks down at the extra chow and is happy for it. So happy she opens up just a little to the man sitting across from her.

"How do you know I'm not a vegetarian, Tuksin?" and she eyes the tag again and hopes her pronunciation isn't too far off.

"Because you're eating special *pho*. And it's got pig snout and coagulated duck's blood in it. Pretty good indication, I would say."

He pushes the plate of spring rolls over to her, sending an unused knife to the floor.

"And you can call me Linx, not Tuksin. Whenever you come in to eat."

Peach dips one of the little crispy delights in the piquant sauce. She rips into it and tastes the mellow flavor of rice noodles, feels the warm, pent up steam on her gums.

Peach chews slowly on a small taste of generosity from a stranger.

WEDNESDAY, THE 13TH OF MAY, 2015

52   RILEY

    Because he has no idea what to do about the astrological symbols and the cards, Riley decides to focus more attention on his finances. He parks along Idaho Street and peers out the window before getting out, heading to the building where his financial manager has his office. He wants to finagle an impromptu meeting with Lars. He's not sure what he's expecting to see outside his window, whether or not anyone is waiting for him in broad daylight, on a heavily-trafficked downtown street. But his neck grows tight and he fights to keep his breath even and deep though it's tending toward quick and ragged.

    Riley eventually gets out of his Nissan and walks west on the sidewalk. The revelation of the sign of Taurus on Simplot Hill has been fertilizer for his paranoia. He passes a man wearing a fedora in deep purple and the oddness of the hat causes him to move as far away on the sidewalk from the stranger as he can get. He steps quickly around doorways leading into wine bars or clothing boutiques. The fear drives his legs toward the office building, where he hopes to talk with Lars about something tangible and real and secure. Money.

He thinks of Sev and Nell. How they are likely in Blaze Lounge right now. One of them dancing nearly nude for leering men, the other stewing in anger, clutching his sore ribs. Riley conjures Sev's image in his mind and despite the poet's unshakable intensity and bad attitude, he's convinced he wasn't the one sending him the cards. Riley is beginning to think the spray-painted Aries symbols on the roadways and the Taurus symbol burned into Simplot Hill could be related to the weird messages. And he can't imagine Sev going to all that trouble to mess with a man who has, no, *had*, designs on his girlfriend.

He thinks it all has to be something bigger, mean something direly incomprehensible from his current perspective. Someone more dangerous, someone close to him is getting off on a new hobby of terror. Or he's completely delusional and the messages have nothing to do with the symbols around Boise. Riley believes in coincidence and its omnipresent ability to color life. He vacillates in opinion, talking himself into one possibility, then another before he steers his mind back to the idea of his financial future.

He's a block away from the glass and concrete behemoth which houses the financial advising business where Lars works. Riley strains to get his body and emotions under control. He wants to see if he can get Lars to figure out a way to slide past the time requirement of five years of marriage before he can touch part of the remaining one half of his deceased parents' estate. Riley is willing to get lawyers involved, maybe even Walker, and make a case that if he's mature enough and committed to someone enough to marry them, that should fulfill the stipulations of the estate plan.

No, he thinks, he only needs to talk Mayra into marrying him. He immediately admits to himself it would be easier to go back to work. Then his brain is spinning, self-doubt setting in and he tells himself there is no way the trust can be altered. He was a contract lawyer, for heaven's sake. He expects his parents would draft something foolproof and watertight because they knew Riley was prone to slacking off and skirting the rules.

The crosswalk signal switches from a glowing red hand to a little white stick person and Riley walks across the street to the building.

He's about to nix the idea of plotting to glean his parents' funds—go home and clean off his wound and get drunk—when the bomb explodes.

53   PEACH

Her hand had been on the remote trigger for fifteen minutes. And those fifteen minutes were agonizingly slow. She had thought to push the button when a gaggle of career girls in calf-length skirts and white tennis shoes had power-walked by the front of the office building on an exercise break. But something had whispered at her to hold back. And Peach had looked up to the blue sky and reminded herself the stars were there, just invisible to her because of the domination of the sun. So she heeded their words.

Then she'd seen him. Riley Wanner. He was walking toward the office building, no doubt to see Lars, his body pitched forward like he was using the breeze to propel him to his destination. His face was stony, his shoulders high and tense. There was a slight limp to his step.

Peach wondered if he was having a rotten time of things and that's when she pushed down hard on the trigger.

Now five, maybe seven car alarms sound monotonously in

the afternoon air because of the blast. The piercing scream of a woman who surely fears death is so intensely loud it drowns out the persistent sirens. The air is hazy with particulate, and she can't make out Riley in the chaos.

Peach stands up from the wooden bench she sat on the first time she made Lars come to her for their initial meeting. This is where she broke the twig in thirds for the little songbird. She looks down and sees the dry wood pieces are no longer there. She hopes the songbird was able to carry them off, that they didn't get kicked into a storm drain. She hopes they were used to make a nest up high in a waving cottonwood, defended against all earthbound hunters.

Emergency sirens drown out the common car alarms. The sharp noise of arriving cavalry moves closer to the scene and Peach walks away, taking calm, measured strides. She does not turn back to assess the damage she has caused. She turns down Bannock and pulls open the door of a clothing store specializing in outdoor wear. Things made of synthetic material. Things meant for action. The employees of the store gather around the front window, their heads pivoting, eyes searching for an explanation to the noises.

One of the employees uses her brain long enough to walk to the register, grab a set of keys and lock the front door. Her coworkers nod in agreement at her action and her small maneuver seems to set them more at ease.

"Might as well protect ourselves and the customers. We should add Siren Armageddon to the employee handbook. Write a checklist for the manual. I wonder what brand of crazy is taking place out there?" The woman's lips quiver slightly and once her act of bravery and verbal posturing is done, she goes back to stand with the other workers and a cluster of shoppers.

Peach slides moisture-wicking shirts around on a rack. The other customers shoot her glances but she goes about her perusal, embodying the attitude of a busy professional squeezing in a shopping trip between meetings. Around the rack clatter the wire loops of the hangers. She chooses to focus on that sound over the reverberation of the deafening alarms outside. She's looking for a top that allows for easy movement. Preferably something in pink.

54   RILEY

He stays with his cheek pressed into the cool sidewalk a
moment longer than necessary. His mind is taking its time to
realize he's been caught in the blast radius of some sort of bomb.
But his body doesn't tell him to run. It tells him to play dead, to
stay down, to avoid the aftereffects of the explosion. He pushes
past the paralyzing fear and gets his hands under his chest, ready
to lift himself off the ground but he doesn't push up his neck like
a rearing cobra or a sunning turtle. He hovers over the sidewalk.
He stays put.

Riley doesn't think he's been wounded.

Except for the fact that he's gone partially deaf.

He reasons the source of the blast must have been very
close to him. There is a loud ringing in his ears, coupled with
what he thinks might be sirens or alarms going off around him.
But he can't be sure of his safety unless he looks at something
other than the hard material under his nose. He finally pushes
himself to stand and checks his body over. He doesn't see any

blood or feel any pain except for in his left foot and the sonorous warbling in his ears, so he figures he's made it through the attack absent any life-threatening injuries.

Then he looks around him, at the others on the sidewalk during the blast. The air is slightly hazy, like Boise air gets during the summer when forest fires plague the area. A man shields an adolescent girl, his back up against the sturdy wall of the office building. He wraps his light jacket around her thin frame, as if he can will away the danger. As if a protective layer of nylon is sufficient enough to keep her out of harm's way.

Another man in a business suit with white hair hanging freely at the tops of his shoulders and skin the color of caramel has his palms up to the sky, his head tilted back. Riley thinks he looks to be praying for rain or an answer from some deity as to why he finds himself in such a predicament. What Riley can't figure out is why the man sports a toothy grin so wide his maw looks to consume the rest of his face.

Then a light rain does come, but it's of particulate matter. A light spattering begins to fall on Riley, and he realizes what felt like minutes of time cowering on the ground were actually handfuls of seconds. His processing of moments is skewed and slowed.

His head still enveloped in a cacophony of pitchy ringing, he sees a woman, her mouth open, her body folded into a fetal position though she remains crouching on her heels. He can't hear her, but her terror is real and he imagines her scream is a fitting match to her body. She suffers, contorted in the middle of the sidewalk like a frame from a silent horror film.

Riley sees then the dark splotches covering her blue dress and tan shoes. There are smears on her face and down the small of her back. He immediately believes it to be blood; the woman is severely wounded and he steps toward her to help.

But then he freezes as the rain of matter gets heavy. It feels like dirt hits his head and piles on his shoulders. He looks closer at the woman and can see what at first he took for blood is actually too brown.

The loud tone in his ears reduces in volume just a bit and as it does, it's as if his nose kicks back to life. He rubs some of the earthy matter off of his shirt and holds it up to his face to give it a sniff. It reminds him of summer drives he'd take to his grandparents' house in Burley, three hours east of Boise. Past the farms and dairies and expanse of endless steppe he sometimes wished he could be lost in and left to his own wild machinations.

"It's cow manure!" he screams but the other people cannot hear him and he cannot hear himself.

55   PEACH

Peach is halfway home when she gets a call from Lars.

"You're not downtown are you? You weren't on your way to my building to surprise me again?" he asks. His voice is terse and his words are quickly spoken.

She feigns mild disinterest into the phone. "No. I'm on my way home to grab some files I forgot this morning. I don't surprise people too often. I hope you didn't get your hopes up."

Lars sighs, his breath making her phone's speaker crackle. "Because there was a bomb set off downtown. Right in front of my building."

"That's horrible," Peach says and does her best to affect a panicked tone. "Are people okay?"

Then Lars laughs for a moment before cutting short another guffaw. She notes how he tones down his mirth and her lips crack into a smile.

"No, that's the thing. It wasn't filled with shrapnel or gas or anything which could kill or maim. It was filled with bullshit.

Literally. Cow manure. It's all over the south side of the first floor of the building. A few people got caught in it, but they're more shaken up than hurt. One of them is a client of mine. I went down and made sure he was okay. But he's a tough guy. He'll probably laugh about it someday."

Peach pulls into her numbered stall outside her apartment building and kills the engine. She stays seated and gives Lars her full attention. "I can't believe something like that would happen in Boise. Did anyone see who did it? Do they have a description of a person or maybe the type of device used?"

"No, Lisa," Lars says, then pulls away from the phone for a moment to say something to someone, most likely another onlooker gazing out the window in his office. "But they're forcing us to stay inside for now. It just happened. Like a half hour or so ago. I personally think it was someone still pissed about the economy. Lost his retirement plan back in oh eight. I mean, you know our company logo is a bull, right? I bet it's a tongue-in-cheek 'fuck you' to our business."

"You know," Peach says, "that's not a bad assumption to make. That really could be it."

Lars is distracted again, says something else to someone other than Peach before clicking back into the conversation. "So hey, listen, about Saturday night. I know I said I was busy with my wife. But hell, after what just happened, I'm having one of those 'life is too short' moments. She and I can talk money anytime. So why don't we get together instead?"

"Are you sure? I wouldn't want to pull you away from anything you need to do. We can hang out another time."

"I mean it, Lisa. I want to spend the evening with you. So get your thinking cap on and take me somewhere special."

Peach says she will concoct a grand plan, that Lars will certainly have an interesting time. She lets him go when she can hear another deep voice beg him to come and see some new situation forming outside the office windows.

She grips the steering wheel tightly and the vinyl squeaks between her fingers. She doesn't want to do it, but she must. And she knew it would work out in her favor. She'd been told as much. She looks over to the passenger seat and grimaces at the bag that holds her new purchase.

"I'll wear you once. On Saturday, like I knew I would," she speaks to the bag, the fabric inside, her fate.

56   RILEY

Once he's checked over by paramedics and once he gives his statement—replete with gestures to convey the look of the man with the purple fedora and written exclamations due to his hearing loss to a police officer who looks a bit like a lovechild of Marilyn Monroe and Pete Townshend—Riley is free to leave.

He gets home and the ringing in his ears finally subsides enough for him to stop worrying the deafness will plague him for too much longer. He showers the manure off of his body and slides on a pair of workout shorts and a tank top. He checks to see if he locked the door after he entered his home. He did, dead bolting it as well, but he continues to check it for the rest of the afternoon, until he's too antsy to be alone and he calls Walker to come over.

By the time his friend arrives with a bag of Chinese takeout in hand, Riley's ears are working as well as if he'd attended an especially loud concert without earplugs. Riley checks to make sure it's Walker through the peephole before opening up the door. He wonders what shellshock feels like, then feels an ass for thinking one semi-harmless bomb could give him the same mental distress as a soldier.

"General Tso's Chicken," Walker says and walks it directly into the kitchen. Riley frowns at the choice in dish, thinks of Sev's affinity for Chinese food, and feels even worse for hurting the man as badly as he did.

Walker busies himself with pulling plates from the cupboard, assembling forks and napkins. "Start talking to me, Rye. I heard about the bomb. One of the interns was across the street from it when it went off. He said it looked like a brown Hiroshima and I told him to cool it on the hyperbole. Won't land him a permanent position at the firm. So you were right in it?"

Riley leans up against the threshold between the kitchen and his dining room and sniffs at his arms. There is a faint fecal smell still there and he decides he'll shower again before going to bed.

"I was in the middle of an actual shit storm. If I weren't so freaked out by the experience I could deliver a slew of jokes about it. What if whoever set off the explosive is the same person who's sending me the cards? I got a new one the other day, Walker. And a package of fried meat to go along with it."

Walker stops his dinner preparations. He gives Riley a puzzled look before opening up the little takeout containers and doling rice and saucy chicken equally on the two plates.

"Fried meat? Do you still have it? You didn't eat it, did you?"

"I'm not actively seeking botulism, Walker. I put it down the disposal. I videoed the whole opening of the delivery on my phone. You can watch it with me after we eat. You want to see the card?"

Riley goes to his study, where he keeps the weird communications, and comes back with the stack. They retire into the dining room to eat on the glass table Riley uses when he has a woman over, trying to impress her with a shoddily home-cooked meal, or Walker as a guest, who prefers formal dining. He'd told Riley on more than one occasion that the customs and eating habits of humans stood as a divide between animals and intelligent life. Walker looks over the new card as he slips bites of deep golden chicken into his mouth.

"You've got to go to the police, Rye. Now more than ever. These messages are getting beyond bizarro."

Riley chews some fried rice and pushes around a wrapped fortune cookie with his index finger. "What if it was the same person who set off the bomb?" He reiterates his worry.

"Okay," Walker says, "what if? Did you have an appointment scheduled today with your financial advisor? A meeting someone could have traced or known about?"

Riley shakes his head. "Actually, no. My plans were spontaneous. I was just going to drop by and chat with Lars," he pauses. He considers telling Walker about his plan to access more of the Wanner funds, but decides he doesn't want a lecture addressing his stupidity. "About money woes. Retirement questions, too."

"Then I think it would be hard to link the explosion to you being there. It might simply have been an instance of being in the wrong place at the wrong time."

The Chinese doesn't sit well in Riley's stomach. He puts his fork down and pushes away his plate. "But what about the other stuff? There are astrological symbols around Boise. And then Double Al's truck. And the tattooist dude who got killed."

"Symbols? Like the painted roads and the big one left by some punk on Simplot Hill? I saw a letter to the editor in the *Idaho Statesman* about it. Guy thinks terrorists are mucking with our minds via our horoscopes. Nonsense. Now the murder, the truck torching, there is something to focus on. You're finally considering it might all fit together?" Walker continues to eat.

"I don't know. Maybe there is a relationship I'm not able to clearly see. Or it's just my crap luck and some weird coincidences messing with my mind. I don't know."

"But it's more than enough concern to take to the police. Really. If you think it could all be linked, tell someone. Do you want this asshole to keep sending the letters? And if he's really dangerous and doing things like setting off explosions or worse, murder, you could stop it. Now."

Riley picks up the yellow, half-moon cookie in its plastic wrapping. He pops the air out of the packaging and then rips it open. He breaks the cookie in half and pulls the fortune free. He laughs and reads it for Walker.

"So generic, but it says, 'Good things come to those who wait,' so I guess I should hold my tongue. Keep up my guard but see how this all starts to play out. Besides, you're a lawyer. I was one. You know I don't have hard evidence for the police to back my fears. What I have is paranoid suspicions. The bomb has me rattled. I need to keep a clear head. Think this thing through."

Walker puts down his own fork and levels a stare at Riley.

"I bet it's just some dude I pissed off. And all the other things are just random, lousy things happening in the city. Because it's life, and life is crazy, cruel, and super chaotic." And as Riley speaks he starts to believe himself.

Walker reaches over and pulls Riley's plate toward him. He tucks into the forsaken food and speaks between mouthfuls.

"You're a stubborn, stupid dickbag, Rye."

THURSDAY, THE 14TH OF MAY, 2015

57   PEACH

Outside the little community arts and recreation center near the road up to Table Rock—the prominent limestone mesa which rises above Boise, capped with a glowing neon cross—Peach carries her creation in a wide-mouthed cardboard box. Complete with a domed theatre for small scale plays and an outdoor softball field, the old, brick building is welcoming and open, people flowing to and from it this Thursday midday. Peach balances the box carefully in her arms, dodging a group of four-year-olds racing ahead of a horde of coffee-toting, gossiping stay-at-home mothers.

One of the moms holds the front door open for Peach. She thanks the woman, slips inside the place. The hallways are dated with squares of white vinyl on the floor and walls covered in dark wood paneling. She checks an old letter-slide style directory behind glass and notes the two places she needs to go. First stop, the pottery room.

Peach locates the room just a few doors away from the main

entrance. She peers inside the window set into the door and thinks no one is around to aid her. Though the room is dim, there is light in a far corner, near a wide window that allows in the afternoon sun. She puts the box down at her feet and knocks before picking it back up and entering, unwilling to wait for permission.

A young woman, college-aged with thin arms and a braid dipping to the small of her back, waves at Peach. She stands from where she was seated at a potter's wheel. The form of a long-necked vase grows from the clay mass resting on the slab of stone in front of her. She picks up a grungy towel caked in gray muck and wipes off her hands.

"What can I help with?" she asks Peach and moves toward her.

Peach keeps the box in her grasp and smiles. "I heard anyone in the community could use the kiln here. For a fee, of course."

"Yeah," the girl responds and points to a rectangular, metal box akin to an oven in one of the corners of the room. It's painted a sky blue and the handle is coated in dried clay. It looks well-used and old.

"I have this project I did at home. And I'm hoping it doesn't take too long to fire. I looked up the information about painting and glazes and all the rigmarole and I'm hoping it will harden evenly. Don't want the thing to crack."

The girl motions her over to a high worktable and asks Peach to set the box down so she can take a look at her project. Peach insists on lifting her creation out of the cardboard and setting it very gently on the surface of the table.

"You made this? If it's your first time working with clay, I'm certainly impressed," the woman says and eyes the form in front of her.

Peach nods and points to a few places she thinks might be subject to cracking in the high heat of the kiln. But the girl assures her it will likely make it out okay. And if not, there are ways of mending mistakes.

"Even if it doesn't come out perfectly, you'll have something you made yourself. That's got to feel good. I know it always feels good when I have something on my shelf made with my own fingers, designed by my own brain."

"It does," Peach says. "And I didn't even think I was that artistic."

She spins her pink sapphire ring around on her finger and looks down at the thing she's made. It's a bit ugly, certainly not symmetrical, but it was propelled into existence by a burgeoning need to create art. More importantly, it was made in ritual, with intent and future purpose.

"So how long will it take to bake? Do you potters call it baking in a kiln? And do the tints look okay on it? I just added bits of different-colored clay in a few spots. That will stay, right?"

The woman points to the clay figure and dips her head around it to look at it without touching it. "It will be fine. The colors will show after the glaze. And you'll be able to come back in a few days and get it. It will be ready for your home. And we say 'firing' though the clay does technically bake."

Peach looks around the workroom—at the wooden racks with drying pots and figurines and bowls—and thinks of the generations of humans who have worked the earth, their fingers in clay, their skin seared by high heat. Just so others could have storage containers and cups for water and representations of their gods. She looks down again at her work and though it's elementary, finds no shame in the end product. It's beautiful. And she wishes she could keep it, but realizes it does not belong to her.

The girl pulls her braid over her shoulder. Her fingers pick at flecks of dried clay holding together clumps of brown strands as she nods to the kiln.

"Do you know how that behemoth works? Well, other than firing the clay?"

Peach shrugs and the woman continues. "The temperature starts out low, and then it rises. Once it gets over six hundred degrees Fahrenheit, the water bonded with the clay begins to evaporate. And then, when it reaches over nine hundred degrees, all the water has been cooked out. At that point, the very structure of the clay has changed. You don't have a clay project anymore. It'll be ceramic."

Peach looks to the closed door of the kiln and wonders what's subjected to stifling, killing heat right now. "So it becomes something completely different. There is no water left. Only pure earth. And it can never go back to what it once was, right?"

The woman picks up Peach's work, finding the best way to grasp the awkward angles of the creation and places it carefully back into the cardboard box. "Yep. You can't un-glaze it or change its color. Plus, it'll shrink a bit. Hope you planned for that."

Peach knows the girl doesn't see the significance she sees in the transformation, and she's glad for it.

"No, it doesn't matter if it shrinks. As long as the form remains."

"It will," she says.

Peach leaves her first name, last initial and ten dollars to help pay for the electricity and attention to turn her creation into one that's solid and permanent. The woman looks down at the little slip of paper and then tapes it to the box.

"Alright, Lisa A., come back in a few days or leave your number and someone here will call when it's ready."

"I'll just come back early next week."

Peach wishes her work a silent farewell. She touches the top of the clay and leaves a very slight imprint of her fingertip in the material. It's next to one of the colored patches and she cannot smooth it away without destroying part of her work. She tells herself it will be all right if a little divot persists.

Peach knows it doesn't have to be perfect. It just has to be what it is. Before she leaves her work in the hands of the young woman, she thanks her and asks her one last question.

"Do you know if there's anyone in the metal shop today?"

58 RILEY

With his decision made about not approaching the police until he has genuine evidence and can be certain the detectives no longer tie him to the dead tattooist, Riley decides he must put more effort into finding out who's sending the letters. If he's not content with going back to his job at High Desert Trommel, his days must be dedicated to more than a bottle of Irish whiskey and internet porn. His goal takes him back to the place he was at just a few days earlier. A place that helps him understand more of the puzzle, even if the sections he currently gathers belong to different box sets. He feels as if he has pieces of a seaside wrought in pastel, a mountain photograph, and a teacup stuffed with a kitten; he's taxed with turning them all into one cohesive, complete jigsaw.

The second floor of the library is warm. The units running alongside the walls under the windows pumping out cool air do little to combat the heat emanating from the people using the rows of computers, reading heavy reference books on high-sided desks and weaving in and out of the towering rows of well-loved books. It reminds Riley of his days and nights spent in the law library at University of Idaho, pouring over case law. He doesn't miss the experience at all.

He sees the same reference librarian he'd talked to on Monday. She's wearing a billowy top which reminds him of the brightly-colored synthetic jumpsuits clowns would prance about in when his parents would take him to the Barnum and Bailey circus. She's aiding a patron, supplying a man with a few photocopied maps of some unidentifiable urban landscape.

Riley waits patiently for her to finish with the gentleman. Another reference librarian puts her hand up and tries to wave him over to her desk, but he sticks to his spot and tells her he'd prefer to talk with Amelia. A minute later the man in front of him leaves and Riley slips into the chair parked in front of the woman's desk.

She eyes him for a moment and he can tell she recognizes him, but can't quite place him. He resists the urge to reach out and mess with a small airplane knickknack near her keyboard. If he picks it up, he'll toss it from hand to hand to help ease his jitters. But the item might have sentimental value. It's likely not meant for public fondling.

The librarian's head bobbles about as she waits for him to speak. He wonders if the incessant motion means she's agreeable to all she senses and witnesses, or if the action is some sort of autistic soothing or exaggerated tick.

"I'm one of the conspiracy nuts who came in here asking about astronomy and astrology. And you told me about the astrological signs in the intersections and the new one on Simplot Hill."

Her face lightens and she wags a plump finger at him, matching the speed of her dipping chin. "Yes, I remember you now. Did you go to the hill and take a look?"

"I did and it drummed up more questions and zero answers.

I'm back to see if any of the books have come in yet that I requested."

She doesn't bother to check the computer. "We call or email when a book is in for a patron. So unless you've heard from us, they're all still checked out."

Amelia looks Riley over and he can tell she can see his desperation. It shows in the bags under his eyes, the way he leans forward in his chair like she's a magnet and he's pure ore.

"Are you sure we can't look up some internet resources for you?"

And this is when Riley considers sharing his strange story with the reference librarian. If he's resolved not to go to the police and knows Walker won't listen patiently to many more anxious, prattling theories, he'll have to tell someone. He wonders if she'll think he's crazy. But then he considers she may be able to take his information and point him in the right direction. To answers.

"So," he starts, looking around the large, open room. "Is there some sort of confidentiality clause between library patrons and reference librarians? Sort of like with doctors and lawyers? Like if I was to tell you something, would you be sworn to secrecy?"

The woman pulls back, her hands gripping the sides of her work chair and she offers up an odd little smirk. "I suppose it depends on what you want to share. I am a civil servant, in a way. And I work for the city. If anything is told to me that's potentially threatening to myself or others, like a description of a past crime or intent to do something illegal, I would be obligated to share that information with my supervisor and the police."

Then she laughs her high-pitched giggle with its punchy rhythm and her entire body rolls along with the mirth.

"But if you want to tell me about some conspiracy theory or about your relationship with your girlfriend, I'm all ears. Until someone else needs my help with a real reference matter. I play counselor to my sister all the time so I can play a bit for you. It would be best if this actually pertains to your research, though."

Riley gives her a smile back and waits for her to finish her giggling. "I don't have a girlfriend, at least not right now. Actually, never mind. I was just curious."

He gets quiet, annoyed he's hit an impasse. He's not sure he can risk telling her anything. She could alert the police. The last thing he needs is to recapture the attention of the detective with the long teeth and the detective with the licorice.

She types something into her computer and looks away from Riley for a moment. He decides as long as he's in front of her, he should ask a somewhat nebulous question. It could lead to some insight about who set off the bomb the other day.

"What if someone were to come into the library and ask about, say, making bombs? You know, the way they work or how to set them off. You would have to tell someone about the person, right? You'd report them?"

And once the words are out of his mouth and he sees the slightly incredulous look on the librarian's face, he realizes she thinks he's the one asking about these things. Not fishing for a tale of someone else who had recently come into the library to learn about explosives.

She stays mum, her lips pressed together and Riley feels he has to explain himself.

"Not for me. I'm just saying, like if someone came in recently and asked about those things, you would report them to the police, right?"

She nods slowly this time and then her eyes widen. "Are you talking about the bomb that went off downtown yesterday? Because we have added security here now. To protect the patrons and employees."

And then she looks over to the stairwell running between the first, second and third floors. A hired security guard with a heavy beard leans against the stair railing and eyes the people who wander around the second floor.

Riley is concerned Amelia will try to get his attention and wave him over or press a distress button under her desk. So he changes tactics quickly.

"Actually, there is something you can help me with. I'm looking for books on private investigation and how to woo women. Like a how-to manual for getting a lady to be in a relationship with you."

And like that, Amelia reverts back to her state of good humor and taps away at her keyboard. She blinks heavily at Riley. "I don't think you'd have problems with the ladies. You're a good looking man."

"It's not the getting ladies I have problems with. It's keeping them. Or rather, wanting to keep them."

"Ah," she says and writes down a few call numbers for him. "All the options are on this floor. Let one of the pages know if you need help."

Riley stands, folds the piece of paper and stuffs it away in his pants pocket. He looks around the room again and sees a man, probably homeless, in a filthy sweatshirt and cut-off jean shorts. The guy is eyeballing him. Riley meets his gaze. The man sticks out his tongue at Riley before opening his mouth into a wide yawn that shows off his decaying teeth. He looks a bit like an aged wild cat. Out of his prime but still dangerous.

As much as he wants to find the books, he's uncomfortable about the man. Is he just some homeless guy staring at Riley, or is he the card-sender? He decides he's relatively safe staying in the library, surrounded by all these people. He looks at Amelia before searching the rows of books for lessons on how to track people down and how to make women commit to someone who doesn't like commitment.

"I really meant nothing by that question," he says to her. "I had other information I wanted to share with you."

She looks up at him, her face doughy, her smile kind. "If

you decide you want to share, I'll be here. But if you get kooky on me, I'll report you."

Amelia nods at Riley and he walks away, the eyes of the homeless man following his path. He delves into an aisle space between shelves housing millions of pages, hundreds of stories.

SATURDAY, THE 16TH OF MAY, 2015

59   PEACH

She dials Lars's number into the phone she uses only for him. It rings once before he picks up.

"Lisa," he says, short of breath. "Hi."

"Hey," she replies. She's sitting at the desk in her living room, missing the company of Roman, but anxious for the event she has planned tonight. "Are you working out?"

"I was doing chest and back," he tells her, his breath still uneven and taxed. "You're not calling to cancel, are you?"

She shakes her head and speaks. "No, not at all. I was actually calling to get you to do something for me. I need you to go to Municipal Park and wait for me there. I'll pick you up and take you on a little adventure."

She can almost hear him smile into the phone. "Isn't that the park we met in? Are you getting romantic on me?"

Peach knew the man would come to that conclusion, even though her intent was to get him somewhere away from his home, where neighbors and friends couldn't watch her pick him up and take him away.

"Yes, it's where we met. Though I recall the blue Frisbee was fresher that day with me than you were. And maybe I can be as romantic as I want to be. So there."

He laughs and his breath begins to even out. Peach tries not to think of Lars lifting weights. She knows he's in good physical condition and she's sorry for it.

"What time? What do I need to bring along?"

"Just get to the park around five. And you don't need to bring anything other than yourself. But dress for something outdoorsy. I guess you can bring along some water."

"Outdoors?" he asks and she can hear the excitement in his voice. "I didn't think I ever told you about my favorite hobby. It fits in with the outdoors theme for our date."

"Oh yeah," she says, "and what is that?"

"I hunt," he says plainly. Then he follows up with, "I hope you aren't against it. I know a lot of women think all hunters are brutes and assholes. But I guarantee you I kill humanely. I build a relationship with the animal I'm hunting and I don't view the action as entertainment."

Peach wishes she could give the same guarantee in terms of a humane death. And while she's not repulsed by his hobby, she would never willingly hunt down and kill an animal. The fact that Lars does this regularly enough to consider it a hobby, and she assumes has some skill at it, makes her concerned for the night ahead.

"I have no moral problems with hunting," she responds. "But keep your guns and arrows at home. No good would come from you packing heat on our date."

"Fair enough," he says and then his voice gets quieter. "I'm really glad I met you, Lisa. I think we can have a lot of fun together. It's been difficult, with my separation. I haven't wanted to move on with the divorce proceedings because I've seen what's out there in terms of partners. You wouldn't believe how many women can turn loony on you. I don't get that feeling from you. You seem true to yourself. Not overbearing or aggressive, but like you're just getting the feel for the woman you want to be."

Peach swallows and does her best to keep her voice from trembling or breaking. "I'm glad we met, too. It's fate. Probably set out in the stars."

He laughs again. "I don't know if I'd go that far quite yet. But I'll see you later on tonight."

And when Peach puts down the phone and takes a look around her empty apartment, she starts to feel dizzy, her throat tightens and her palms sweat. She puts her head between her knees and takes in long, measured gulps of air.

"Who said this would be easy?" she reminds herself, her voice sounding louder, flesh squeezed against her head. "Who said he'd be a simple sacrifice? Who said he wouldn't be a hunter?"

And she stays like this, nearly in a fetal position until her body relaxes and her lungs stop their labored pumping. She nestles her head down deeper and curses herself for not being more thorough with her research. She promises herself that next time, for the others, she'll be a better investigator of character.

"But," she reminds herself, "there is no controlling the signs on this one. They flare across him like comets across the nighttime firmament."

Peach grits her teeth and flips her head up. Her wig goes flying from her scalp, revealing blond fuzz and the patch of new, prickly hair that springs up from the black V with its curly tops.

60   RILEY

Because the afternoon is pleasantly warm, accompanied by a gentle wafting of cool air, Riley decides what might be best for him is a walk. His foot feels better today than it has since he kicked Sev and he urges himself to keep testing his balance and stamina. To keep moving. So that someday he might be able to run.

He locks up his house, something he would have never done before the cards just to take a stroll around his neighborhood. But now, with the psycho knowing where he lives and being brazen enough to come to his doorstep at least once, he doesn't chance making it easy for the man to get inside his personal space. Riley draws the line at the front porch. The man will get no farther.

He starts down the street and eyes every car he passes parked on the road and even the ones in the driveways of houses where he doesn't know the residents. He has his old Hacky Sack tucked into the toe of his running shoe and it's working as ballast for the time being, though he figures it'll get uncomfortable if he walks too far.

Riley allows himself to consider all he's seen and been through in the last short while. The pieces dally around his mind. He sees the sheep downtown, numbers in red on their wooly sides. He recalls the way his ears felt, useless and assaulted after the explosion. He tries to call the tattooist's face to mind, but he'd only met the man once, long enough for him to put a line of black ink near the juncture of his ankle and foot. Riley looks down to his left foot cradled in its shoe, his wound and his barely-begun tattoo hidden from sight.

"It's all odd," he whispers to himself, "but it could all be odd, randomly."

He passes by the house of the divorcee, the man whom he talked to the day before Easter. He had been seeding his front yard with vividly-colored plastic eggs. The man is not outside, but a teenager is washing a Lexus in the driveway. He wears a heavy sweater, shorts and flip flops. It's a typical outfit for a young man raised to be hardy against the Idaho cold. His hair is shaggy, in need of a cut and it covers his ears. His body looks as though it has just experienced a gangly shot of growth.

"Your car?" he asks the boy as he continues to walk.

"Nah, I wish," he replies and scrubs at a bit of dirt on the back window.

Riley remembers when his own father would make him wash his beige-colored Saab. Riley would dream of owning his own car, something fast and low to the ground in cherry red. But the desire for speed and automotive muscle had faded once he could actually afford to buy his own sporty vehicle. He'd gone with an SUV instead. But he'd never been sure of why he'd made that choice.

As he walks, Riley becomes acutely aware he's never really quite sure of why he makes most of his choices. He blames habit and laziness and programming. He does not blame himself. Not really.

He walks, passes a few streets in his neighborhood, sticking to the smooth surface of the concrete sidewalk. His wound begins to ache and he decides to turn around and make it back to his house before he's gimping his way to the couch. He hears the sound of a door slamming shut and his eyes snap in the direction of the thud, his nerves on edge.

Out of a dark blue two-story house walks Nicole Trey. The woman he exchanged greetings with the night Double Al's truck was set aflame. The best friend of his ex. The woman he slept with anyway.

Riley can't move fast, doesn't have the option of fleeing before he's seen. So he stands his ground and puts a smile on his face. Nicole winds down the front walk of the house, fumbles for the keys to her car and catches sight of Riley. She's wearing a tight-fitting blazer with designer jeans clinging to her long legs.

"You again?" she says to him and he nods. She abandons her poking around for keys and walks down the driveway to the sidewalk. She keeps her distance but her body is relaxed, her face calm, framed by mousy-brown hair.

"I guess Boise is still a small city, right? No matter if those population signs on the outskirts of town keep ticking up. How are you, Nicole?"

"I'm okay," she responds and then she looks down the street in the direction Riley had been walking. "Do you live around here?"

"I do," he says and leaves it at that. "You live here?"

"No," she says, equally evasive.

Riley checks her out casually, not wanting to leer. She still has the same shapely legs that seem to take up two-thirds of her body. He remembers how soft they were wrapped around his ears. The image embodies their relationship: great physical chemistry with little to actually talk about. He recalls he didn't even know her last name until his ex-girlfriend Kristin had spewed out Nicole's full name to him long after he'd stopped having sex with the woman, but before Kristin had stopped making him pay for his mistakes.

Both Riley and Nicole look uncomfortable, caught off-guard at the impromptu meeting. Riley thinks to ask her about her life the past few years he hasn't seen her, but then he decides the question would come off as disingenuous because he doesn't actually care. And while he wouldn't mind another go with her in the sack, he's resolved to find a woman who might become his partner. A woman like Mayra, or preferably, just Mayra.

It's Nicole who speaks next. She looks at Riley's feet and points.

"There's something wrong with how you're standing. You're not putting all your weight on your left foot."

Riley looks down, too, and notes he's leaning to his right.

"You're observant," he tells her. "I had a little accident. My foot got hurt. That's all."

"I tend to pay attention to details now," she says. "Unlike I did in the past. But bummer about your foot. I hope it heals completely."

He doesn't tell her that it never will. That his five toes from his left foot are rotting in some toxic waste dumpsite by now. Or long since incinerated in a giant oven. He wonders what happened to the parts of him he lost and he's suddenly mad he never thought to ask. Or thought to keep what belonged to him.

"It's fucked, actually. But thanks. Maybe we'll run into one another again," he says, turning away from his old mistake.

"We could only be so lucky," she says quietly and goes back to searching for her keys.

61   PEACH

He's waiting for her at the entrance of the city park as she
pulls into the lot at five on the dot. She keeps her seat and waves
at him to get in. While he walks toward her car, she cranes her
head around to see the tree, the giant oak that had helped her out
with meeting Lars in April. She says a silent thank you to the old
hardwood and smiles when Lars slips into the passenger seat.

"Are you ready for this?" she asks him and puts her car into
reverse.

"More than ready," he tells her, cradling a hiking bag on his
lap. She eyes it before pulling out onto the main road and
making for Warm Springs Avenue, one of Boise's oldest roads
lined with stately mansions.

"What did you bring?" she asks and hopes he doesn't
respond with an affirmative on weaponry.

"Just some snacks and a change of clothes. A few survival
things. I like to be prepared. Never caught off guard."

She keeps her eyes on the road, twisty and sparely traveled

as it transitions into Highway 21. Lars points at bikers out on the Greenbelt and when they curve past the dam, its side printed with the command to *Keep Your Forests Green*, he finally starts asking questions.

"So where are we going exactly? Or is it really a surprise? Because I sort of hate surprises."

"Do you? Well, it's not that big of a surprise," and then she answers him, to put him at ease. "I wanted to show you a site I found a while back. Near Idaho City. Thought we could mess about and then get some dinner in town. Trudy's has amazing huckleberry cheesecake."

"Cheesecake isn't dinner," he says and turns toward her. "And what do you mean by 'mess around'?"

"I mean exactly what I said," she smirks and then changes the subject.

"Did you know Idaho City was once the biggest town in the Pacific Northwest? There were opera houses, with emphasis on the plural. Boise doesn't even have *an* opera house. And it had several saloons and groceries and a huge population of Chinese gardeners to boot. Out of the first two hundred people to be buried in the pioneer cemetery, only twenty-eight died of natural causes. Can you imagine if those odds still held today?" Her nerves cause her to take on the role of tour guide as she drives onward, words slipping from her mouth so quickly she slurs some of them together.

"Geez," Lars responds, "did you do some research for our trip or what?"

"I like to be informed about places I visit," she replies as they crest a hill that gives them a supreme view of the Boise foothills, the bridge that spans Mores Creek, and the swath of blue known as Lucky Peak Reservoir. Peach thinks of all the boats that will zip across the water come the summer, tubers and water-skiers in their wakes.

Lars cranes his neck above the dashboard to watch a hawk

play on the current of air above the highway. Peach has noticed the bird of prey keeping pace with their car, ruddy wings showing up in her peripheral vision every few minutes of the drive.

Peach goes on with her rambling off of knowledge, determined to keep him occupied.

"Even though it was a hard life for the residents of Idaho City, they had the promise of riches to keep them there. That bit I thought you'd like. The fact that most of them were miners in search of gold. So many of those men came out west to improve their financial situation. They were driven by money, just like a lot of people today."

"Ah," Lars says, sitting back. "But not you. I bet you won't do even a fraction of the things I've suggested in order to pad your retirement portfolio."

"Then teach me something right now," she prompts him. "Even if I choose to be ornery and ignore your wisdom."

He flips on the air and adjusts the vents to point at his body. "Let's see. Okay. How about we learn a term, a definition? Do you know what a bull market is?"

Peach had been holding the steering wheel lightly, her hands on the underside of the circle. She puts them up at ten and two and grips the vinyl tightly until her knuckles turn white.

"No," she finally replies. "Tell me."

"It pertains to stock markets. Basically, a bull market is one where there is a high level of optimism and confidence on the part of the investors. They make the price of shares go up, whether or not there is a rhyme or reason to it. The belief in the strength of their convictions is enough."

"I could get behind that," Peach answers and smiles. "The optimism and confidence leading to success, I mean."

And then she presses for more, because she's curious and she's anxious to know the origin of the term for her own sake. "But why is that a bull market?"

"It has to do with the way a bull attacks its opponent. There is a bear market, too. Which is the opposite of the bull market. Pessimism and fear controlling the moods of investors. So while the bear swipes its paws downward to hit its prey, the bull lifts upward with its horns. Get it? The bull acts with an upward attack. Hence, bull market when things are looking good."

"I like it," she says as they twist through the dry, sagebrush-dotted hills that eventually give way to mountains covered with blankets of pine. Currant bushes and willows crowd against a creek to the left of Peach's Honda. "Thank you for telling me."

Peach allows herself a bit of silence and time to think about the attack of a bull. She imagines how it must feel to be gored or trampled. She says a silent prayer to her friends overhead to keep her safe.

The rest of the drive they talk more of Idaho City and finances, swapping tales with one another, until the small town comes into view. They pass a few restaurants settled into the old pine lodgings left from the late 1800s and keep on driving through the remains of the nearly-abandoned mining town. She slows so Lars can eye the little jail, the foundation blackened by fire. He also takes in the structure at the end of the main street covered with old metal signs and knickknacks from bygone years. After a few more turns, Peach spots the forest service road she needs. They drive off onto the rocky, dusty lane.

"We really are going outdoorsy, aren't we?" he chuckles.

Peach nods and glances up to the side of a hill she knows leads to the old town's pioneer cemetery.

"We're going to have an experience," she promises.

They drive a half hour farther into the mountains. They pass several people on ATVs, most of them in tank tops with large armholes and ball caps. Some wave. Others don't. Peach prays none of them remember her anyway.

After climbing a small summit and pitching back down to earth, she pulls the car onto another dirt road, this one barely big enough for her little Honda. She drives a few yards onto the rough path and then pulls her car over into a thicket of leafy brush. She kills her engine.

"We're here. Almost," she says and gets out to be greeted by a plume of dust. Lars steps out of the car as Peach digs around in the vehicle's trunk. She stands up and slams it shut, a backpack of her own in her hands. She sets it down on the dirt next to a pool of muddy water and Lars walks around to her, picking up the bag.

"Wow," he exclaims, weighing it in his palms. "Did you bring enough canned food for the apocalypse? What the hell is in this thing?"

He kneels down, ready to pull the zipper on the pack when Peach snatches it up. Swinging it onto her back, she grazes the man's chin with her zealous motion. He rubs at his skin and frowns.

"I'm sorry," she says. "I didn't mean to get you. You okay?"

"Fine," he replies and regains his composure. "I guess you should lead on, Lisa."

The straps of the bag dig down into the tops of Peach's shoulders. She immediately wishes she'd been practicing with the weight of the pack. All she can do now is carry the burden the best she can and hope it doesn't zap her of too much energy.

Peach points down an embankment and smiles. In the far off distance, she can almost make out the sound of water.

"We're going there," she says and takes her first step downward.

A hawk, perhaps the same one who journeyed with them from the low valley, swoops overhead. He lets out a keen shriek, dives for something earthbound. Peach watches him vanish from her line of sight, lost in his zeal to kill.

62 RILEY

He can only check the locks on his windows and doors so many times. He chides himself for the new habit, not wanting to become an obsessive-compulsive neurotic. But his desire to feel secure in his own home compels him do three whole rounds of the place before he stands still to eat Oreos over his kitchen sink.

Riley twists off the chocolate cookie and licks at the cream filling which is more shortening than anything dairy. Eating half of the inside, he smashes the cookie back together and plops the entire disk onto his tongue. He chews with his mouth open, letting crumbs fall from his lips into the waiting sink basin.

He gets through half the bag before realizing he's stress eating. He looks down to his hands, smeared with cookie and a slight bit of grease, and quickly washes them off and dries them on a dish towel. He smoothes back his unwieldy locks and decides they need to be trimmed before he gets mistaken for a Phish groupie. He sorts through a pile of junk mail on his kitchen table. He dusts off his dining room buffet. His toilets start to sparkle. His books are reorganized by both genre and alphabetized by author's last name.

And when he finally becomes tired of killing time and expending energy, the thoughts are allowed in and they take him for a spin.

Nell. Kristin. Nicole. He thinks of each woman, everything from their smells to the sounds they made during sex if he can call those auditory memories to mind. Only Kristin supplies enough memories of things like favorite meals or preferred dresses. Nell is a void dotted with snippets of remembered sensations or images of that big mole on her breast. Nicole is just hot, intense chemistry, wet sheets and fucking done in secretive locales.

Riley considers his inability to see them as more than sexual conquests might be why he doesn't miss any of them. He doesn't yearn for their warmth in bed or the sound of their voices. Then his mind spins back, snagging on the faces or general auras of the other women he has been with or taken out once or twice. Some still have names, others are just hazy recollections. By the time he numbers them past eighty-three, he can think of only a few more though he knows his true count is much, much higher. And those numbers signify general notions of femininity in the forms of women. Some brunette with heavy bangs. A woman with small tits and wide thighs.

But he thinks of her last. His one real chance of a healthy relationship. Mayra. Unlike the others, she is more than her sex. She is simply and wondrously Mayra. The field biologist. The Mexican-American with strong roots in her heritage. The woman who tried and failed to play the piccolo for a new hobby. Her smell moving from that of cinnamon and citrus to gardenia. Deep brown eyes. Skin soft and warm except for on the heels of her feet.

He wants to cry, to physically excise the emotions ruling his mind, but he doesn't. Instead he takes up a pen and scrawls a note on a piece of paper. He gathers his keys and puts a little square of Scotch tape at the top of the sheet. He leaves out his front door and locks the deadbolt. He tapes the paper up on the door. It reads:

Hamal and/or Aldebaran. If you're reading this, go fuck yourself.

He starts his Nissan, pulls out onto the road ready for his early evening to get better. He heads back to Locust Street, to potential comfort and love, to Mayra's house and to Mayra.

63 PEACH

Cool water tumbles over rounded river rocks and gadflies amass by the thousands. Once they reach the banks of the creek, Peach slips off her pack and unzips the biggest compartment. She pulls out two green pans made of plastic and a small hand trowel used for digging in gardens. She drops them to her feet and winks at Lars.

"We're panning for gold," she says with enthusiasm. He picks up one of the pans and feels around the bowl of the concave object.

"I guess you should have told me what you had planned. I could have brought up my own pan."

Peach's face droops and she tells herself to close her mouth. "So you already know how to pan for gold? I guess I shouldn't be surprised. Outdoorsman and into money. Now it all makes sense."

Lars drops to a squat and pulls Peach down next to him, his hand wrapped around her wrist. He asks her to run her fingers over the plastic surface and she does, finding it smooth and just a bit grainy.

"I do know how, yes. My father taught me when I was a preteen and we'd mess around on some gold mining club-owned claims during the summers. Haven't done it since, but I do remember a few tricks. Like getting the pan roughed up. So the gold will stick."

Lars takes both pans and dunks his hands into the creek, pulling out fistfuls of sand and rock. He puts a pan in front of Peach. "Use those rocks to scratch up the plastic," he commands and then demonstrates with his own green pan.

Once she's put fine lines and a few gouges into the unused surface, he takes it from her and dumps the contents back out into the stream. She watches him work and keeps an eye on her pack behind them.

"You like to take charge of situations, don't you?" she asks as Lars rinses the pans in the slow-moving current.

"This is your thing. I just jumped in and started barking orders. I'm bad at backing down when I feel I know better." He lifts the pans out of the water and sets them in front of Peach, balanced on rocks just touching the liquid in the creek.

"No, it's good. Because I have no idea what I'm doing," she admits and nods down to the pans. "Please, continue."

Lars smiles and motions for her to come closer to where he crouches. Using the spade, he moves aside some of the larger rocks at the little bend in the creek and digs up the earth underneath them for material. Lars plops a shovelful of the rocky soil and sand in Peach's pan.

Once both pans are full, he stirs the rock and sand around with his hands. Peach mimics all of his actions, a water skipper catching her eye as it jumps by on the water's surface. After the stirring, he shows her the trick of getting the silt moving around with centrifugal force so that any gold present will shift to the bottom of the pan. The cold water and the motion make Peach's wrists hurt a bit; she puts her pan down to watch Lars finish the process.

When he's down to just fine, tan sand, he allows a small amount of water back into his pan and slowly moves it about, forcing the light grains to one side. As Peach watches, a line of black sand studded with what look to be miniscule, dark-purple garnets appears at the top of the pan. He moves this aside eventually with his measured stirring and a tiny speck of gold is revealed.

Peach gasps, the glimmer of the ore making her forget her true intentions if only for a moment. The solitary flake in the pan is the only thing dredged up and worth something. Lars sets aside the plastic bowl, out of the reach of the water on a pine stump.

"Do mine," Peach begs. As the black sand is revealed in her pan, she grows nervous, anxious for the sight of gold. She's crestfallen when she sees something globular and silver instead.

"Mercury," Lars says. He starts to toss the pan of water, sand, and liquid metal back to the creek when Peach catches his arm.

"That's toxic. Mercury. There was a reason for the miners' madness and it wasn't just gold fever. In fact, some people believe gold fever is due to toxicity affecting the brain and not some state of glamour in the presence of a pretty metal." Peach stretches an arm to her pack to retrieve a little Ziploc sandwich bag. She uses a stick to shift the small blob into the plastic and seal it away.

"You can keep the gold," she tells him and tucks her find back into her pack. "Since you're so good at getting wealthy," she finishes.

Lars smirks and puts his small find in his water bottle. He tells Peach he'll be careful not to drink it down.

"And you probably knew all the stories about the miners and Idaho City I told you on the way up here, didn't you?" she presses.

"I did not. Well, some of them, but they were mainly new," he replies.

Both Lars and Peach stand up and stretch. Lars tosses the worthless rocks and sand from his pan back into the creek and smiles at Peach.

"Again?" he asks. "The way the sun is dipping low behind that rise means we probably don't have much light left."

Peach looks down the creek and then to the line of a hill running behind them, curving north, bending out of sight. She shoulders her pack again and asks Lars to rinse the pans off for her in the moving stream.

"I have something I want to show you, actually," she says as she takes the pans back, water dripping from their rims. She tosses them into the little footpath they used to get down the embankment. "I'll pick them up later," she explains and then reaches for Lars's hand.

He takes her hand in his own and lifts up his own small pack. They walk, Lars a bit behind Peach, toward the mounded earth in front of them. The air is dry and smells of pine and Peach breathes in deeply. They weave around stands of spindly aspen, clusters of willow with sparse leaves and dull yellow pollen heads. Lars knocks his foot against a sprawl of downed deadwood. Peach tugs at him to move on.

A few feet farther toward her destination, in a clearing of dirt and a mat of pine needles, Lars points to the ground and whistles. In front of him are the remains of a large bonfire, the ash cold and some of it undoubtedly carried away by the breeze. Only a few blackened logs remain.

"Someone's been up here recently. I guess we aren't the only claim jumpers, Lisa."

Peach stops, eyes the remains of the fire, and thinks for a moment she can see some of the videotape. A bit of glossy, filmy black shimmers in the center of the spent wood she set alight.

But she turns her head, looks harder, and can see she did her job right. Nothing remains of the things that could link her to the death of Roman the Tattooist.

"Come on," she pulls at Lars. "That's old news. Onward to something new."

64   RILEY

When he parks his SUV on one of the side streets close to
Mayra's house, Riley tells himself it won't be a repeat of two
weeks ago. He convinces himself, as he takes the sidewalk
around the corner to her little bungalow, that she will hear him
out and be receptive to his visit. He imagines her alone, perhaps
in a ratty pair of sweatpants and a soft shirt riddled with holes
from years of wear. He'll interrupt her from watching television
on her couch. He imagines she'll welcome the intrusion. Maybe
she's even been waiting for him to return to her home and bring
passion in his wake. To make her life interesting and dynamic
and complete.

He thinks all these things until he actually sees her house in
front of him. The lights are on inside, gleaming yellow and
strong against the disappearing sun. Then he sees someone move
in front of one of the living room windows: a man with a
military-style buzz cut. He decides instead of turning away, he
needs to press on. The man could just be a friend. But if he's a

date, or a boyfriend, Riley can make that inconvenience disappear if he sees even a spark of interest in Mayra's deep auburn eyes. He'll do so by showing her the contents of his heart. The talk of finances will come later.

He passes her little patio in her front yard, a blossoming lilac offering up its heady smell as he brushes by its tulip-shaped leaves. His eyes move from the lighted doorbell to the brass knocker, shaped like the head of a bull, the ring through its nose the heavy-weighted knocking mechanism. He takes the hoop in his fingers and raps it sharply three times against the wooden door.

Then Riley steps back a few feet and waits.

Mayra answers, her hair swept up and off her neck, held high by a silver clip. She has a tray of bruschetta balanced in one palm and her face is glowing, her head turned to say something to someone within the house. Only when she turns to see Riley at her front door does her mouth turn down and she shuffles the tray of hors d'oeuvres to a small entryway table.

"You came back," she says and opens her door wider. Riley can see a few people milling about in her kitchen. She's clearly hosting a small dinner party, perhaps with the same friends he saw when he drove by two Saturdays ago. And as much as he would like to behave and leave her to have her fun, he's desperate for her attention. It's an action he can perform instead of lingering in his home, frustrated about the letters and the odd happenings he cannot control nor decipher.

Riley holds his ground and decides he won't leave her house until he's determined whether or not she'll be his once again.

"I am back. You're not imagining me," he replies. He tries to focus on her instead of the men and women sipping on white wine and shouting out answers to trivia questions behind Mayra.

"I just thought we left things a little weird the last time I drove by your house. I had a feeling you didn't get a chance to say what you really wanted to say." He hopes his subtle prompt is enough to fortify her, get her to confess to years of missing Riley's hands and lips.

Mayra crosses her legs at the ankle and leans on the doorjamb. She shakes her head. "No, I said what I wanted to say when I last saw you. Nothing else I can think to talk to you about."

Another light flips on—a retro-looking table lamp in the living room beams out long rectangles of illumination— and the party makes their way from the kitchen to sprawl across the couches and the easy chairs. Miniature plates decked in salami and slices of havarti pinched between fingers lead the procession. Riley notes the man with the buzz cut again. He doesn't sit by any of the other ladies and when he presses a pillow to his chest his biceps bulge out, veins lifting up his skin like tiny snakes.

Riley tries not to think of the man touching Mayra or at least not touching her the way he did. He wonders if the man knows about her fondness for foot massages and a gentle blow of air across her upper back.

"Then I guess maybe I had something else to say," he says as a woman from the party breaks away from the group and comes to stand next to Mayra. She's petite with a smattering of freckles along her cheekbones and at the tops of her shoulders, exposed in her strapless, springtime dress. She is shorter than Mayra, the crown of her head in line with his ex-girlfriend's chin and her lips are so devoid of pigmentation they are almost the same color as her pallid cheeks.

The friend smiles at Riley and speaks to Mayra. "Oh, I thought it was Mitch at the door. Sorry, I don't mean to intrude."

Scooping up the tray of tomato and basil-topped bread abandoned by Mayra, she meanders back to the group and Mayra watches her go.

"You were saying, Riley?" She blinks hard, checks the

corners of her mouth for stray crumbs left there from snacking.

"I was just going to tell you thank you, for the words about my parents. I'm sorry I drove away. I guess I was just caught a bit off guard." Riley steps a bit closer to Mayra and she doesn't budge. He leans a hand against the doorframe and smiles wide, keeping some of his weight off of his left foot.

"And I wanted to tell you I like the way you smell now, just like I did back then. Now you're more floral in scent. More delicate, though I can't imagine you've gotten rid of any of your battle axe tendencies just because you smell like a flower blossom."

Mayra laughs at this and scratches at the back of her neck. "Well, thank you, Riley. Is that all you wanted to talk about, because if so, I should probably get back to my guests."

He's aware she won't invite him inside. It's not her style to feel obligated to someone who shows up unannounced and uninvited. It's a brand of harshness, stiffness Riley didn't appreciate much in the past. But he thinks if they were together now, it would keep him honest and on the straight and narrow.

Spying the handsome man on the couch again, Riley notices him eyeing Mayra's back, his face calm. It could be a mask of indifference, Riley thinks, and decides there is only one way to find out.

The freckled woman comes back to the door with a nearly empty tray of bread in her hands and puts it down on the little table. Riley decides his next move will establish, in front of all her friends, whether or not there could ever be a future for the two of them.

He pitches forward on his right foot and as he moves his face in toward Mayra's, he puts his lips in a loose bow. Mayra doesn't move but her eyes open wider and he can see her throat gallop with a heavy swallow. Closing his eyes, Riley waits to feel her soft, plump lips against his own.

What he gets instead is something hard and bony. When he

opens his eyes he sees the hand of the small woman next to Mayra planted firmly between their sets of lips. Riley removes his face from her knobby knuckles and watches Mayra move a few feet back into her house.

The pixie frowns at Riley, the top of her chest flushing red. When she speaks her voice is tight and high.

"Who the hell are you? And why are you trying to kiss my girlfriend?"

65   PEACH

Hand in hand, Peach and Lars walk around the mounded
earth and the tall, sappy pines to arrive at a dark, small hole in
the side of the protruding hill. Something catches the man's eye
and he walks over to a grand ponderosa. A yellow placard made
of metal, as big as his hand, is nailed onto the trunk of the
conifer. He points to it and speaks to Peach.

"I knew we had to be on somebody's mining claim. I
wonder how many other signs are posted around here,
threatening off people like us?"

"It doesn't matter," Peach tells him, digging two headlamps
out of her bag. She tosses one to Lars and he slips it onto his
head. The blue plastic around the bulbs of the light nestle into
the middle of his widow's peak. He's reading the sign with the
help of the light, studying the name of the claim and the name of
the claimant.

"As long as we don't get caught taking any minerals out of
here, we'll be fine. I guess," he says and moves next to Peach.

Pulling her own headlamp down onto her forehead, she tells Lars to lead the way into the mineshaft and he laughs. He doesn't move.

"That's a questionable idea, Lisa. We don't know what's in there. Or how stable the rock is within the shaft. We don't have hard hats or ropes. When I said we'd have fun together, I wasn't imagining spelunking or claim jumping."

Peach makes a show of rolling her eyes and sighing loudly at his trepidation. "I thought you wanted to have an adventure. We came all this way and this is what I wanted to show you. I never intended for us to pan for gold once and then leave. I've been in this tunnel. I'm sure it's solid. I didn't die, now did I?"

Lars adjusts the headlamp on his forehead. "Then I'm going first. Seems like the manly thing to do here."

"I agree," she answers and readjusts the hefty pack on her shoulders. Her scalp is itching, burning, the sweat pouring from her head making the nylon netting of the wig unbearable against her skull. She rubs at the hairpiece with her palms and waits for him to move.

When he steps forward, she follows a few strides behind. Their headlamp lights bob in tandem, shining against the dimming evening light. He stops at the entrance to the shaft and feels around at the gray rock. The mouth of the fissure is only big enough for them to walk in single-file. He runs a finger over some of the rocks cut away at the opening, their angles sharp and rough. They dare enter the maw of a stony beast.

"I didn't take you for a daredevil," he says and looks back at Peach before ducking his head and stepping into the manmade cave.

She pauses for a moment to glance upward before exchanging sky for hard earth. They walk slowly, their bodies moving in queue through the narrow shaft. Lars taps his feet out in front of him before moving the rest of his body forward, checking for loose rock or camouflaged holes. Peach didn't think he would be so methodical and reasoned with his movements. But she'd just learned he was a hunter. And he was surely a more adept and experienced one than she.

Her voice is squeaky when she begins to talk but she coughs to set it right and mask her rising adrenaline. "Have you heard of the Mithraic temples of ancient Rome? They were all manmade or converted caves. Underground. It's where the initiates in the cult of Mithras would hold their rituals in secret. This place reminds me of one of them."

"Oh?" Lars responds, keeping his face and light pointed ahead. His skull just skims the ceiling of limestone and granite. Their small light sources illuminate bits of the damp cave. Otherwise, they are surrounded in darkness. Water plinks against stone somewhere in the distance. Peach's nose is filled with a moist musk.

"Did you travel to Rome and see one of them? What are they called?"

"Mithraeum. That's the modern term. And no. I've actually never left the country. I just like to learn things about ancient religions, especially those practices native to the Mediterranean. Things most people consider myths."

Her foot catches on something and she looks down to see a bit of rusted, iron cart track on the ground of the mine. It's bolted into the rock, a few feet long with a slight curve in it to the right. But it leads to nothing; it's a relic of an era long past.

Peach goes on, unprompted. "And the followers of Mithras, they had their rituals in these caves because of a heroic act for which Mithras was known. See, he had ridden a rampaging bull, worn it out, and decided to drive it underground into a cave to slay it. And he did. He held it by the nose and stabbed it in its throat. There are still images, plaques of this in museums. It's an example of tauroctony, of the sacrificial killing of a bull for sacred matters."

Lars ducks his head to pass underneath a dipping shelf of

rock at the height of his earlobes. Peach passes it too, her hands held high to feel her way clear from the hard overhang.

His voice is muffled by the rock encasing them both. Other than their movements and breath, the passage is silent. The dripping water is somewhere behind them now. Peach notes the heavy mineral taste which slicks her tongue from the stale air.

"Underground? In the earth? That's like the worst place to kill a bull," he says. "But good on the god, or whoever Mithras was, for getting it done. A bull would be quite the opponent. That's why I only kill predators when I hunt. Not sure if I mentioned to you that I'm focused only on animals adept at hunting animals themselves. There is a kinship there I respect and a challenge far more rewarding than dropping a buck with a compound bow."

She stops abruptly and closes her eyes to gather her courage. "No, you didn't tell me you killed other hunters."

When she resumes her gait, she goes back to her little speech. The one she practiced over and over again, to slight variation, over the past two weeks.

"And Mithras wasn't the only god who demanded bull sacrifices in his or her honor. There were many deities who expected taurobolium to be performed. Many weren't Roman or Greek. But some were. For instance, Venus."

"Like the goddess or the planet?"

"The goddess who inspired the name for the planet," she answers. "Celestial Venus. Venus of the Heavens. *Venus Caelestis* was her proper name."

Lars stalls for a moment and turns his head left to right. Peach peers over his shoulder and can see the shaft splits. One passageway leads straight forward, its mouth wider and smoother than the other hole which pitches a sharp right. The low clearance of the second tunnel would force them to duck down as they walked.

"I vote on straight," he says and wipes a bit of moisture

from his upper lip.

Peach feels something move past her toes and looks down just in time to see a small snake, nearly the same color of the rock surrounding them. It slithers quickly past her and Lars and straight into the wide-mouthed passageway. She smiles as it undulates away into the black.

She is grateful she has given herself to a life purpose so resplendently guided by signs.

"I agree. We move on the path of least resistance," she whispers and Lars goes ahead of her. Peach watches him step into the circular opening, her headlamp light beaming onto his upper back and head.

There is muscle and tight connective tissue at the nape of his neck, cloaked in skin damp with perspiration. There is a man who hunts predators. There is a man with his flank exposed not to a predator, but to a blessed vassal. One dedicated to the burgeoning existence of Perfect Peach.

66   RILEY

He runs a red light as he drives as far away as possible from Mayra's house in as little time as he possibly can. She'd tried to stop him, calling after him as he hustled away, putting too much weight on the ball of his left foot and swearing at the pain under his breath. With other women, the promise of girl-on-girl sex would have made Riley more resolved to be a part of the experience, or at least negotiate an option to watch. But Mayra is different. Riley believes she is his one shot at a real relationship. He isn't interested in trying to find someone new. He wants her.

He was lucky there wasn't a police car near the traffic light to catch his transgression. He floors the gas pedal and makes all the greens down Idaho Street, until it turns into Fairview as he travels west. He pulls his car to an abrupt stop in the pot-holed parking lot of a place he thought unlikely he'd ever frequent again. The neon flames run across the roof of Blaze Lounge, blinking on and off in waves of dazzling color.

What he needs now is a fix of pure sexuality. And since

Nell worked for him in the past, he figures she will prove a fitting distraction from his current confusion and the physical pain in his foot.

The bouncer lets him in with a nod of acknowledgment and Riley spots Sev at his usual place at the bar. Riley doesn't try to hide from the man but walks straight up to the runway stage in the center of the room and stands in front of Nell working a silver pole. She grasps the metal with both hands and kicks her legs into the air, holding her body perpendicular to the ground before letting her heels make contact again with the catwalk.

Nell sees Riley gazing at her. She stumbles a bit in her routine before resuming her slithering motion, running her hands over her breasts covered by a scant bit of purple sateen. The woman is uneasy with Riley in her vicinity. He knows she remembers something of their night together though the memories may be mired in a mental fog.

Riley waits for the familiar twinge to hit his groin but nothing happens. He thinks of the dancer flat on her back, her bare genitals open and ready for his cock. Still nothing stirs and he closes his eyes hard before walking over to the bar and Sev.

The man is writing on napkins again. Riley pulls a poem away from Sev without permission. He doesn't read the poetry but instead focuses on the print. As he looks at it in the dim light of the strip club, he makes out differences in Sev's handwriting versus that of Aldebaran's firm print. Sure, there are similarities, but the messages from Aldebaran are far from facsimiles of Sev's writing. He wishes he'd focused on the differences earlier on, when he had first compared the writing, instead of narrowing in on the scant likeness. Maybe then he wouldn't have wasted so much time fighting a man who isn't guilty of anything other than being a controlling asshole.

Sev snatches the napkin back and clicks his pen closed, tucks it away into his leather duster.

"I hope you're not here for another fight," he warns Riley,

"because this time I won't be caught off-guard. Broken ribs or not, I'll throw you in the skip."

Riley reaches into his own jacket pocket and Sev shuffles his bulk off the barstool, hopping up to his feet, keeping his eyes on Riley's hands. But all Riley produces is his wallet and a checkbook tucked inside a plastic liner.

"Can I have that pen?" he asks Sev and the poet hands it over.

Riley opens up the checkbook and writes out a check, to the amount of three hundred dollars. He stops his scrawling but doesn't look up at Sev.

"Your last name?" he asks, his arm resting in a spilt pool of what looks like Sprite and maraschino cherry juice.

"Ross," Sev replies and waits patiently, his eyes still studying Riley's movements.

With a rip of paper, Riley tears the check from its copy and hands it over to Sev along with the man's blue pen.

His former competition looks at it before tucking it into a pocket on the inside of his dirty coat. He glares at Riley. "At least now I can get an X-ray of my chest. After you kicked me when I was down like a wanky petrol sniffer."

Riley takes a look around the strip club. Nell is still writhing on stage. Now the woman is on her knees, her torso bending backward slowly, controlled by the muscles in her stomach. An elderly man tucks a dollar into her panties, not at the waistband, but where the fabric stretches tight over her genitals.

He shakes his head and thumps the bar before turning to leave.

"Sev Ross," he says to the man he cuckolded, the poet, the guy who surely would have put him back in the hospital if Riley hadn't caught a break during the fight.

"Sev Ross," he repeats, "you're an asshole. Have a great fucking life."

When he leaves the strip club, Riley pauses to watch the neon dance about on the roof. If only it were real flame, a true fire, to burn away all of his mistakes.

67 PEACH

She thinks of the man in front of her—his outline moving farther away from the light of her headlamp—as an animal. But just for this moment, just to make her work easier. Because as soon as she sees him as the animal of Mithraic myth, as a bull, she no longer feels the twinge in her stomach and the fire racing through her fingertips. She can sympathize with animals too readily if they are indeed animals. Lars is a bull in spirit, in purpose, so her perspective on killing animals shifts with this knowledge. And though she likes Lars, she must see him for who he is. Or rather what he is. A sacrifice: needful and timely and poised to make her life much more complete and satiating.

He mumbles something about the path narrowing ahead but Peach doesn't pay attention to his words. She slips one of the straps of the backpack off of her shoulder and swings the bag around to her chest. The supplies inside squish against her breasts and she unzips the middle compartment. From the backpack she pulls three small lances, their tips ending in sharp points.

The metal shop guy at the community center had gladly cut one of the metal stakes she'd found out near the pastured bull into thirds. She hadn't asked him to do more than one, not wanting to draw too much attention to her work or have him asking too many questions. She then had three well-balanced lengths of metal she had taken home and sharpened with a metal file to while away hours left absent of Roman the Lamb.

If she couldn't kill Lars in three throws, with all her practice over the month, then maybe she didn't deserve to gain his power and steal the energy from his dying body. And if she failed, she was certain his hunting instinct would kick in and she would be the one tasked with thwarting death.

She swings her bag to her back and slips her arm through the loop. She tucks two of the lances, both the length of her forearm, into the front pocket of her cargo pants. They put a smear of grime down the front of her pink athletic shirt she bought for the occasion. The metal reaches high up her pelvis and prods lightly at her stomach. She grips the other lance, the first of three in her hand. Peach looks ahead at Lars.

Her headlamp still illuminates his neck. He stops briefly to run a finger along a vein of lighter stone trailing up to the ceiling of the shaft. He studies the earth and stone above him.

"I wish it could have been someone other than you. But the signs were on you. I will fail at my efforts if I start ignoring the importance of divine omens," she whispers under her breath.

Then she lets the lance fly.

It glances off of the top of his small pack and nicks the back of his neck. He slaps a hand to the spot where the metal sliced his skin and then looks around at the ground. Lars spies the make-shift weapon a few feet ahead of him up the passageway when his beam falls on its dull sheen.

"The hell?" he screams out and turns toward Peach.

Before she can speak or slide another lance from her pocket

he's on her, pushing her up against the rough stone wall of the mine. Her throat slams into a sliver of rock protruding from the wall and puts a ragged gouge into the front of her neck. She screams out in alarm more than pain and clutches at the torn skin at her throat, slowly oozing blood.

Peach twists violently, Lars's grip on her slipping just enough for her to bolt back the way they came: to the entrance and the forest and the night. As she struggles to see the path and get away, she realizes her headlamp shattered when she impacted with the rock. She reaches up to find it a mess of broken plastic. She's left to retreat without the aid of light.

Lars is behind her, his operational headlamp trained on her back. She can just make out how he keeps a palm pressed to the back of his neck to stop the blood from seeping too quickly from his wound. She chances a look at his face, but his features are hidden behind the blinding light of his lamp. She imagines his face has gone as hard as the rock around them, stolid and fixed.

"You're a psycho, Lisa?" he asks as if she would readily accept the title. Peach scurries over the rocky floor of the mine until she finds a little outcropping of rock to squeeze her body behind. She catches her breath and notices then that the other two lances have ripped a hole in her pink shirt with her movements and are scratching at the skin over her abdominals.

She gropes at where they lie against her stomach and works both lances from her pocket. Peach places them on the ground where she can pluck them up quickly. After she does this, she looks up to see Lars's headlight moving back toward the lance that had been meant to kill him in a single shot. Peach knows if he takes up the metal, at the very best she will be marched from the cave and driven to the nearest police station in Idaho City. At worst, she will die.

No, Peach thinks, the very worst would be that Lars would not die. And then she would be left without his bit of essence, his energy association with *that* man unsuccessfully regained to put to use in her own ascension. And the entire endgame would collapse. And come February, she would not have enough strength and energy to do what she must.

Lars's headlamp beam bounces around the dark cave as he moves swiftly back to the sharp length of metal. Peach plucks up one of the lances at her feet and whispers a prayer to Europa. The maiden was captured by Zeus when he was in the form of a bull and taken to the isle of Crete to be molested. Eventually Zeus had gifted the woman with a few fantastical presents, one of which was a weapon Peach imagines she has in her hands this moment to give herself strength of mind and steadiness of hand.

It was the most remarkable of gifts given to Europa: a javelin which never missed its mark.

"Please, Europa. Please, Mithras. Please, Taurus."

All Peach can see now is the light. So she aims her lance just below the white ray and lets the second length of metal sail off her thin fingers.

68   RILEY

The whiskey tells him nothing. It just goes into his gut and makes him horny and angry and neurotic. Riley realizes he's back at square one. His gut, full of booze, tells him he was completely wrong about Sev. And that definite realization forces Riley to admit he has no idea whom the stalker could be. Then he thinks of Mayra touching the short woman, brushing her nipples, lifting her skirt, and it makes him livid. He loses his horniness immediately and swigs down another three fingers of Jameson.

The nighttime is quiet on his backyard deck excepting the shrill call of what Riley thinks might be a barn owl or a Great Horned with those tufts of feathers capping its head. It does not release hoots to fit Riley's stereotypical notion of noises made by owls. He considers calling Walker but he's sure his friend would just make more demands about seeing the police or doing something logical. Riley thinks of all the horror movies and thrillers that rely on characters not going to the police to detail their predicaments. But Riley doesn't think he's in one of those movies. Riley believes he's in an adventure tale. And he's the star: the swashbuckling rogue who gets the girl and bests his enemy in the very end. He holds to the idea of being a cliché for a while longer before turning his mind to the paper in front of him.

The cards sit on the little glass table murky with calcium buildup from rain and snow. Five cards in total. He imagines handing all five to a cop and the cop snorting and asking him if he's serious or if he's just bored or insane. There are no overt threats. Who would Riley file a restraining order against? The night sky? The constellations of Aries and Taurus?

Then a thought enters Riley's head and he pulls his phone from his pocket. He blinks heavily to clear his vision and keys in the word *zodiac* into his internet browser. He takes another sip of the amber alcohol and nestles back into his chair while the search results load. Clicking on the top result, he's taken to a page that lists the zodiac cycles.

He scans it, noting that the traditional procession of the zodiac begins with Aries and ends with Pisces. Taurus comes after Aries, followed by Gemini. Riley taps on the screen to make the font bigger and notes the bookended dates of each zodiac month. He looks at Taurus's dates and sees the cycle will end in the coming few days.

"Then on to Gemini," he says to his phone and clicks it off. He tosses it on top of the stack of cards. He figures when he's sober and less angry he'll look up the constellation of Gemini. He wonders if he'll get a new card in a week or so. Maybe it will be signed with the name of another star.

But then he considers what another card would really mean to him. It would just be another strange communication to pile up with the others. Likely it wouldn't be aggressive enough to constitute a threat. And it wouldn't be enough to force him to take it to the police. So his pile would just get taller, cardstock layers growing. He wonders for how long? For a year? For his life?

"I'll have enough of them to make up a scrapbook," he says and laughs and imagines himself cutting little stars out of sparkly ribbon with safety scissors. He takes a sip of whiskey directly from the bottle and then returns it to rest next to his missing toes.

Then his thoughts move unbidden back to Mayra. He tries to remember her perfume, call it into existence within his nose. The whiff he dreams of is her spiced citrus aroma. But all he gets is the heavy fragrance of gardenia. He smells the white petals in his booze and in the air and it's a change he decides he doesn't want before he passes out in his deck chair—the call of the bird insistent and piercing and unable to rouse him from his lack of consciousness.

69   PEACH

Lars's gurgling cry tells Peach her lance hit its mark.

She keeps her little hiding spot for a full minute, her breath quick and loud in the cave before she decides to inspect her sacrifice. She picks up the last of her sharp pieces of metal and grips it soundly in her palm before stepping quietly in the direction of the downed man. She can see the light from his headlamp is muted and low to the ground. It's likely he fell directly onto his face when he was pierced.

Getting close enough to tell if he's moving proves to be a feat. Peach is hesitant to get within striking range of the man's hands so she stays with her back to the entrance of the forward passageway—one hand pressed against the stone wall for security and to make her way safely in the true dark, the other holding the lance like a dagger. Another few minutes pass before she is willing to touch Lars. She reaches out a foot and prods at his leg. He doesn't move but she knows it might be a trap. He is a hunter, after all.

Something within her gives her the strength to kneel down and feel at his neck for the homemade lance. She wonders if it's Perfect Peach, her future self egging her on. When she finds the metal embedded securely in the back of Lars's neck, just to the left of his spine, she sighs and thanks Europa, Mithras, and the stars.

Grasping him by the arms, she heaves up with her legs and flips him over onto his back. The headlamp light beams into her face. She works it off of his forehead and holds it over his wound and the sharp point of metal impaled through his flesh.

When a spray of blood shoots past Lars's lips, Peach takes to her feet and trains the light on his face. His eyes are closed and his lips barely move, but she can tell he's trying to speak.

"I'm sorry about this," she says to him. "I want you to know what's happened tonight isn't your fault. It's someone else's fault. We're actually both victims, in a way. And I didn't kill you for Mithras or Venus. I swear it. Your death has higher purpose to me and to others."

The blood from his neck and his mouth pools into a thick puddle of dark liquid under his black hair. His eyelids flutter but his lids stay closed. Peach resists bending close enough to his body to hear what he wants to say. She stands her ground and stays silent, her ears waiting, straining to make out his mumbling from a place out of reach.

Then the words come, barely audible and Peach catches them.

"Don't hurt my wife," he mutters.

Once Peach understands the words, she can make out his saying them three more times. Then she does the only thing she can think to do for the man who so graciously gave her his life.

"I won't," she says. "I promise she's safe. She's not connected to him. I won't hurt her. I promise."

The thing which tells her Lars has died is not the slackness in his jaw or the tilt of his head to the side. It's the way her body feels as she's bombarded by energy, raw and heavy. The current hits her straight in her pelvic core and she bites her tongue to keep from screaming out in elation. Peach has no desire to celebrate his death with excessive cheer. She'd gotten to know this man at her feet and truly liked him. She's determined to give him a moment of respect.

It will take her time to get used to this absconding with life. She knows she will have more practice at it, until her decorum is a mix of solemnity and joy acceptable to the standards of Perfect Peach.

A few seconds later, the feeling of new life and energy mixed with a sexual current is gone. Peach bends down and takes a large plastic Ziploc from her backpack. She pulls the lance clean through Lars's neck and drops it into the bag, the metal coated in his thick blood. Then she pulls something else from the bottom of her bag, and she's immediately thankful to have the weight taken off her shoulders.

It's a mining pick, a tool she found used at a thrift shop. She grasps the handle with the sleeve of Lars's shirt and wipes off her prints. Then, with the fabric still wrapped around the worn leather binding, she pushes the length of the pick into the long wound made by the lance.

A shock of pain races up her own neck and Peach remembers she's been wounded. She does her best not to touch the cut, not wanting to smear any of her fresh blood on Lars's body. In a panic, she uses the light to look at her own hands and is relieved when she sees the blood from her throat that had made its way onto her hands has already dried.

She sticks her hands in her pockets and briskly rubs off the flaking blood into the insides of her cargo pants. Then she produces a pair of rubber dishwashing gloves from a small pocket on her pack and pulls them over her fingers.

Putting her broken headlamp into her bag, she slips on the working light, lifts Lars by his armpits and drags him toward the end of the passageway. She had known the path only went on for another forty feet or so before ending. She'd scouted out both junctures weeks ago.

When she gets his bulk to the back of the mine tunnel, she lifts up his left hand and wraps it around the handle of the mining pick. She hopes as his body becomes stiff, the fingers will grip tightly to the tool. She'd taken pains to notice if he was left-handed or right-handed the day he brought her brochures to study and a beetle flew into his open mouth. The day Riley Wanner had been in Lars's office. Then she busies herself with piling rocks over his face, torso and legs. She had made sure there was a large pile of spent stone nearby. With the mini quarry her work is quickly finished.

"There is powerful meaning to all of this. Thank you for your role in it all," she speaks to the corpse.

On her way out of the mine she checks for any shards of plastic from her headlamp and scoops up a few errant pieces. The place where she thinks Lars pushed her into the rock seems clean of blood. Peach figures she must have started bleeding a moment after pulling herself away from the stone.

When she clears the entrance of the cave, she's greeted by the crystalline stars of a deep night sky. The pines look like pointy lances, their tips tilted skyward. She makes a straight line for the stream on the site and washes the rubber gloves in the running water before pulling them off and rinsing her fingers up to her elbows in the cold brook. She uses sand to scrub the dried blood from her skin and the cold water leaves her flesh numb.

Her headlamp illuminates a drip of dark liquid plinking into the water from her neck and she touches the wound gently to find the bleeding starting anew. She looks around and finds a patch of thick mud near the creek bank. She scoops up a handful and mashes the earth into her neck. It will dry and provide a temporary seal over the cut.

She uses a stick to smooth over the imprint her boots left

near the water and then she tosses the twig into the current. Adjusting her headlamp, she makes her way back to her car, stopping to scoop up the gold pans at the path up the embankment.

The memory of the tiny flake of gold in Lars's water bottle makes her smile.

"Really, I wish he hadn't been marked with all the signs," she says to the dome of bright stars, to Aldebaran and the planet Venus. "But if not him, then another."

"Another," she says. "Another."

70   RILEY

While his body lies in the deck chair of plastic and painted metal, Riley's soul takes a trip. Some might call what happens to him a dream. Some might call it slipping between levels of consciousness. Riley doesn't put a label on it while it happens. Because to him, it is a natural phenomenon in a different world operating under different rules and different constructs.

He stands in a hospital room. The bed is older, non-electronic, with high metal sides and a thin mattress covered in scratchy, blue sheeting. The top of the sheeting is turned down and rumpled, as if someone has just left the bed and vacated the room. He's the only soul in sight and he turns about the room, checks the hook on the wall with the blood pressure cuff, gazes at the little boxy-screen meant to monitor a heartbeat.

The display shows the zigzagging pattern of an erratic heartbeat though no one is in the bed. So Riley wonders if the heartbeat is his own. He looks down at his arms and there are no needles, tubes or bands touching him, listening in on his vitals.

He wears nothing, in fact. In the nude, his only covering is a layer of gelatinous goop over his skin. On his inner thigh, back of his hands and around his left pectoral are cloying, caking globs of blood. He presses in at one bloody spot and his fingers come away awash in a deep pink.

There are no windows in the room, and when he thinks to check, there is no door either. The walls look like white cinderblocks, but when he walks to a corner of the room and depresses his palm to the wall, it gives a bit. He pulls his hand away. The wall springs back to place.

Riley never questions where he is and what is happening. He feels a lack of judgment concerning the experience. He merely notes what he can sense: room, sparseness, medical machinery.

And when he looks back to the bed balanced on a wheeled frame, he notices something newly arrived. It's a sack of white fabric; the edges have been gathered together and tied closed with a neat bow of fair ribbon. It's big enough to hold a roast or a basketball or a baby.

He goes to it and though he has no curiosity, his fingers do the work of pulling the trimming away from the cloth. As the material slips to the bed, he sees what's been delivered in the neat, quaint sack.

It is a stack of greeting cards. He opens the first card on the top of the pile. It's a belated birthday card signed by someone named Hamal. He recalls seeing this card before. Once he finishes reading this card, he opens the next and the next, until he doesn't recognize the cards anymore. There are new cards for future occasions he has yet to experience.

When he puts down one of the cards in the stack and acts to pick up the next, he notices the next item in the heap isn't a card at all. It's a picture. Of a person's face.

He shuffles through the remaining glossy papers. All pictures of people. He studies each face shape, the line of the nostrils, where the hairline starts. He doesn't wonder whether or not he knows these people. To him, now, they are just simply faces.

Riley reorders the cards, stacking them back up with the birthday card on top and nestles them into the center of the textile. He does up the fabric with the ribbon.

Then he stands in the middle of the room. The bed remains messy, the package still there. The monitors are monitoring someone or something. There is no way to escape. And Riley, he just keeps standing.

71 PEACH

She's careful to drive slowly back to Boise from Idaho City. Though night is full on, and it's unlikely she'll be pulled over, she winds back down out of the mountains two miles below the speed limit. Her mind is surprisingly clear. Peach doesn't think too much about the process of Lars's sacrifice. She's becoming good at compartmentalizing her experiences. His death is tucked into a little spot of her memories already gathering a coating of mental dust.

With her air set to blast from the vents in the Honda, the mud around her neck has dried to a tight bandage. When she turns her head to look out the rearview mirror, flakes of clay soil land in her lap.

Once she's home, she pulls her pack out of the car and heads inside, looking around for nosy neighbors or people returning home from late dinners or first dates. She hasn't seen the older woman, Mona, who lives next door in weeks. She makes a mental note to check in on her soon. When she slips inside her home, she deadbolts the door behind her and wastes little time.

Carrying her backpack, she moves to her bedroom and yanks open her closet door. Peach dives in for the dark green duffel and comes up with it in her hands. She puts both bags down on the counter in her bathroom and pulls off her wig before looking in her mirror. The fresh air is a delectable boon to her scalp dirtied with old sweat. She breathes out in pleasure and then takes a look at herself.

The mud did its job and sealed off the bleeding, but there are streaks of dried blood running down the pit of her throat to her collarbone where they peter out like desiccated rivers. She decides the best way to deal with the dry clay is to turn it back to mud. Peach peels off her pricey shirt with the tear at the belly and the dirt and blood stains on it, slips out of her shoes and shimmies out of her cargo pants.

She steps into her tub and pulls the shower curtain, the metal rings clacking against the metal rod. She's still in her underwear, a set of cotton underclothes in rose, and turns on the water. It's warm immediately and once her bra and panties are darkened with the water and heavy, she peels those off as well and holds her throat under the stream of water.

As the mud comes away, the extent of her wound is revealed. Soon the jet of water causes her neck to convulse and prickle with sharp jabs of pain. She shuts off the tap and steps out onto the rug, her breasts and belly still covered in a slick of watery muck.

She goes back to her mirror and sees the ragged tear beginning to ooze dark red blood once more. She prods at the slice gently and finds the gash is about three inches long, the tear uneven. Gritting her teeth, she lifts up a corner of her skin to check how deep the cut runs. All she sees is pulpy, crimson flesh and she's suddenly acutely aware of how lucky she'd been. It could have easily been a nicked artery or a cut into her larynx.

From what she can tell, she's just suffered a deep laceration. And as messy as it looks, it will heal.

"As long as I sew it shut," she says to herself. As soon as she speaks she regrets it, for the muscles flanking the abrasion pull sharply at her hurt.

From under her sink she produces a brown, rectangular bottle of hydrogen peroxide. She holds her head and neck over her sink and unscrews the bottle before dumping the chemical straight into her injury. She lifts up the skin as she pours and allows herself to whimper at the biting pain of the liquid on her raw flesh. A wash of bubbling, pink blood rushes from the wound, carrying with it a few flecks of dirt and a miniscule pebble down into the sink basin.

Peach tosses the empty bottle into her bathtub and holds the sides of her counter, pressing into the woodwork with her fingers. A minute later, the bulk of the burning has dissipated and she unzips the large compartment on her backpack. She produces the lance that felled Lars, tucked away in a thick, plastic bag.

Most of his blood that hasn't dried onto the piece of metal stake has settled in the bottom of the bag and she notes that it is viscous, but still liquid enough. She sets it aside and opens up the duffel readied on the counter. From this, she takes a different plastic bag. It's the sack emblazoned with the green-skinned, oval-eyed face of an alien.

It's folded in on itself, hiding away something long and thin and another item squat and cylindrical. She unrolls it and looks into the sack before pulling out her stolen goods. They are the only things she kept from Roman's tattoo parlor. They'd been necessary to hold on to.

Thrusting her hand into the sack, she pulls forth a jar of jet black ink and a tattoo gun and its power supply. The same one used on her head by Roman. While she could get her own, new tattoo gun and needle and ink, Peach is a stickler for ritual. She wants the same one to deed her with this tattoo, the same one that marked her with the symbol of Aries.

The same gun for the tattoo she plans on inking directly into her open wound.

She plugs in the tattoo gun's power supply and flips it on, watching the sharp needle tap away at the air. Peach unscrews the cap on the ink and puts a small amount into a cup she keeps next to the sink. Then she picks up the Ziploc with the bloody lance and holds the bag stiff to drain some of Lars's blood into the cup as well. She stirs the ink and fluid with her finger, not sure on proper consistency. As long as there is enough ink to make the tattoo, even a drop of the sacrifice's blood will do.

When the gun and ink and her courage are ready, she tilts her head in the mirror to get a good look at her wound. She lifts up the skin again to see the crevasse of red, angry flesh cut across her throat. Then she decides on the best place for the tattoo, the sign of Taurus. Raising the gun, she turns it on. The buzzing makes her entire hand vibrate until she finds the right hold on it.

The first prick of the needle is like ice married flame, in union only to torment her. She screams but does not pull back. She holds the needle where she needs it, dipping down for more ink when necessary, and fights the flow of blood escaping her throat. She understands this tattooing is all about ritual; without skin to hold the ink, the design likely won't stay on the meat of her muscle. But it's the process that matters. To her. And to the masters of Taurus whom she aims to please.

She decorates her wound with a small circle capped by horns and as she draws the last tip on the last horn, only then does she switch off the gun and begin to breathe again. She watches as the ink mixed with Lars's blood dallies with her own. The horns of the bullish sign begin to run, and she thinks of what Lars told her of the way a bull attacks. Prongs down so they may be lifted high to gouge.

She knows when she pulls her skin over the splotchy attempt at a tattoo—the cut sewn shut or mended with a thin layer of Krazy Glue—any ink left in her flesh will be invisible. She'll be the only one who knows it's there. In a way, it will be hiding in plain sight.

Just like Peach.

SUNDAY, THE 17TH OF MAY, 2015

72   RILEY

He finds night to be the worst time. It's when he feels most alone and most vulnerable, with his mind prone to wandering to thoughts of work and money and Mayra and the cards. Riley lies awake, watching a play of light and shadow on his ceiling from the tree moving in the breeze outside his bedroom window. The shadows of the limbs and leaves look like girls in hula skirts, dancing, shaking their hips.

When the doorbell rings, he freezes. Then, he has the thought that if he moves fast enough, if it's another card or package, he might be able to catch his stalker. And with that, Riley bolts out his bedroom and down his flight of stairs, moving as fast as his foot will allow. When he gets to his front door he fumbles with the locks and swings it open quickly. It smashes into the wall and takes down a framed picture of a young Riley with his parents—their sweaters all matching, arms folded and resting on carpeted boxes, the product of a mid-90s photo shoot.

He steps outside, emboldened and unafraid that he might be

attacked. But there is no one there. He walks down his path and doesn't see a car. There are no dogs barking in alarm, no security lights over garages switching on to shed light on dastardly doings.

But there is a package. A cardboard box of dull brown. And there is a note taped to the top.

Riley drops down and sits his butt on the metal threshold of his door. He pulls the package toward him. He wishes he'd brought a baseball bat downstairs with him, but now that he's outside, he thinks he's unlikely to meet the stalker tonight. He figures the man rang the doorbell to signal a delivery, just as a UPS man would do, and then left.

He pulls his phone from his pajama bottoms, used to having it on his person at all times and flips on the video option. This time he decides to open the box first. He removes the paper from the container and finds the sides taped up. He runs a fingernail through the clear tape and pulls up on the top of the package.

Under his porch light, in the bottom of the box, sits a handmade figurine. It's the size of a large coffee mug if tipped onto its side. He lifts it from the carton and sees it is a cow, a bull, in fact. The legs are of varying sizes, the body a bit undefined and bulbous. But it is clearly a ceramic steer.

The bulk of the figure is dark brown, but there are spots of color around the animal and he turns it over in his hands to eye each symbol. There is a small, white triangle over the bull's brow. On his flank, a crescent moon in light yellow. The tip of his tail is a fork of hair in black and a little, blue beetle is placed just under its chin. And on its back is the feathered wing of a bird in dark gray.

The bull itself is expressionless.

He makes sure his phone's camera captures all the designs on the statue and then his slow act of opening up the note and a quick scan of the words before shutting it off.

The paper is simple and white, what one would find in a

printer tray or copy machine. But the handwriting is the same staunch, thick font he's seen over the past few weeks. He reads it to himself, starting over a few times as his eyes dart so quickly over the words that he misses some of their meaning:

This is your very own figurine of the Apis bull, Riley. In very ancient Egypt, people worshipped a bull deity known as Apis. Part of their rituals required finding an earthly, mortal bull that had all the appropriate signs indicating it was Apis incarnate to house and feed and worship. These signs were a white triangle on the forehead, a vulture's wing on the back, a double-haired tail, the outline of a scarab under the tongue and a crescent moon on its hindquarters. Once the bull was located, it was given a life in a temple, to be prayed to for good harvests and just verdicts and general happiness. And then it was sacrificed. And then another Apis bull would be searched for, and until found, the followers would wonder if Apis had abandoned them. But another bull was always found. And the followers would begin the cycle again.

Riley, I am not a follower of Apis. But I thought this statue would be a useful reminder for you. Of your limitations and losses and failures. It will also encourage you to try and understand my position. To see what it is I aim to do, what I mean to become.

Riley Wanner. My dear nemesis. It's time for you to get in the fucking game.

With love,
Aldebaran

FREE Secret Chapters

There are more than two sides to the story!

Get exclusive chapters from the perspectives of other characters in THE BLOOD ZODIAC Series!

ACKNOWLEDGMENTS

To the humans who have always looked to the stars and seen stories written there, I am proud to carry on your work and share your myths. To my family, friends and support team that cheered me on and worked with me to bring this second book in *The Blood Zodiac* series to life, I cannot thank you all enough. And lastly, but in no way least, I am indebted to my guides. A hearty round of applause to you all. I raise a glass to the heavens. Another one down and many more to go.

CONTINUES...

BECAUSE

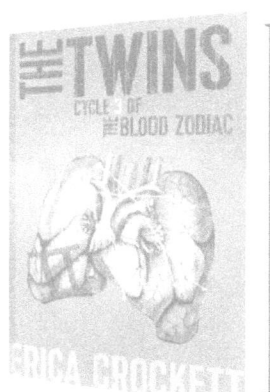

DOUBLE TROUBLE

MEANS MURDER.

THE TWINS: CYCLE 3 OF *THE BLOOD ZODIAC*

AVAILABLE FALL 2016

www.ingramcontent.com/pod-product-compliance
Lightning Source LLC
Chambersburg PA
CBHW020409260626
47156CB00007B/2296